A
SECOND
CHANCE
AT FOREVER

BOOK TWO OF THE DARK KISS TRILOGY

BY LIZ STRANGE

Her vein throbbed, and I drank in her warmth and softness against my body. I pressed my mouth to her throat, savouring the moment. Her demeanor was perfectly compliant to my needs, and the rush of her blood called to me. As my fangs sank into her flesh, she gave a small murmur of surprise. Her heartbeat quickened, and the blood flowed easily into my waiting mouth. As the liquid slid down my throat to my stomach, to be absorbed into the rest of my body, I swooned with a satisfaction beyond reason. Soon I felt her legs begin to buckle, and I withdrew my mouth, easing her gently to the ground.

Eli was already finished and waiting back at the car. He leaned with lazy nonchalance against the hood, and I smiled at how wonderful he looked under the moonlight. His long legs stretched out before him, and his cobalt blue eyes pierced the unforgiving darkness. A twinge of unexpected sadness gripped me as I realised all traces of the little boy I had loved as my own were gone.

Yet I couldn't deny that becoming a vampire agreed with him. He had always been an attractive man, but the change seemed to enhance the best of what he already possessed in life. He smiled as he caught me looking with appreciation in his direction. In a blur he was at my side, holding me in an intimate embrace.

PROLOGUE

FOURTEEN MONTHS AFTER LEAVING ENGLAND

It's been more than a year since Giovanni died, but a night hasn't passed that my first waking thoughts aren't of him. Though, as the months have gone by, my sleep has been less punctuated by nightmares of his death and more dominated by dreams of happy times spent together. On the darkest days, I find myself seeking comfort in Eli's arms, knowing those actions can only lead to a different kind of pain, but I am unable to stop myself. I can give to him my body, but my heart will always belong to Giovanni, no matter how many years I may exist without him. Yet, some days, Eli's unwavering love and dedication are the only things keeping me going.

The three of us, Eli, Charles, and I, have slipped into an acceptable rhythm in our new town. We have our difficulties and our conflicts for sure, but for the most part things are comfortable between us. We are undeniably bonded by a terrible past.

Eli has blended with the university scene in our new town with ease. He is respected by his peers for his incredible mind and has been welcomed socially because of his charm and wit. The change has only enhanced the physical appeal he always had. The young women are attracted to his looks, and the men are good-naturedly jealous and appreciative of his strength and popularity. I suppose he could continue with this charade for any number of years, as the student body around him passes on from the world of academia to the "real world," but, eventually, we will have to move on from here as well.

That Charles has remained with us is a surprise. He makes no demands on either Eli or myself, quietly living a life that is both a part of and separate from ours. His power still frightens me, knowing that if he wanted to, he could crush us both like bugs under his shoe, but he has never been menacing. In fact, he is quite the opposite, like a silent, yet ever-watchful guardian over the weaker members of his flock. Will he stay indefinitely? I cannot say, but I do think that no matter what twists our lives may take, he will always be an ally.

The evenings of waking to a pillow soaked with blood-tinged tears are growing fewer and farther between. The vise-like pain of my love's loss against my heart grows fainter with each passing night. I have even started to smile again.

I go on because I know you would want me to, Giovanni. I will do my best to be strong and to look after Eli as he struggles through the first trying years after his change.

And, if ever I can, I will take revenge on those who stole you from me.

I love you still. I love you always.

CHAPTER 1

NEW BEGINNING

The music thundered. It was too loud and heavy for my personal taste, but Eli had asked me to accompany him tonight, so I didn't have much say in the matter. He had developed a serious interest in the whole nightclub scene, with alternative music his current personal favourite, and, if there was a live band playing, no matter how obscure, he couldn't be kept away. It made sense, I guess, as there were always hundreds of attractive young women at these types of places—women who would be open to spending the evening in Eli's company. Tonight it was retro night, and a vamped-up version of "The Devil Inside" by INXS blasted through the club. I thought the song was appropriate for our purpose there.

I sat at a ledge stretching the length of a twenty-foot banister and looked down onto the dance floor. Hundreds of young, intoxicated patrons were moving suggestively to the music. The heady mixture of sweat, blood, and sex saturated the air like fog. *Eli*, I thought, as my exasperation grew. I cast my preternatural sight out over the throng of milling bodies until I found him on the far side of the building, sitting at a small table in a darkened corner. He had three young women with him, all made up and dressed in what could have easily passed for lingerie. I groaned inwardly. He must have caught my thought, as he looked up and gave a brief nod in my direction.

A few minutes later he was at my side, with two of the three girls in tow. Once they were all close, he pressed a cool kiss to my cheek. I watched the women for a reaction, and when there was none, I knew they were under Eli's influence. Over the past year we discovered he had superb mind control, so much so that he was easily able to control and influence those around him. He could also completely block other vampires from seeing into his mind, or from projecting their own thoughts onto him—at least the vampires we'd been in contact with.

Charles and I had stumbled across this fact accidentally. In one situation or another, we had both attempted to make contact with Eli when he was out of our sight, only to discover blankness. Charles, because of his age and strength, had a great ability to block out others, but not even he had the complete, iron shutdown that Eli possessed. I feared I was on the near opposite end of the spectrum, being a completely open book to the two of them when they wished to know my thoughts. As for the control of others, all vampires had some level of glamour to use over their victims, but Eli's talent seemed to reach the level of complete elimination of memories. It was a powerful tool—one that could have far-reaching and frightening possibilities.

I followed him and the women out to his car. We drove to a secluded area up in the hills, which overlooked the dark ocean below. It was a place that at night attracted teenagers wanting somewhere to make out and smoke dope, and in the day was frequented by nature lovers, hikers, and the like. Eli parked the car, and we all made our way into a small clearing. There was only one other car nearby. I hesitated for a moment, but the sounds coming from it indicated the occupants were too busy to have noticed our arrival.

As he took the hand of one of the women, he gave me a sly smile then led her a little ways away. Almost immediately they lowered themselves to the ground and embraced passionately. He winked at me over her shoulder, giving a brief flash of fangs. The other woman turned herself toward me with an expression so blank it was disturbing. I went to her, using one hand to cup her chin and the other to pull at her long hair until her head was forced over to the side far enough to allow perfect access to her throat. She was very pretty and couldn't have reached her twenty-fifth birthday yet.

Her vein throbbed, and I drank in her warmth and softness

against my body. I pressed my mouth to her throat, savouring the moment. Her demeanor was perfectly compliant to my needs, and the rush of her blood called to me. As my fangs sank into her flesh, she gave a small murmur of surprise. Her heartbeat quickened, and the blood flowed easily into my waiting mouth. As the liquid slid down my throat to my stomach, to be absorbed into the rest of my body, I swooned with a satisfaction beyond reason. Soon I felt her legs begin to buckle, and I withdrew my mouth, easing her gently to the ground.

Eli was already finished and waiting back at the car. He leaned with lazy nonchalance against the hood, and I smiled at how wonderful he looked under the moonlight. His long legs stretched out before him, and his cobalt blue eyes pierced the unforgiving darkness. A twinge of unexpected sadness gripped me as I realised all traces of the little boy I had loved as my own were gone.

Yet I couldn't deny that becoming a vampire agreed with him. He had always been an attractive man, but the change seemed to enhance the best of what he already possessed in life. He smiled as he caught me looking with appreciation in his direction. In a blur he was at my side, holding me in an intimate embrace.

"You look lovely tonight," he murmured in my ear.

I pressed my palm to his solid chest. "Save it for your conquests."

He relented with a shrug and moved to open the car door for me. "Whatever you say." The door had just closed and he was already seated in the driver's side. "Where to now?"

I looked out over the dark landscape. "Are you just going to leave them here?"

"They'll be all right in a few hours. They'll be a little weak, but there will be no lasting effects and no memory of how they got here."

"Okay. I don't care where we go, but maybe somewhere a little less frantic?"

"What about your place? What's going on there?" He swung the car onto the road with a soft purr of the engine and headed back in the direction of downtown.

I looked over to his profile. "I didn't think you liked my place."

"I didn't say I didn't like it. I said it was a little tame."

I rolled my eyes at his easygoing tone. The last time he had accompanied me to Carmilla's, he looked as if sticking pins in his eyes would be more enjoyable. My establishment was a far cry from the huge, crowded nightspots he usually frequented. It was a discrete, subdued type of club, which couldn't hold more than three hundred patrons at a time. Most of the time, the nights passed with less than half that number of paying customers. We did get quality performers, though I tended to book them in the blues, jazz, and rock-type categories.

"I have a new act tonight. She's a local girl, and she kind of reminds me of Amy Winehouse before all the drugs."

"Why not?" he responded easily, steering the car in the direction of my club. It was in the downtown entertainment district, just a little off the beaten path. About fifteen minutes later, he pulled in behind the building to my private parking spot, and I let us in the back entrance.

The door opened inward onto a narrow hallway with blood-red carpet. Openings led to the storage area, my office, a small dressing area for live acts, and an employee break room with washroom. I only employed three bartenders and a handful of wait staff. I kept the books myself, and an outside cleaning agency came through during the day when the place was closed.

We followed the hallway to its end, where a door led out into the space behind the bar. I nodded at Jared, my only full-time employee and de facto second-in-command, as we came through. I knew if I didn't manage to make it in one night, the place would be in capable hands. He smiled as I passed and nodded in Eli's direction.

We took a table against the wall, near the back of the dimly lit club, which was essentially one long oval-shaped space, with a small stage at one end and the bar and washrooms at the other. A series of booths and tables extended from the bar to about three-quarters of the way to the stage. Off to one side of the stage, on a slightly raised platform, was the DJ area, but tonight there was no DJ. All eyes were on the stage.

There, under a soft light, stood a delicate young woman, with waves of medium-brown hair hanging nearly to her waist. She was dressed part hippie flower child, part 1940s glamour, and wore almost no makeup, except for a dark-pink lipstick. Her features were child-like, and she couldn't have stood more than five feet tall, but her voice was larger than life, deep and soulful, and powerful enough to fill the space. The soft caress of her voice crawled along my skin, and I could see the other listeners were equally affected. Wordlessly, Eli placed his hand on top of mine.

We sat there through the remainder of her set, feelings of joy and heartbreak invoked by the caliber of her performance. Mary-Jane's time on stage meandered its way through everything from Nina Simone to Pat Benatar. She performed a particularly gut-wrenching rendition of "Total Eclipse of the Heart" that had the hairs on my arms standing on end. When finished, she gave a simple bow and left the stage to thunderous applause. I made a mental note to book her for a regular gig, before her talent received so much notice she would no longer play at small venues like Carmilla's.

"Wow, she was great! You don't hear singing like that much anymore. She's a real throwback." Eli's words were full of enthusiasm and appreciation, and I was in complete agreement. She was just what the place needed. "What's her name again?"

"Mary-Jane Stillwater."

He gave me an incredulous look. "You're kidding?"

"Nope. I even saw her driver's license. That's her real name."

"Sweet. You're going to have to introduce us." His blue eyes twinkled at the suggestion.

I raised my eyebrow and frowned at the implication of his words. "Let's go try to catch her before she leaves, but listen to me, hands off. She's working here, and I'd like to keep it that way. She could be the catch this club needs."

Eli looked back at me with mock innocence. I couldn't help but smile at the puppy dog eyes he gave me. "Oh, course. I only meant that I'd like to express my appreciation of her singing talent."

"Uh-huh." I walked away, leaving the conversation at that.

Eli followed at my heels as we made our way back around the bar to the employees' hallway. Jared's gaze tracked our progress, and I wondered fleetingly if he was picking up on something from us. He was one of the few humans I interacted with regularly, and being in close contact like that was bound to have some effects. Even the most closed-minded of people got some "vibes" from being in the presence of vampires. God forbid if he might be attracted to me, or Eli, for that matter. It was San Francisco, after all. I gave him a small smile, and he returned to the customers sitting at the bar.

Just as we were about to pass through the doorway, I caught the peripheral image of a young woman sitting near the far end of the bar. Her profile was to me as she sipped at a drink in her hand. Her attention was directed at two other women standing by her side. I didn't have a clear view, but she looked startlingly familiar. Something about her jaw line and the high cheekbones reminded me of a member of my family I hadn't seen in almost twenty-five years. I shook my head at my own silliness and realised Eli was regarding me quizzically. I continued, but the incident buried itself somewhere in my mind.

We found ourselves back in the narrow hallway, and I could see that the door from the adjoining hallway connected to the stage was open. I heard movement in the small dressing room and knew the songstress was packing her things to leave. I tapped lightly on the closed door and waited for her to answer. When she opened, I had one of those rare moments as a short, adult woman where I got to look down on someone. God, she was tiny, even more so up close than she had appeared on stage.

"Oh, Rachel, hi. Come on in." Her voice was surprisingly deep for such a delicate-looking creature and had a wonderful raspy quality to it. The door opened a bit wider, and the two of us entered the small room.

Mary-Jane's eyes quickly flicked to Eli, and as I looked back in his direction, I found him smiling. "This is my cousin Eli. He helps me around the club." It was the latest story we had developed to explain our connection and living arrangements.

"Nice to meet you, Eli. Did you enjoy the show?" She took a few steps back into the room and lowered herself onto a chair covered in red crushed velvet. With the lacquered furniture, the hazy lighting and splashes of red, the room reminded me of an Asian-themed bordello.

"Loved it," he said and flopped down on a black leather sofa close to the door. His attractiveness didn't fail to register with me or Mary-Jane.

I remained standing. "It's why we're here, actually. We were wondering if you would be interested in some type of regular performance here. I'm not sure what your schedule is like, but I'd love to see you here weekly, or at least a couple of times a month."

A soft blush spread across her face, and her heartbeat quickened. "Really? I can't believe it. Um, this is great. I'm pretty flexible. I mean I play at a couple of other places, but nothing regular. What are you thinking?" I could see a sprinkling of tiny freckles across the bridge of her nose.

"What about Saturday nights?" I suggested.

She didn't hesitate a second before answering. "Perfect. Shouldn't interfere with school or my job."

"What are you taking?" Eli interjected from the couch.

"I'm a liberal arts major, part-time for now, and I work at a delivery service. I'm trying to save up to be able to afford full-time schooling next year, you know if the music thing doesn't work out well enough to keep the bills paid."

"Aren't your parents helping out with your tuition?" I asked.

A tight look crossed her face. "They're not really in the picture."

I decided to let it slide. It really wasn't any of my business. "Well, we should settle on a price then."

We spent a few minutes working out the details, including her fee and the use of back-up musicians. Eli even offered to fill in on the piano if needed, something that he had become skilled at under Giovanni's tutelage. Mary-Jane seemed impressed, both with the fact he could play and that he offered his services. With a shake of hands, the deal was sealed, and we left the girl to pack her belongings.

Eli gave one last lingering look then followed me back out to the car. "She smells wonderful," he said once we were inside.

"Remember what I said."

He smiled slyly. "Of course. Where to, my lady?"

By then it was nearly one in the morning, and I had had enough of the club scene for one night. "Why don't we just head home?"

He nodded in agreement and revved the engine to life. As we pulled out of the parking lot and around the corner of the building onto the main street, I caught another glimpse of the woman who had been seated at the bar.

This time I saw her full on, since she turned in our direction as the car neared. It felt like time slowed down; our movement stretched out from the actual mere seconds it took to pass her. I knew the windows were too darkly tinted for her to be able to see me, but I had a clear, unobstructed view of her. A cold shiver ran down my spine as I looked at a face that was so much like the young niece I'd left behind all those years before. I pressed my hand against the dark glass, seeing but not quite believing.

Eli immediately noticed my reaction. "What's wrong?"

I snapped my head back at the sound of his voice. I blinked, and Giovanni's blue eyes appeared in my mind. My eyes flew open again. "Nothing, I think. Just the weirdest sense of déjà vu."

"What do you mean?" The tiniest note of concern had crept into his voice.

"That woman we just passed, she looks just like I imagine my niece Danica would look now. She was seven when I left almost twenty-five years ago. She has the same features. It's just a coincidence, I'm sure." Though to myself I didn't sound so sure.

"Do you want to go back, maybe talk to her?"

Did I? "No, forget about it. I'm just being silly. The resemblance just sort of spooked me out. It can't be her. She's back in Canada somewhere. Let's go home. I got a new book in that I wanted to show you." I knew the mention of new information would distract him, as he was almost as obsessed with the pursuit of knowledge as I was. How many countless hours had we spent pouring over books, taking private audiences with top academics, and searching the internet?

Minutes later, the road to our house came into view. We lived just outside the city, in an area populated by business moguls, movie stars, and other well-to-dos. Our home was hidden from view by a naturally occurring hillside common to the local geography. The almost two-mile drive to the house cut through the hillside toward an electric fence running the perimeter of the ten-acre property. We stopped at the console, where Eli punched in the current code, and the gates swung inward. Once inside, we punched in another code and waited until the gates closed again. The funds allocated to our security was money well spent. It was nearly impossible to approach the property without detection. Sheer walls of rock over two hundred feet high and electric fences surrounded the house, with cameras, motion detectors, and a regular patrol by our security service providers.

Eli parked the car in the garage, and together we entered the main house. Inside the front doors was a grand foyer with double, curved staircases rising to the second floor. The walls of the main hallway were adorned with precious pieces of Giovanni's art, a link to keep us close to the loved one we had so tragically lost. I stopped, as I often did, at the portrait of Eli and myself, which Giovanni had drawn on the first night we took him into our lives as a boy. I saw the features of the garden in the background and was reminded of a house and a country I loved so dearly. The sight of Eli's sweet boyish face was a stark reminder of all that had been sacrificed for our current moment in time.

"I'm going to have bath, and then we can take a look at that book," I called back over my shoulder as I headed to my bedroom at the back of the house. We all had rooms on the ground floor, which had underground access to the garage and another outbuilding on the far reaches of the property. The upstairs ones were really just for show. We had even converted two of them into a home office and library.

I punched in the code to open the door to my bedroom, and began to pull off my clothing as soon as I entered. I smelled of blood and smoke from the club, and I felt the irrational tickling of being "unclean." A hot bath would certainly get rid of the lingering aromas and help to soothe my tender psyche. Even after these months since Giovanni's death, I still felt raw, as if there was something broken inside of me that could never be fixed. Some days I could push further than others, but today was not one of them. I was drained.

My bathroom was one of my favourite things about the whole property. It was larger than many homes' entire floor space and verged on being a work of art. The previous owners had spared no expense or effort. They had used the best marbles and travertine and installed faucets made of gold. An enormous vanity took up an entire wall, and mirrors rose to the top of the ten-foot ceiling. I took a moment to look at my naked body before filling the tub with near scalding water. I added luxurious oils that smelled of rose petals and vanilla.

An appreciative sigh escaped my lips as I lowered myself into the heavenly comfort of the hot water. I closed my eyes and let my mind wander to pleasant memories and fantasies that couldn't possibly come true. I let myself experience *his* kisses and *his* smile, not wanting to open my eyes to a world where they no longer existed. Then, as something dark began to edge its way into my thoughts of our time in England, I forced myself to the present. I grabbed a sea sponge from where it rested on the tub's edge and began to scrub at my skin, which the heated water had tinged with pink.

"Why don't you let me get your back?" Eli's husky voice sounded from the doorway.

I turned to find him clad only in jeans, his hard, pale upper body exposed to the soft lighting. His hair had grown out—something that does actually happen to vampires, and it just brushed the top of his shoulders. A smile tugged at the corner of his mouth, and his eyes smoldered.

"Eli, this has to stop..." I turned away, a lump of shame catching in my throat.

I had barely moved when Eli's hands slid down my arm, reaching for the sponge clenched in my hand. I let him pluck it from my grasp then felt him rubbing it across my shoulders. I moved forward to allow him access to my back.

There were so many things about our relationship that

bothered me, yet I was weak in putting a stop to what I knew was inappropriate, and I was conflicted because of my own need. I knew I did and would love him as much as I always had. I just couldn't give him the part of me he was so desperate to have. That part had died with Giovanni.

His fingers brushed aside the long, wet tendrils of my hair, causing them to spill forward over my shoulder. He pressed his still-warm lips to the spot where my shoulder met the base of my neck, lingering there. His mouth softly pulled away, and I heard clothing hit the floor. He eased his lanky body into the tub, and a small lap of waves washed over me as his weight displaced the water. I found his smiling face across from me in the hot and sweet-smelling tub.

"Why do you keep pursuing this, Eli?" My voice was heavy with emotion.

He shrugged one shoulder and gave me a wistful look. "Because I love you, and because I know you're still hurting and that you need comfort. I don't want you to continue with your life in misery when the chance for happiness is right in front of you."

"You know I love you, too, that you are a part of me. It kills me to think of not having you in my life, and of not being close to you, but no matter what, my heart will always belong to Giovanni."

For the first time since any of this had come up between us, real anger flickered across his face. "Giovanni is gone, Rachel, but you're still here."

"I can't help how I feel." I echoed the words he said to me after Giovanni's death.

Silence settled between us for a long time, and I could feel his struggle to gain control of his anger and frustration.

"I could make you happy," he said very quietly.

"You do make me very happy, but it's not the same thing as love, not the kind of love that you want anyway. Jesus, Eli, you could have any woman you want, and I don't mean by using your power over them. You're beautiful, kind, and intelligent. You're fiercely loyal. Any woman would be lucky to have you."

"You're the only one I ever wanted." He was looking at me

with that savage, unabashed longing I knew all too well. His body moved with fluid grace as he closed the space between us. His hand slid up my waist to my breast, and his thumb rubbed over my nipple until it was hard and erect. Looking directly into my eyes, he focused on me while his other hand found its way between my legs. His fingers slipped inside my body. "Tell me you don't want it," he said with a husky, seductive voice.

I was powerless against his touch. My body betrayed me, responding with eagerness to his hands on my flesh. Slipping his fingers out of me, he moved my hand over to his own body, where I found him hard and ready. His lips pressed down onto my own before I could respond. I loathed myself for my weakness, but I needed some kind of pleasure, however fleeting, to take me away from the everyday emptiness that filled me. His strong arms lifted me up and out of the tub. He carried me to my bed with a trail of water dripping from our naked bodies onto the floor.

He dropped me onto my back, his body landing firmly on top. I wrapped my legs around him, making myself open and available to his penetration, and when it came, I could not suppress a satisfied moan. His mouth and tongue moved hungrily over my neck up to my lips. He pounded into me as I said his name over and over again.

"Tell me this isn't what you need?" Eli's voice in my ear was tight with arousal.

"Eli, please," I managed, despite the incessant throbbing need that rocked my body. He brought me up to and over the edge of fulfillment twice before letting go. He stayed tightly pressed against my body, hands running through my hair.

"This isn't right. This isn't the way things were supposed to be." A tear slipped out of the corner of my eye.

He pulled himself up onto one elbow. "Maybe not, but this is reality. This is how things are, and there's no reason we can't make the best of it, make each other happy." He pressed a soft kiss to my cheek and as he pulled away wiped the tear from my face.

"But sex isn't love." As soon as the words were out of my mouth, regret bit me.

He leapt from the bed with lightning speed to disappear into the bathroom. When he returned, he was redressed in the jeans he had worn in earlier. He leaned against the doorframe, and it pained me to see such hostility on the face of someone I cared so much for.

"I'm not a child anymore, Rachel, and I certainly know the difference between sex and love. Sex is what I get from the women I pick in the clubs or at school, and love is what I feel for you. You love me, too, at least part of you does. You just won't let yourself be open to it. You feel like you'll betray Giovanni if you let anyone else into your heart, and it's not true. I know that he will always be your true love, but I could happily settle for second best! If you would give just a little, I would drop everything else…. I want to be your one and only." His voice dropped from a thunderous outburst to a chilling quiet. Without question I was hurting him terribly.

"I'm sorry, I don't mean to hurt you. I just can't give you what you want, and I don't know if I will ever be able to. How can I ask you to hold out for something that may never happen?" I started to sob in earnest, and his face softened in reaction to my pain. "And I know that I lean on you and expect you to be there when I need you. I know that it's wrong to let you into my bed, but the times with you are the only ones where I feel something other than grief or emptiness."

He returned to my side on the bed and pulled me into his strong arms. "I'm sorry, too. I shouldn't have pushed you. I know you're still hurting. I can wait. Let's face it, if there was ever someone who has the time to wait, it's me."

I cried quietly against his chest for a few minutes before I was able to pull myself together enough to speak again. "You really are the most important thing in the world to me, and I'm honored to have your love. Right now, I'm just not deserving of it."

"It is what it is." He squeezed me tightly to him then stood to leave. "I think you need some time to yourself. I'll be in the library if you want to join me later."

I watched him walk from my bedroom and knew, despite his kind words, he was both hurt and completely frustrated with me. I curled into a ball on my enormous bed, pulling the silk comforter in around my naked body. But I didn't break down completely, a first in the many similar moments since Giovanni's death. The tears I spilled during my conversation with Eli did not continue.

I felt irritable and impossibly alone, even though there was a man upstairs willing to pledge his eternal life to me. I stared up at the incomplete portrait of myself Giovanni had been working on when he was killed. It hung over my bed as a constant reminder of everything that had happened, and could never be again. I let my eyes slip shut, and in my mind saw the beauty of Giovanni's face.

I sighed, and tried to push away the painful past for the present. Just as I made the decision to dress and join Eli upstairs, a sickening wave of unease washed over my body. A strange, achy prickling raced along my spine. An incredible pressure flared in my brain, pushing phantom tendrils outward against my eyes and ears. A horrible, shrill keening filled my mind, and I fell over the edge of the bed to the floor from the suddenness of the attack.

Rachel!

In seconds both Charles and Eli were at my side, and the pain abruptly vanished. I found myself sprawled across the gold carpet of my bedroom floor. They both knelt—Charles wearing his ever-present mask of blankness, with only the slightest touch of tightness to his emerald eyes, and Eli obviously concerned, all signs of the anger that had been there only moments before now gone.

"What's going on? You were screaming like a banshee!"

Charles handed me a throw from a nearby chair as I pulled myself into a seated position.

Dizziness and confusion gripped me. "I don't really know what happened. I was just getting up to dress, and then there was this terrible pain in my head...I guess I fell off the bed."

Eli helped me to my feet, and I felt like a complete fool with the two of them standing there staring at me. "Well, you scared the crap out of me," Eli said.

"Sorry, I'm okay. Give me a sec and I'll be up to the library."

Eli nodded and left the room. Charles lingered by the door, eyeing me with concern.

"Seriously, Charles, I'm okay. I was just thinking about Giovanni, and I was really upset…"

"Yes, of course. Giovanni." He paused, thin lips pursed in thought. "You know I could not help but hear the conversation you just had with Eli." I cringed inwardly. Of course he heard. His hearing was even better than ours. "And I do not mean to rub salt in the wound, as they say, but he has a point. I do not think for one minute that Giovanni would expect you to carry on with the remainder of your existence in misery. He would want you to find happiness again."

"What can I say, Charles? I'm doing the best I can." It was the absolute, unrestrained truth.

"Maybe some night soon we could have a talk, just the two of us?" His eyes were bright, but his expression frustratingly unreadable.

Before I could even open my mouth to answer, he was gone from my room. I didn't know what to make of his request. He had never been one for conversation. Though I knew he was making the effort, expressing himself and sharing concern were not his strengths. Yet, he had a point. If the three of us were going to continue to live under the same roof, then Eli and I would have to learn some discretion.

I joined Eli in the library, and aside from an awkward first few minutes, it seemed the incident was behind us. We spent the remaining hours of darkness reviewing an ancient text I acquired through the black market. It dealt with an obscure legend from an Indus Valley Civilization about a woman, who conquered death after ingesting the blood of a dying "great cat." The details were vague, and the particular translation I purchased, though genuine and extremely old, was many generations from the events in question—another tale that may or may not mean anything.

CHAPTER 2

The next few weeks passed by without incident. Some strain remained between Eli and me, as evidenced by the increased amount of time that he spent away from me. I didn't begrudge him that. If anything, I was pleased he was being more independent and proactive with the course of his own existence, and we still saw each other every day, and sometimes spent time together like we used to. I needed to not rely on him as much as I had been, and he needed to let go of his fantasy.

Charles and Eli were both correct in their own right. Giovanni was gone, had been for more than a year. I was still here, and being miserable wasn't going to help anyone, and it certainly wasn't going to bring him back. I made an internal decision to focus on my club, write, and to pick up where I had left off in the search for the origins of our kind. It was something Eli and I could work on together, something to focus on that was more than just our relationship.

When I awoke, I bathed and dressed for a night at the club. I came out into the main house and discovered, as I did most recent nights, that the men were already gone. I made my way to the spotless kitchen and into the pantry, where there was an additional hidden section to store our personal type of sustenance. Charles had secured a provider for freshly taken blood donations—I didn't ask how, and he didn't share—and we kept enough on hand to feed us all for several weeks, if needed. I tried to use it several times a week, leaving my feedings from humans few and far between. I could have taken my nourishment this way exclusively, but my predatory nature tended to come to the surface even when I didn't want it to. I needed the control and dominance, and yes, sometimes I needed to feel another's fear. The fear I invoked in others, and Eli's touch, were the only things allowing me to feel anything deeply. Everything else passed in shades of grey.

I arrived early enough that the club was not yet open. Inside, Jared was in the stockroom taking his weekly count, which I knew I would find on my desk by the end of the night, along with an order for whatever we might be low on. Business had seen a decided upswing since the introduction of Mary-Jane as Carmilla's house act. Through word of mouth, I was approached by other local bands wanting to audition, and even landed a well-known comic for a series of appearances. Things were definitely looking up on the business end.

I stepped in behind Jared in the cramped storage room, enjoying how singularly focused he seemed on the task at hand. "Hey, Jared, how's it going?"

A bottle he had been holding slipped from his hand and crashed on the bare stone floor. "Jesus, Rachel, you shouldn't sneak up on a guy like that." He bent down to retrieve the broken pieces, and the fumes from the spirits filled the space between us. "Look at what I did."

"Don't worry about it. It was an accident." I lowered to help him and noticed for the first time how long and nimble his fingers were, like a pianist's.

He snatched up a large chunk of the glass, slicing the edge of his outermost finger in the process. A line of blood welled up from the wound, and its scent erased all of the liquor from my notice. He pressed the wound to his mouth, sucking at the cut lightly. He gave me a strange look, and I realised I was staring at him with a fierce intensity. "You should make sure to get that cleaned properly."

"I will. I think I'll use the broom to get the rest of the mess." He moved away from me to grab the broom from the rack where all the cleaning instruments hung. As he returned and started to sweep, he asked, "Was there something you wanted to talk to me about?"

I shook my head. "No, not really, I just don't often make it here this early, and I thought we might take the opportunity to talk. I mean you've been here almost a year now, and I don't really know much about you."

He bent down to move the pile of glass onto the dustpan. "What did you want to know?"

I couldn't be sure, but it sounded like the tiniest bit of unease had crept into his voice. I laughed softly. "Don't worry, it isn't an interrogation. I just thought since we work together, that it would be a good idea to get to know one another better."

The tinkling of broken glass falling into the waste basket could be heard before he spoke again. "Okay."

I was picking up on some strange images from his mind. A series of emotions, suspicion, annoyance, and interest, overlapped with disjointed and seemingly random images of various people and places. His mind was often closed off or completely focused on what he was doing moment by moment. He was a very unique individual, who gave me neither good nor bad "vibes." A lot of the time, the things I did pick up on didn't make any sense, at least not to me.

I couldn't actually read minds, nor tune into people's internal dialogues. Some people were very open, but most were available only to varying degrees. Strong emotions like lust, anger, and fear were easiest to pick up on, and some people possessed different levels of psychic awareness, from clairvoyance to empathy.

I gained the impression that Jared picked up on others' emotions, and more importantly *intentions*, quite easily.

"Why don't I let you finish up here, and we can talk in my office when you drop off the forms," I said.

He met my eyes then, and I noticed his were such a light brown, they verged on being yellow. I had been expecting blue, I think, to match the pale colour of his hair. He was one of those rare people who retained their blond hair into their adulthood. Jared was a nice-looking guy, in an understated, California surfer-boy kind of way. He was of average height, well-defined muscles in his arms and a nice smile with a slightly chipped front tooth. "Okay, I should be done in about fifteen."

I tried one last tug at his mind and received a cold mental flutter in return. I saw an image of what appeared to be Jared as a small boy and a woman with the same odd-coloured eyes. He flinched, and his one eye twitched ever so slightly. "See you then."

After entering my office, I closed the door behind me and settled down to the paperwork Jared had piled in my inbox—bills, bookings, deposit slips, and a few weeks' worth of daily receipts. I decided to start with the latter, as I knew the books did not accurately reflect the club's current financial status. I worked through them quickly and was just starting on reconciliation with the bank statement when Jared knocked at the door.

"Come in," I called out and pushed the pile of papers off to the side.

Jared entered and closed the door behind him. He moved to the chair opposite the desk from where I sat and lowered himself into it with a fluid movement. Strange, I had never noticed how graceful his movements were before—not that he didn't project a masculine front, because he did. He just had a nice way about him, no overly-done machismo or strutting about.

He took a moment to look around the small space before giving me his full attention. "Oh, so here are the counts and an order for next week." He handed over the sheets of paper, and his fingers brushed the side of my hand. He recoiled as if he had received a nasty shock.

I decided not to comment on his reaction. "Thanks. I'll look at them after I get through all this other stuff." I waved to indicate the piles of paper. "Thank you also for keeping everything so organised for me, it really makes the bookkeeping much easier."

"No problem."

He was making it clear that it was not going to be easy to get information out of him with his short, concise answers. I leaned back in my chair. "Well, I guess we could start off by me telling you a little about myself. I think you're aware that I just moved back to the States last year, from Europe, where I had been living for several years. I came over with my cousin, Eli." Jared gave the slightest reaction at his name.

"I bought the club about a year ago. What else can I tell you?"

He shifted slightly in his seat. "Why were you in Europe? You don't sound European."

"No, I'm not. I'm Canadian, actually. Well, originally at least. I was in Europe with my..." My voice trailed off as my eyes moistened in reaction to my pain. I cut the crying off cold. It would be difficult to explain blood-tinged tears. I came back with a much stronger voice. "I was in Europe with my husband, but he was killed in an unfortunate accident. So, I thought it might be best for a fresh start."

I felt as much as I saw a noticeable change in his demeanor. "I'm sorry, I didn't know."

"There's no way that you could have." I smiled through my grief, though the image of Giovanni under attack was burning its way to the surface.

"You seem very young. Were you married for very long? I'm sorry, that sounded real insensitive."

"No, it's fine, kind of a compliment. So, to answer you, yes, we were married for quite some time, and I'm older than you probably think I am."

"Okay. So how do you like San Francisco?" He tapped his one foot lightly against the Persian carpet.

"I love it, actually, lots of interesting people here, and what about you?"

"What about me? Not much to tell I'm afraid." The tapping increased in tempo.

"Well, were you born here? Go to school here?" I met his eyes, and he licked his lips. His heartbeat picked up.

"Yep, born and raised. I went to school here, finished high school at least, and have been bar-tending pretty much ever since."

My voice remained friendly. "And your parents? Any siblings?"

He was visibly distressed at the mention of parents, but I didn't acknowledge my observations. "Siblings, no, not biological ones anyway. Um, I never knew my dad. I guess he took off before I was even born, and my mom, well, she died when I was still a kid. I was in foster homes afterwards, and I haven't stayed close to anyone I knew through that stuff." His attention shifted to something beyond where I sat.

"I'm sorry. I didn't mean to stir up any bad feelings, but I get it, I'm an orphan myself. All my family has been gone for some time now." I looked at him, until he met my eyes with discomfort.

"That so? What about Eli?"

Nice catch. "Well, he's a distant cousin, but family still, I guess. Anyway, I just wanted to let you know that I've been very pleased with you and the way you stay on top of things around here. As far as I'm concerned, this job could turn out to be very rewarding for you. I take hard work and loyalty very seriously." I never had the level of effect on humans that Giovanni, Charles, and Eli did, but I saw a slight slackening to his mouth when I stressed the word "loyalty."

"Well, good, that's great. I really like it here, too, good customers and good music."

A slight tingling whispered along my scalp, and I had to fight against turning my attention in the direction of the hallway. "Okay, well, I'm sure you still have things to do before we open, so I'll talk with you later,"

"Cool." As he opened the door, I caught sight of Eli and Mary-Jane chatting in the hallway. For some reason, the sight of their easy exchange soured my stomach. Eli looked up and winked in my direction. As he turned to enter the office, he touched Mary-Jane's arm, and she shivered.

The door closed behind him, and Eli sat in the chair Jared had just vacated. He never seemed to tire of being able to move with his preternatural speed.

"To what do I owe the pleasure?" I asked, taking in the slight flush to his cheeks and knowing he had recently fed.

He twirled a lock of hair absently about one of his fingers. "Nothing. I just haven't been here in a few weeks, and things have been somewhat strained." He stopped playing with his hair and turned his piercing baby blues in my direction. "I don't like the way things are between us right now."

"Me neither," I answered. "You're my best friend, but I feel like there's a wall between us."

"So, can we make a conscious effort to get past it?"

"Yes, I'd like that."

"Good." Then he was standing at the door. "I have plans to

meet up with some guys from school. I'll see you at home later?"

I met his half smile with one of my own. "Of course, don't do anything I wouldn't do."

"Never." And in my mind, *I love you.* Then he was gone, before I had the chance to respond.

After about another hour alone in my office, the books were up to date, and I was pleasantly surprised to have found a significant increase in the numbers of customers and a rise in profits. While the club had never been a lemon, it hadn't been the most lucrative of investments either. I was pleased to see that perseverance and some chances had paid off. No small part of that had been Jared's single-minded attention to details, and his dedication to the club's smooth operation. The Christmas season was sneaking up rather quickly, and I could envision him finding a nice cheque in his stocking this year.

Mary-Jane had started her set a few minutes before, and now that business was taken care of, I decided to go out and enjoy the music. I took a glass of chilled white wine to a table, where I sat alone. The wine was more for appearance's sake, though I did allow myself a few sips. The club was almost full to capacity that night, something I had never seen since the first night of my ownership.

The crowd was completely absorbed in Mary-Jane's performance, swaying and singing along. A full band backed her up this time, not just a guitar player and pianist like the first time I saw her perform. The bassist caught my eye, and I found my focus drifting back to him throughout the set.

He was wearing low-slung, skinny jeans and a plain white wife-beater with a black leather vest over top. Every square inch of skin on his arms was covered with tattoos. He appeared to be in his late twenties, but his face had a boyish quality to it. He was definitely attractive, what I would call a "pretty" boy. The odd time that he smiled, his whole face lit up and made him almost breathtaking. I wondered if he and Mary-Jane were involved.

As the last song wrapped up, a cool hand touched my arm. I looked up, expecting Eli, surprised to find Charles standing there instead. He'd never set foot in the club before. "I thought we might have that conversation now. You have an office, I presume?" His green eyes were cold, his demeanor stiff.

"Yes. Follow me." I stood and felt him at my back like the cold breath of death. Charles still had moments where he freaked me out a bit, though I don't think it was his intention to affect me that way. He simply was who he was, and old habits die hard.

We made our way through the crowd like salmon fighting their way upstream. As we finally reached the nearest end of the bar time seemed to slow down. I nodded in Jared's direction, our eyes meeting briefly as Charles and I made our way past him. I heard disjointed snippets of conversation and laughter, the tinkling of ice cubes in glasses. Then I saw her again.

The woman I saw about a month previously, the one who reminded me so much of my niece, Danica, was seated on the second-to-last stool from the office end of the bar. I stopped short, and Charles pressed against my back. Slowly the woman turned, as though in response to my stare, and I saw her clearly. The sense of familiarity I experienced was like a slap to the face. She resembled not only the niece I had known as a child, but also myself. We shared the same eye colour, the same slight body, and narrow shape of the face.

Then with a whirl, the motion of the room fast-forwarded back to a normal pace, and the woman quickly looked away. I turned to find Charles also watching her intently, his usual blank expression locked in place. His gaze slid sideways, and he frowned. When I took his hand, he flinched, and I led him to the employee side of the bar. The woman noticed our movement and leaned in to speak with another woman on the stool beside her. Without being obvious, she glanced in our direction; then they both stood to leave.

"Follow her," I whispered in Charles's ear. Without waiting for his reply, I moved toward the front door. Stepping out into the cool, fall air, I was overwhelmed with the melancholy memories of the same season so many years before. The climate was different, but the feeling was still the same.

I looked up and down the street, searching for the woman among the crowds. A natural break in the passage of bodies occurred, and I caught a glimpse of her and her companion as they rounded a corner two blocks down. I didn't look back, but I knew Charles was close on my heels.

I stopped at the corner to peer down the street, hoping to remain off their radar. Charles and I kept a safe distance as the two travelled about a mile away from the club, moving farther from the crowded business district to a residential area close to the university. They stopped in front of a series of townhouses, and I watched as the other woman gave the one I was following a brief hug and a wave goodbye. The woman who held my interest continued for another few blocks before stopping in front of a beautiful three-story building that had been a single residence once upon a time. Then it was broken into three separate flats, as had many similar buildings in the area. It appeared as though all three units were accessible by the main front entrance. She unlocked the massive door and gave a hesitant look behind her before pulling the door closed.

Charles and I remained safely out of sight, lurking in the shadows like stereotypical creatures of the night. After remaining there for several minutes in silence, Charles put his thoughts into words. "What are we doing here?" Since we had been cohabitating, he very rarely projected his thoughts onto me or tried to communicate with me telepathically.

I didn't really know, so I just stared back at him as I tried to formulate a reasonable explanation. "I'm not sure, to be honest. It's just that the woman we followed here seems so familiar to me..."

Charles nodded. "She does look remarkably like you."

It got my attention. "Do you think so? So, it's not just my imagination?"

"Not at all; it's the first thought that came to mind when I saw her in the bar." He looked up at the building, and I experienced a chill as some sort of emotion washed out from him. "Do you suppose she's a relative?" His emerald green eyes flashed like lasers in the cool, dark night.

"I don't know. I mean, I'm not aware of any relatives who live in this area. I had a very small family to begin with, and all members I knew about lived in Canada."

"You've been gone a long time, and things change."

All too true; a quarter of a century had flown by in a heartbeat, and I really couldn't be certain about what happened to the remains of my family. I hadn't checked in a long time, as I always thought it was best to let all of that part of my life go. Maybe it was finding its own way of creeping back in. "You're right. I can't honestly say whether that woman is a relative or not."

A gust of air fluttered across my skin, as Charles's sudden movement caused a vacuum in the space between us. "Wait here," he called out as he left, and I had no choice but to remain where I was. He was gone less than five minutes before returning, uncharacteristically pleased. "She needs to remember to lock her windows."

I tapped my foot impatiently. "And?"

"And her name is Danica—"

"Armstrong," I cut in.

He didn't indicate any surprise at my interjection and continued. "Yes. She has a university employee ID pass, and several degrees posted on her walls. She lives alone, has a cat, and is very tidy. It's about all I got in that quick a perusal but shouldn't think it would be too difficult to find out more, if you wish. So, she is someone you know, I gather?"

"Someone I knew. She's my niece, my brother's daughter. The last time I saw her, she was seven years old. I wonder what she's doing in San Francisco."

"There are several good schools in the area, and she seems academia-directed. Perhaps she came here to study or simply for a job. Secure teaching positions in post-secondary education are few and far between."

To say I was rattled was an understatement. "Let's go. I'm going to have to think about it."

Charles stared back blankly, and I took it as his answer. His silences could speak volumes. We moved swiftly through the night, making it to the house in a matter of minutes. Eli had not yet returned, and I didn't expect him for several hours. When he was out with "friends," he didn't appear until close to sunrise.

Once inside, I followed Charles to a sitting room just off the main foyer. It was a little-used room. I hadn't even bothered to redecorate since we took possession of the house. I sat stiffly on a satin-draped loveseat with Charles opposite me and was eerily reminded of the first night we met. He leaned back and looked off into space. "I'm not sure how to begin." His voice was like melted butter, but sometimes the cadence of his impeccable upper-crust accent wore at my nerves.

"Well, I have no idea what this is about, so I'm not much help."

He paused, green eyes meeting my own before he continued. "As you are well aware, both Giovanni and I have a large number of contacts and business associates throughout the world. Well, I have been tapping into these since we established ourselves here a year ago. I have gone through all of Giovanni's personal papers, accounts and so forth, and have compiled a list of contacts separate and above the ones I already possessed. From it I have systematically contacted everyone and have set into motion all of these people to one common task."

"Okay, but I still don't know what you're talking about."

He stood suddenly and, with hands clasped behind his back, began to pace the length of the room. "I think it is time for us to go on the offensive, and by that I mean, I think it is time that we began to pursue the Desmarais ourselves, instead of waiting for them to catch up with us again."

I found myself on my feet also. "What do you mean?"

"I have set all my contacts to tracking this group down. I have people infiltrating their leagues, engaging in surveillance and studying the group's every move, and I have managed to secure the current location of the group's leader, Jean-Claude, and also the location of their two main meeting places and research facilities. By having our allies in all these strategic places, I think that we could develop a plan to wipe them off the face of the earth in one fell swoop." His face became quite animated as he spoke, showing more expression than I had ever seen from him.

I sat again, mulling over the information and letting it settle in my brain. Turning the tables on the Desmarais? Could it work? The more I thought about it, the more I liked the idea. "So, what did you have in mind?"

"I think we should take the next six months and watch these places, day and night, recording every movement, getting every name. And, in doing so, we will surely find a flaw of some kind, some weakness we can exploit to our advantage, and then we will strike. There may need to be a few subsequent sweeps to make sure everyone is eliminated, but I think it will work."

"And you think that you can count on all these contacts to keep quiet and to pull through when needed?"

"I think that both Giovanni and I have been extremely careful in choosing our allies, and I have called in a couple of favours from our vampire counterpoints as well." Charles appeared somewhat miffed that I would question his judgment.

That statement surprised me. "Really? I thought you didn't mingle with others of our kind?"

"I said that I didn't believe in love and long-term companionship, but I do know others of our kind, and I am on reasonable terms with a few."

That statement reminded me how little I knew about Charles. Other than how he was changed and where he had come from originally, I knew next to nothing. Charles wasn't big on sharing. "Wow, it's a lot to take in, especially after what we discovered tonight with my niece and this situation with Eli."

Charles sat beside me and patted my hand awkwardly. He wasn't one for affection, either, and that simple touch was a huge gesture on his part. "I think it will be good for all of us. It will give us closure, and maybe we can show others of our kind out there that we can be allies when the times call for it."

I think it was the most we ever conversed with each other at one time in all the months we lived together. "So, those times when you disappear for a day or two, it's what you have been doing?"

"Yes. I wanted to be certain that it could work before I dared breathe a word about it to you or Eli. No sense stirring up unnecessary pain."

I couldn't help myself. I threw my arms around his thin frame, squeezing him tightly, and though he did not return the embrace, he didn't pull away either. For the first time in a year, the pressure on my heart eased, and I experienced the first real moment of happiness I could recall since witnessing Giovanni's murder. I pulled back, and he instantly relaxed.

"Thank you, Charles. It is amazing, and it has to happen. It has to. You know that Eli and I will do whatever is needed?" I couldn't help but grin when I added, "And I want to be there to crush that bastard's skull with my bare hands!"

Charles gave me his icy smile. "I expected nothing less."

He left me alone then. I sat by myself for several hours, playing out scenario after scenario in my mind, until I heard the approach of Eli's car. Soon the familiar sound of the security code being punched in touched my ear, and I drew comfort from the fact that he was home and safe.

"What are you doing in here?" he asked from the doorway. I turned, warmed by his familiar smile, and motioned for him to sit with me.

"I have a lot to tell you."

CHAPTER 3

Several weeks passed after Charles and I discovered Danica's identity, and Charles shared his plan for the destruction of the Desmarais with me. I didn't see Danica again after that night and crossed paths with Charles little more than that. I was content to let him go about things as he saw fit, knowing he was smart, sly, and ruthless. If anyone could bring down the Desmarais, it was Charles.

Carmilla's continued on its upward swing with more and more new faces every night. The previous Saturday had been so busy that, for the first time, we actually had to refuse entrance to some would-be customers. Mary-Jane was a definite draw, and she never failed to put on a good show. I noticed that, more often than not, she was accompanied by the bass player, who caught my eye, and a few other regular back-up players. Eli even sat in for a night when the pianist was sick.

Jared continued to stay just out of touch. I managed to pick up a few memories from him in the times when we were close, but for the most part he remained unreadable. I mentioned my experience to Eli, and he informed me that he also found the man difficult to read. I suspected some terrible trauma that his mind kept locked away somewhere, leading him to build up an ever-present wall around his feelings and thoughts. It happened sometimes, as it did with Eli after the murder of his mother.

One evening after I had bathed and dressed, I wandered into the main area of the house, expecting to find it empty as I did most nights. Instead I found Eli sitting on a chair he had drawn up to the island in the kitchen, and in his hand he swirled about the sanguine contents of a delicate crystal wineglass. He looked up as I entered and made a face to express his obvious displeasure. "How can you drink it? It tastes awful."

I took the glass from his hands and downed the remaining blood, now cooled to room temperature. "I don't notice anymore. I just don't have the urge to hunt like I used to. I'm only concerned with meeting my needs adequately enough to be healthy and refuelled."

"'Refuelled.' It's one way to describe it."

"Why are you here? Are you waiting for me?"

"I am, actually. I was hoping that you might go with me somewhere tonight."

"Where?"

"There's a lecture on campus. It's about creationism stories from around the world. I thought you might be interested." He gave me a winning smile, and I had to laugh.

"That's it. No ulterior motives?" He hesitated, and I knew there was more than he was owning up to.

"Okay. We haven't done anything together, since, well, that night. I miss you, and I'd like to spend some time together. So, sue me."

"Well, it's sweet, and I can honestly say it's the best offer I've had in a long time. Sure, I'd love to go."

"Cool, let me go change, and then we can head out. It starts at eight." He rose and stopped just as he reached the entrance to the hall. "I almost forgot. Here's the flier. I know how you like to Google people, so you have time to check it out if you want."

I took the flier from his hand, and my fingers lightly brushed his. An instant parade of tingles marched up my arm, and I tried to be nonchalant as I moved my hand away. I let my gaze wander over the paper, taking in the photo of a nice-looking man dressed in typical professor's attire: dark suit, plain shirt, and tie. I read over the lecture title, "Similar Themes in the Origins of Humanity across the Borders of Geography and Time, presented by Micah Lazenby." I scanned his credentials, publications, and biography. He seemed remarkably well-educated and knowledgeable about the subject. I was intrigued.

I was just finishing up my internet research of Dr. Micah Lazenby when I caught a whiff of Eli's cologne. As he came into view, a small lump caught in my throat. He looked amazing. His dark hair was still damp, hanging in soft, shaggy tendrils to his strong shoulders. His smooth skin was slightly pink from the warmth of the shower. Dark jeans fit like a second skin, and a long-sleeved shirt with stripes of navy, charcoal and white was open at the collar, exposing his pale throat. I felt like a goofy schoolgirl then, overcome with melancholy as I remembered feeling the exact same way about Giovanni. I had to stop being so hard on myself. Admiring Eli's attractiveness was not a betrayal of the love I would always have for Giovanni.

Eli offered his hand, and I took it willingly. We left in a Mustang convertible, a new toy of Eli's, and I enjoyed the wind whipping through my hair. Soon, we pulled into the parking lot on the west side of the campus, where a number of vehicles had already accumulated.

"Good turnout," I said as I closed the car door.

Eli was instantly at my side. I looked down as his hand slid into mine, but I did not comment. "I think that Dr. Lazenby has quite the female student following."

"Is that so?" I asked. I flashed back to the flier, remembering an attractive male face then experienced a moment of strange familiarity.

"Oh, yes, his classes are always full, not that there's anything wrong with that. I took one of his courses last semester and have another, this one. He's quite brilliant and well respected among his peers. He also has an enviable number of published articles for one so young."

We were whisked into the building with the others already lined up at the door. Inside, signs directed us to one of the building's lecture theatres, and Eli and I took a spot near the back of the seating space. I happily watched people as the theatre filled to capacity, and though the crowd was predominately female, there was a good mix of young and old. Just as the light started to dim, I thought I caught sight of Mary-Jane sitting almost directly in front of the podium.

For the next two hours, I sat mesmerised by the tales of human origins from the perspective of peoples from different times and places. We were told how the Iroquois believed that the spirits of the Sky World came down and looked at the earth, and finding it to be beautiful, they created people to live on it. They eventually called the earth "Turtle Island," and the turtle remained a sacred symbol for many of the aboriginal groups of North America.

We heard the Norse legend of Odin and Ymir and how life was created from the drops of thawing ice. It was Ymir, and he was the first of the frost giants. Odin descended from a man who was licked to life by a cow, made from the same drops of thawing ice that created Ymir. They had stories to explain the existence of the sun, the moon, and the stars.

The Maori believe all humans descended from one pair of ancestors, Rangi and Papa, who are also called Heaven and Earth. Rangi and Papa had six sons: Tane-mahuta, the father of the forests and their inhabitants; Tawhiri-ma-tea, the father of winds and storms; Tangaroa, the father of fish and reptiles; Tu-matauenga, the father of fierce human beings; Haumia-tikitiki, the father of food that grows without cultivation; and Rongo-ma-tane, the father of cultivated food.

There was talk of the Jewish creation story of Yahweh and how on the day He made the heavens and the earth, the land was dry and barren until a mist came up and wet the land. Then Yahweh took dust from the earth and shaped it into the form of a man, and He breathed life into that form. Many other religious and cultural stories were touched on, accompanied by an extensive slide show of ancient texts, pottery, and ceremonial relics.

The lecture began to wind down, and my mind reeled with the enormous volume of information I just absorbed.

"Just as an interesting side note," Dr. Lazenby offered to the group in his rich, eloquent voice, "I have discovered through my years of research an interestingly similar concept throughout the various cultures and groups that I have studied. In every culture, from the most primitive right up to modern times, there is a similar story depicting some type of creature who is not alive and yet not dead. It is a creature who can be a spiritual or a corporeal entity, and who subsists through a parasitic relationship with humans. It may need fear, sexual energy or, most commonly, blood. We know it here in North America as the vampire, born of legends in Eastern Europe. It has always seemed odd to me that, of all the things our ancestors felt needed explanation or personification, a creature of death was common to all. And on that dark note, I thank you. Good night."

People stood and began to mill about. Some approached the podium to express their appreciation, while others made a beeline for the door. I turned to Eli, who sat with the most irritating of smirks plastered on his handsome face. "What is that about?"

"I've heard it before, when I took his course last semester. It's one of his personal interests. I think he plans to write a book on it one day."

"And I suppose that you find this immensely amusing, considering that we're in his audience tonight?"

He didn't answer; instead he stood and grabbed my hand. He made his way down the set of stairs cutting through the center of the lecture's seating area. Maybe a quarter of the attendees remained as we reached the bottom, the vast majority of whom were college-aged woman. Eli emitted a strange feeling at uneven intervals, which touched me with a weak, sexual energy. This effect intensified as we approached the object of our attention. The feeling was intimately familiar and somehow different from anything I felt from Eli before.

Up close I had an odd sense of déjà vu, suddenly certain I saw the professor before in some other setting. I was just turning to ask Eli about it when someone spoke to me.

"So, how do you like him, better? Stuffy, button-up type or bad, rocker dude?" I turned to find Mary-Jane standing before us, her long waves of hair pulled back in a tight ponytail.

Both she and Eli were smiling, but I didn't get the joke. "I don't know what you mean?"

Mary-Jane gave Eli a conspiratorial look. "Didn't you tell her?"

"Tell me what?"

"Dr. Lazenby is also Mary-Jane's bass player, a fact that he tries to keep from his throngs of adoring students." I could have smacked the smile off of Eli's face; he was so pleased with himself.

I had a quick flash back to the man dressed in jeans and

his tattoo-covered arms, rocking out on stage. I looked at him closely, and our eyes met. I hadn't noticed before, but they were a rich, chocolate brown, and so close I put his age in the thirties, a few years older than I previously pegged him. He smiled and nodded at Eli and Mary-Jane. He returned his attention to the group of women he had been addressing, and after a few minutes they left with some reluctance. Dr Lazenby and the three of us were the only ones who remained.

He loosened his tie as he approached our group, looking relieved to be shed of his admirers. "So, what did you think, Eli?"

"Wonderful. Very informative. May I present Rachel?"

As Eli indicated in my direction, Dr. Lazenby extended his hand toward me, and his flesh was warm against my icy skin. As our eyes met, I experienced an outpouring of sexual energy and heard one word very distinctly in my head. *Beautiful.* I smiled. "Very nice to meet you. Dr. Lazenby?"

"Please call me Micah; 'Dr. Lazenby' makes me feel old." He smiled, and when I saw a snaggled, front tooth I could have swooned. I couldn't explain my attraction to crooked teeth, it was just one of my little quirks.

"So, any plans, Micah?" Eli asked with a strange easiness, but I noticed he was standing close to me, as though guarding a valuable possession. I also picked up on a brief, but intense non-verbal exchange between the two men I didn't understand. Eli touched my arm with his hand, and an image flashed through my mind too quickly to connect to it. I was left with a vague impression of a naked male body and intense need.

"Not really. Thinking about heading home and cracking open a beer." He smiled warmly, his attention lingering on Eli.

"Why don't you and Mary-Jane come back to our place for a few drinks?" Eli asked.

I cast Eli a dark look. *What are you doing?* I knew he understood, but he just continued to smile pleasantly while the two made up their minds.

"Sure, why not?" Mary-Jane answered happily.

"Sounds good to me. Eli tells me that you two have quite the CD collection, and I confess that I am a serious music junkie. I'd love the chance to poke through it. So how do you want to do this? Should I follow in my car?"

"Sure."

"I walked. Can I hitch a ride?" Mary-Jane looked in Eli's direction as she spoke. He stepped from my side and offered her his arm like something a man from an old black-and-white movie might have done. She giggled and linked her arm with his. I shrugged in Micah's direction, and we followed them out to the parking lot.

Up at the house, our strangely assembled group settled on the back patio with the French doors leading to the large first floor entertainment room thrown wide open. The men spent nearly thirty minutes going through the CD collection, which took up almost an entire wall of the over-sized room. Micah was like a kid in a candy store when he saw the thousands of disks waiting to be heard. The two of them pulled out enough CDs to play for days while I fixed us all drinks from the well-stocked bar.

Micah let out a comfortable sigh after taking a sip of his drink. "I have to say that I truly appreciate someone who knows their music." Then he indicated the glass in his hand. "And their scotch."

The CD changed, and *Led Zeppelin III* spilled out into the night.

Eli was enjoying Mary-Jane's undivided attention, though he stole furtive glances in my direction every few minutes or so. Micah and I talked easily about a variety of topics from the superficial to the exotic. He seemed impressed with my knowledge on any number of subjects.

"You know, Rachel has a whole library upstairs full of ancient texts, one-of-a-kind documents, first editions, you name it. She also has a penchant for history, mythology, and all that stuff. It's why I brought her to your lecture tonight," Eli offered into the conversation.

Micah's eyes lit up at the mention of my collection, and I felt both perturbed and confused at Eli's obvious attempt to get us alone together. Or perhaps it was an attempt to be alone with Mary-Jane, and from the signals she had been sending all night there would be no protests on her side. I was looking at Eli when Micah excitedly inquired about the contents of my personal library. I turned away from Eli, after sharing with him a look to show how *not* pleased I was with his orchestration of the situation, and forced myself to smile at Micah. "Come with me. It's something to be seen, not told about."

As Micah followed me back into the entertainment room, I felt Eli's gaze boring into my back. I didn't understand why he was acting in such a way. I already warned him off Mary-Jane, and if it was just a matter of feeding, he could have waited until they left, or he could have not invited them back to the house at all.

I smiled at Micah's appreciative looks at Giovanni's art, the beautiful furniture, and architecture of the house as we made our way upstairs. I stopped outside the library to punch in my code. He gave me an odd look but didn't comment. Once we stepped inside, he understood the need for extra security.

The room was climate-controlled to aid in the preservation of some of the pieces I owned. Under glass, I kept several papyrus scrolls, parchments, and broken pottery from eras dating from pre-Biblical times to the Middle Ages. I had shelves of books, written from just about every era of recorded history. It was an impressive, almost unbelievable collection, and one that to a trained mind such as Micah's must be incredibly enviable. It felt peculiar to have a stranger in there with me. I had never been in that space with anyone but Eli and had never shared my collection with anyone other than Giovanni and Charlotte. There was a certain amount of my personality and self-worth trapped within the pages of the many volumes lining the room. It had become a personal sanctuary of sorts.

Micah walked from display to display in awe. Several times he reached out to touch something then quickly drew his hands back. I laughed and encouraged him to take out any of the books he liked. "I only ask that anything under glass not be touched, as there are special precautions that must be taken when handling these items. I do have translations that I can show you if anything interests you."

He looked at me, shaking his head and grinning from ear

to ear. "*If* anything interests me? I could stay in here for weeks. You have works in here that I have only heard of and never imagined that I would get chance to review personally." He pulled one volume from the shelf, handling it as if it were made from the most delicate crystal. "How is it that you could have this incredible collection, and the world is none the wiser?"

I sat, suddenly aware of just how much the contents of that room meant to me. "Because it's how I want it."

He looked through several pages before meeting my eyes again. "I don't mean to be personal here, but you seem very young to own a collection like this. Is it something you inherited?"

I paused before deciding the truth was not going to hurt. "Yes, from my husband. He had quite an extensive collection to begin with, and then I added to it over our years together. He passed away last year." The truth—just not the whole truth.

He put the book down, and gave me a look that was both sincere and heartfelt. "I'm sorry. I had no idea. I don't know Eli all that well, certainly not well enough to discuss something so personal." A funny feeling associated with his mention of Eli's name caught my attention, as though something almost escaped, but he quickly forced it back somewhere deep in his mind. The feeling was oddly reminiscent of the warm, sensual sensation Eli passed to me earlier.

"Please, don't be sorry. It's been rough, but Eli has been a good friend to me and really helped me through the darker days." Again, the warm flare at the mention of Eli's name.

"I'm glad. I know personally how hard it can be to get over the hurt when someone close to you dies. I had a girlfriend in college who died in a car accident, and there were times when I didn't think I could go on. I only made it because I had some good friends and my parents to lean on." As he spoke, he unknowingly allowed me glimpses of the dead girl's face and bathed me in his old pain.

"Well, I'm certainly lucky to have Eli as I have no other family to speak of." He reached across the table to pat my hand lightly, and I was uncomfortable with the ease at which he offered his sympathy. Yet the fact that I didn't want to pull my hand away from the warmth of his flesh bothered me even more. Giovanni's passing left a chasm of need and hurt within me, and I was afraid I might allow myself to fill what was missing from somewhere I shouldn't. He had a strong mind, which didn't seem to work like most of the world's population. He had many thoughts on the go at once, some fleeting, some intense. They danced about each other, intermingling at times, and were not easy to follow in a reasonable, linear way. I pulled away, feeling strained from trying to make sense of the inner workings of his brain.

I felt an uncontrollable urge to change the subject and steer us both away from areas that could lead to trouble. I was allowing myself to be too affected by his sympathy and the fact that he was a kindred spirit, of sorts. It was also intoxicating to be in a human's presence like that, uninterrupted and intimate. His scent was wonderful, the sound of his rushing blood like music to my ears. It had been a long time since I took a life, and it would be all too easy to take this one. I choked down that dark desire, forcing myself to draw back from the situation I was allowing myself to be drawn into. I was too vulnerable, and I could not afford a mistake.

An interesting thought popped into my mind, and in my haste to avoid dangerous subjects, I jumped on it. "I was reviewing some of the courses and such with Eli recently, and I came across a name that sounds familiar. Do you know a Danica Armstrong? I believe she works in the same department?" I tried to make my inquiry seem as casual as possible.

He pulled his hand back, resting it on the top of the book. "Yes, I mean, I don't know her all that well, just as one colleague to another. I don't have much occasion to talk with her. She specialises in Women's Studies and Art History, if I'm not mistaken. I believe she's working on a book right now."

If I raised any alarm bells, he wasn't showing it. "Maybe that's where I've heard her name. I'm quite interested in art as well. It was a passion of my husband's."

"I noticed the pieces as we came up the stairs. I'm no expert by any stretch, but I think I recognised some names. The ones in the hallway though, I don't think I'm familiar with that artist."

A coldness spread out from the pit of my stomach. "They are my husband's work. He was an artist. You'll have to look more closely when you go back down. There are several of both Eli and myself."

A quiet, yet intimate moment of understanding passed between us, solidified by words that remained unspoken. Loss was a curious thing, something so unique to individuals that it became a part of them, silently hovering in the background of every action and reaction to come after its appearance. Though people may heal and, in fact, move on to wonderful things, loss leaves its mark deeply. Only those people who had experienced true loss could ever empathise with another's, though even those people who were similarly affected could never truly understand another's pain.

We spent another hour in the library, carefully talking about books, research, and various schools of thought. Micah brought a fresh view and a unique interpretation to records and accounts I had studied many times over. He pulled my mind along trains of thought never considered before, causing me to feel intellectually provoked and stimulated in new ways. Eli was certainly his equal, if not his superior, in intellect and volume of knowledge, but Micah brought with him an undeniable passion. His thinking was wide and creative, not as rigid and linear as Eli's. I felt myself responding to his way of thinking, connecting with him in a most satisfying way.

During a brief lull in our conversation, Micah glanced down at his watch and winced when he saw the time. "I should get heading home. I have a huge pile of papers to mark tomorrow, and I still have some prep for next week." He looked back longingly at the books he had not had a chance to review. "I hope that I might be invited back again."

"Of course. It's not often I find someone with interests so close to my own."

He had a small pile of books before him, which he scooped up carefully and placed under his arm. "Thank you for the loan of these. I will use the utmost of care with them."

With a twinge of despondency, I realised one of the volumes he chose was the book of mythology Giovanni gave me during our time in Japan. It made sense that it would interest him, considering the topic he touched on in the closing of his lecture, but seeing it was like picking at a painful scab. "Yes, please keep them safe."

We found Eli alone on the main floor when we returned after our time in the library. He was stretched out on a couch in the entertainment room, listening to some music I was unfamiliar with. I noticed the doors to the outside were closed and locked. The alarm system's light blinked, indicating that it had been engaged.

"Where's Mary-Jane?"

Eli smiled and sat up. His movements were languid and easy but seemed almost too casual to my scrutiny. "Oh, she went home. She was tired, so I called her a cab." His eyes were piercing as he spoke, yet I didn't detect any sign of deceit.

"And I should head out, too. Thank you both for the hospitality, and again, Rachel, thank you for the loan of the books." Micah extended his hand, which I took and shook lightly. His fingers tensed at the coldness of my touch.

Eli watched our exchange thoughtfully. "Let me walk you out, Micah."

When the men had left, I lay on the same couch where Eli had been stretched out moments earlier. As they disappeared from view, I experienced a sharp jolt of a peculiar emotion: jealousy. Internally I chided myself and quickly pushed the feeling aside.

Their inconsequential conversation was audible to my sensitive ears as they made their way to the door, followed by the diluted sounds of Eli disengaging the alarm system and the soft rumblings of a car engine. Almost instantly after the reengagement of the security system, I felt the fabric of Eli's shirt brushing against my bare arm. I lazily opened my eyes, before moving over enough to allow him to lie comfortably beside me.

"What was going on tonight?"

The corner of Eli's mouth twitched, hinting at a smile. "I thought you might find the good professor interesting."

"Really?"

"Yes, really. I saw you admiring him one night when he was

playing at the club, and it planted a thought in my head. Then when I saw he was going to be speaking at the university, it seemed the perfect opportunity to introduce the two of you. I know how you like smart men."

I gave him a playful swat at that comment, but couldn't help but be amused. "And I suppose that being left alone with Mary-Jane was just a convenient accident?"

He pressed a hand to his chest and made a face of mock innocence. "You've already made it clear that you don't want me getting involved with her."

"Yes, but what about feeding off of her? I know how talented you are in making your conquests forget the details of your encounters."

He turned so our noses were almost tip-to-tip. "Well, I might have had a little taste, nothing that would cause her any harm. And what about you and our dear Dr. Lazenby?"

"Not a chance."

"But not for lack of interest, that's for sure. Even Mary-Jane picked up on it." His nearness was calming and comfortably familiar.

"I'm not looking for anything so intimate right now, but he is quite interesting, a very knowledgeable man. He has some unique interpretations of some of the legends and stories that I've studied, and I think that he could be immensely helpful.... What?"

Eli was regarding me, his amused smile irritating me. "You're smitten," he teased, and I happily joined in his laughter, "and I'm not disagreeing with you. He's extremely intelligent, and his interests are very close to your own. He could be a good resource and perhaps a friend?"

"Just please don't push for anything more, and maybe I'm not the only one who finds the man...interesting?"

"He's not my type," he answered quickly, but there was a strange tone to his words. He pressed a soft and easy kiss to my lips. "I only want your happiness, and you know you always have me, for whatever you may need." His words were as tender as his voice.

I returned the kiss, lingering a little longer than he had.

"I know, and if I were to ever open my heart to anyone again, Eli, it would only be to you." I saw the surprise and joy on his face from my words before he was able to conceal them with a mask of control. He pulled me into his strong arms, where I always felt safe and loved. If only I could love him in the way he wanted me to, things could be so amazing. Perhaps time would heal all wounds.

CHAPTER 4

"*Rachel, Rachel!*" My name was being screamed with such ferocity, the sound was an actual force, travelling though my body like an electric current. My mind swam with bright pain and confusion, and my eyelids were so heavy they would not open. I thrashed about in cold terror, my unseen attacker ripping away at my unprotected flesh. Then someone beside me in the darkness reached out for me with hands as icy and strong as my own. I clung on to them like a lifeline, desperate to stay afloat in the darkness. "*Rachel!*"

I sat bolt upright, moving so quickly I smashed the back of my head against the mahogany headboard. My eyes snapped open. I felt the hands again, and I turned to Eli, staring at me in panic. His blue eyes were furiously bright; his mouth, tight with worry. I was trembling, and, as I began to recover my senses, I realised the hands held out to me for help were covered with blood.

Instantly, I became aware of a vicious throbbing from my arms and torso, and, looking down, I found the pale silk sheet lying across my body crimson with blood. I pulled it back to discover jagged, violent wounds snaking across my naked flesh. I pressed the fingertips of my shaking hands to the wounds to find them sticky and damp. The room swirled in nauseating shades of grey.

Eli lifted me with his strong arms and carried me across the room, the whisper of his footsteps like butterflies in a gentle wind. With care he placed me in the tub, the empty space feeling impossibly large around my traumatised body. Soon the emptiness was replaced with warm water, cocooning me with its comfort and façade of safety. I drifted in that hazy place between reality and dreams, unable or unwilling to accept the truth as evidenced by the damage to my body.

"Sweetheart, are you okay?" Eli's voice was an angelic whispering near my ear. The sound hovered just above the pain. It floated on the air, heavy from the water. I turned toward the voice, knowing in my mind it was Eli, but feeling in my heart it was Giovanni attempting to soothe me with his velvet voice. My eyes drifted open, and, at first, all I saw was the steam rising from the tub. Then a pale face began to take shape, surrounded by a mass of dark waves and eyes as blue as the sky. A hand brushed my cheek.

"Giovanni..."

"*Rachel!*" The voice was no longer kind; it was frightened and urgent. I slammed back into the present with a sensation akin to having the wind knocked out of me. My chest tightened with anxiety. Eli's face was but an inch from my own, tense and worried. A smile slipped across my lips. His hands dropped in reaction, and he went down on his knees, lowering his face to rest atop his arms, positioned on the tub's edge.

"Rachel, what just happened?" His voice was so quiet, and the concern with which he released the words squeezed at my heart.

"I don't know exactly... I was in the darkness..." I murmured, trying to recall the moments leading up to finding myself a bloody mess. I felt so terribly scared and somehow angry with myself, as though there were something incredibly important I'd forgotten. "Come in here, please, I need to feel you close to me."

Eli slipped into the water without another word. He tenderly slid an arm around my shoulders, pulling me alongside his firm body. His other hand moved across my stomach, and I flinched as his fingers made contact with one of the strips of damage on my flesh.

"That must have been some dream you were having," he said quietly.

Then it rushed back into me: the darkness, the pain, and the panic. I had been trapped in small space with a blackness so complete even my immortal eyes could not penetrate it. There was nothing except the sound of my struggles and the unrelenting pain coursing through my body. I felt myself clawing at my own skin in a pathetic, desperate attempt to make the pain stop. As my nails raked against flesh, I realised that's all there was—flesh stretched tightly over bone. My body was emaciated, and my throat, so dry. I was mad with thirst! All I could think was: *I need blood!,* but there was nowhere to go, and there was no release from the pain.

"It wasn't a dream," I said with sudden certainty.

I looked into Eli's tender face as he asked, "What do you mean it wasn't a dream?"

I shook my head, not entirely comprehending myself. "It was too real; it was as if I was experiencing someone else's pain or reliving their memory. It was so awful; I could feel their pain and their terror. It was real..."

"I'm sure that it felt real, Rachel. Dreams are like that sometimes. They can be very powerful." His tone was kind, but I knew he could not understand what I had experienced.

"I can't make you understand."

"I saw you clawing at yourself! And you were screaming Giovanni's name over and over again. This is about guilt and grief, Rachel. You're finally allowing yourself to let me in just the tiniest bit and you're scared."

"There's more to it than that; this is not just about guilt! I know I can't make you understand, and I know it sounds crazy!"

Eli just looked at me sadly and said nothing. He pulled me gently into his embrace and pressed his cool lips to my forehead. "I knew this wouldn't be easy, and I am willing to wait as long as it takes. I love you, Rachel, with everything that I am. I can live in Giovanni's shadow to the end of time, if that's what it will take."

"Your love is the only thing that keeps me going," I said with honesty, knowing it was easier to let him believe what he would, and maybe he was right. God knows grief and guilt can eat at a person like a cancer, spreading their blackness out to every area of life. I simply wasn't ready to let go yet.

I looked down to see the wounds already beginning to

heal. The deep furrows in my skin were knitting themselves neatly back together. By the time I got to the club, there would be nothing but my memory to confirm the incident had ever happened.

"I won't push. I will give what you ask for and take what you are able to give me." The sadness in his voice was as terrible a torture as anything else I had experienced.

I pressed my lips to his, drinking in the eagerness with which he responded. "You already give me everything."

I was just about to go to the club when the urge to head out in an entirely different direction overcame me. Eli had left before me, needing to get to class. He lingered longer than he should have because he did not want to leave me in what he considered a fragile state. I assured him many times that I was fine, even though I didn't feel it was exactly true. My brain was full of turmoil, with conflicting thoughts and memories intermingling into a nonsensical and exhausting parade of images. I felt pulled in a hundred different directions, each destination making less sense than the one before it, but I was tired of being a constant source of worry. I was not the only one who felt the effects of Giovanni's death, and the grief I felt had become not only self-destructive but just plain selfish.

I found myself heading down the street toward Danica's apartment, without a clear plan or purpose in mind. I parked about a block away and casually made my way toward the building. The streets were quiet, with neither traffic nor humanity in evidence. I opened the outer door, stepping cautiously through to what served as the entrance to the building's three units. In another life, the space would have been a grand front foyer; the only remnants, the winding staircase that led to the second-floor unit. I paused outside the door to Danica's apartment until I was certain the place was empty. Then I picked the lock and slipped inside.

I didn't need to turn on the interior lights to see the space clearly, saving me from drawing attention to my breaking and entering. It was moderately-sized, consisting of a living room with fireplace, a small dining room, and a kitchen with a beautiful bay window that overlooked the street below. There were two bedrooms, the smaller of which had been turned into an office. In this room, the walls were covered with articles, maps, certificates of educational accomplishments, and many awards. Two of the walls held overflowing bookshelves; the remaining two held the desk with a computer, a small couch, and a TV and DVD ensemble. The room spoke to being well-used, and it brought me a strange comfort to see titles on my niece's shelves matching ones I had at home.

What I didn't see were personal touches or mementos of any kind. It was not to say the space was not inviting—it had been decorated nicely and painted with warm, earthy tones, but there was no artwork, no knickknacks on shelves, no plants, nothing to show that there were any interests outside the world of academia. I wandered into the bedroom, catching the scent of musky cologne.

Underneath the window was a low, narrow table that held a series of framed photos that instantly piqued my curiosity. There were several of Danica in different stages of her childhood and adolescence, some with her brother or parents. One showed her sitting with my mother at what appeared to be a Christmas celebration. Then there was the traditional graduation shot with Danica in cap and gown, where I saw my brother showing the visible signs of the years we spent apart. I was just about to turn away, pangs of regret clawing inside my chest, when a small, almost unnoticeable photo caught my eye.

I picked it up and made an audible sound of surprise to find my face reflected back at me. It was from a family trip to an amusement park in the summer before I met Giovanni. The picture caught Danica and me laughing and unselfconscious with the sun bright in the background. Physically, I appeared just as I did now, but with a touch of sun-kissed colour to my cheeks. I replaced the picture carefully, more upset than I could rationally comprehend.

I left quickly, not stopping until I was back in my car. I realised how hard I was gripping the steering wheel when a terrible snapping sound began beneath my hands. I released my grip, flexing my fingers to try to shake off the intense hostility I was experiencing. On a certain level, I knew that I was feeling the sense of regret so deeply because of the real loss of Giovanni from my life. I had not had even one moment of remorse in leaving my previous life behind during all the years we spent together, but since he was gone, it seemed everything in my existence was measured against a sliding scale of loss. The only certain and unshakable thing I seemed to have anymore was Eli and his love for me.

For some reason, that personal epiphany jarred me into action. I tried Eli on his cell phone, and it went to voicemail. He always turned it off when he was in class, and it was especially important tonight; they were writing an in-class essay. I left him a somewhat cryptic message to let him know I was not going to the club as planned and would try him again later. I could perhaps get him with my thoughts, but it wasn't urgent, and I didn't want to distract him. And it wasn't always easy to get through to him anyway, especially from a distance. For whatever reason, closeness always made our silent communication with each other so much easier. Who knew, he might pick up on my presence after I made my way onto the campus.

I didn't know exactly where Danica's office was, but I knew she was in the same department as Micah, so I figured my best bet would be to head to the building where we attended the lecture. If her office wasn't there, it would be close by. The doors were unlocked as there were still classes being taught, and labs were open for students to work and prepare. An intense but pleasurable energy existed in the building. It was life in its simplest presentation. The students and staff left their marks in releases of pride, worry, excitement, and disappointment. It was as if I could taste their feelings in the air, lingering ghosts of the paces they went put through.

As I wandered the halls, I attracted quite a few approving and somewhat lustful stares from members of the student body. Very few reactions to my presence were undercut with fear, though, which I found very curious. People might not rationally know what I am, but often their internal alarm alerted them in the presence of creatures like me. Yet, at the same time that we might be feared, we were also desired, but here, among the many ethnicities, cultures, and personal presentations, I was just another face, albeit a very attractive one.

Even my pale skin was not a cause for scrutiny, with the populations of Goth and Emo students milling about. Some looked much stranger than I did with their intricate black makeup, wild hair, and piercings in every conceivable part of the human anatomy. At that moment, I understood Eli's comfort completely and his attraction to that environment. The closeness of all those warm, inviting bodies aroused me more than I would have thought possible. It was easy to blend in, and it would be easy to hunt.

I caught a familiar whisper in my brain, and I knew Eli must be close. I peered in the next door I encountered, finding him seated among a flock of adoring females. *Eli*. He looked up as he caught my silent communication and gave me a quizzical look. I waved and continued past the door, catching sight of Micah leading the lecture. He was dressed in a button-down shirt with long sleeves and a tie loose around his neck. I smiled as I had a visual of him in his other identity of musician. I picked up on his train of thoughts, alternating between the information he was presenting and a piece of music he had been having trouble with. Then, unexpectedly, I caught a flash of Eli in his mind, and an intensely warm feeling attached to the image. What did it mean?

As I rounded the corner, I arrived at a crossroads of sorts, where a main hall continued at a ninety-degree angle to the one I came from. Two narrower halls ran across the main thoroughfare, and I suspected they contained offices and storage spaces. A reference board at the mouth of the nearest of the two narrow halls seemed just what I needed, and I quickly scanned it until I found the name I was looking for. I headed down the hallway, anticipation prickling at my scalp.

Most of the rooms were dark, and I did not pick up on more than three individuals in the hallway at that time. Danica's office was of the type with a central space opening right off the hallway, which generally held a desk for the secretary or assistant and a small sitting area. Off of it were several doors that led to individual offices and possibly a storage or a copy room. The door to the front office stood slightly ajar, and the light was on. I hesitated, wavering between what I wanted to do and what I should. After an internal pep talk, I pushed the door wide with a solid smack from my hand and stepped inside.

I took in the mammoth-sized desk pushed up against the wall opposite the door I just entered. It was piled with mail, file folders, binders, and more. Stands of books and magazine filled the rest of the office, with two sagging loveseats pushed into a corner of the tight space. Three of the four doors leading from the main room were closed and dark. With a spark of adrenaline, I observed that the open one belonged to my niece.

I was just at the office, having moved as silently as possible, when she appeared. She stopped short, the bundle of papers dropping from her hand to flutter to the floor around her feet. Her heart thundered in response to her shock at finding another person in the near-deserted space. We stood there for a long, tense moment, regarding each other without speaking.

After the initial reaction, she seemed resigned to the encounter about to take place. I took in her dark hair, the same blue eyes as my own, and a strikingly similar figure. The faintest sprinkle of freckles covered her nose and cheeks, and the beginnings of age lines formed around her eyes and mouth. In all, she was lovely.

I bent down and swept up the mess of papers with a movement much quicker than I should have executed. Her lips twitched as I handed her back the papers, yet she did not seem frightened or even all that surprised at my presence in her office. With papers in hand, she returned to her chair behind the battered work surface that stood between us. The room was so tight; the desk divided the space in half. The clearance was perhaps three feet at the one end to allow access to the sitting side. Much like her home office, the walls were covered with shelves, maps, and articles. A series of awards from various academic publications were displayed on a narrow shelf above her monitor.

I was still standing in the doorway when she indicated the only other chair in the room. "Are you going to sit down?" Her voice was soft and made her sound much younger than she actually was.

I sat, still observing her calm outward demeanor. Her pulse

picked up, but she held herself confidently. I immediately liked that about her. "You don't seem all that surprised to see me?"

She seemed to think that over carefully before responding. "Well, I am, and I'm not, if it makes any sense."

"It makes perfect sense, considering the situation we find ourselves in."

She leaned in across the desk, and I was touched by the same musky scent I picked up on in her apartment. "Who are you?"

I mirrored her actions, placing my hands atop the desk and stopping mere inches from her. Her eyes flicked downward then quickly back to my face. "You know who I am."

"But it's not possible. You can't be who I think you are. She's been gone since I was a child."

"And she is?" I prompted.

"My aunt, Rachel. She disappeared, and no one in the family ever heard from her again. One day she was there, and the next she was gone." Her mind shuffled about a series of thoughts and memories, jumbled and hazy. The tiniest crack in her resolve began to show.

"And why can't I be her?" I tried to keep the tone of my voice as neutral as possible, but it was difficult while being so close to a part of my past I had not experienced for so long.

She blinked rapidly and cleared her throat. "Because you look exactly the same as she did twenty-five years ago. She would be in her fifties by now."

"So, then who do you think I am?"

"I don't know. Another relative possibly, her daughter, or just someone who looks remarkably like her? I mean, I was a child the last time I saw her, and maybe my memory isn't as solid as I would like to believe. Maybe I'm just seeing what I want to see?" Her eyes clouded over as she thought back to the last time she had seen me.

I remembered it as well: a Thanksgiving dinner at my mother's, with all the family in attendance. After we had eaten, Danica and I slipped away to the basement to watch a movie. It had been a nice, easy time. It was strangely intense not only to relive my own memory but also to be absorbing the feelings and visual images she associated with that time. I thought back to a similar experience with Giovanni and Charles, though that memory had not been a pleasant one.

"And why would I not just simply present myself as this other person or relative as you're suggesting?" I smiled, and she trembled ever so slightly.

"I don't know, but if we want to be clear here, you haven't presented yourself at all."

I had no idea where I was going with this encounter and no thoughts about the outcome when we got there. I was being reckless, and I realised belatedly, selfish again. "You're right." I reached across and took her hand in my cold grip. "I'm Rachel."

She snatched her hand back so abruptly she smashed her elbow into the arm of her chair. I knew it must have hurt, but she didn't flinch, and she never broke eye contact, a strong woman. "You can't be, and it isn't funny."

"I agree. It is not funny. It is a very serious situation for the both of us. There could be a terrible fallout, and the consequences for me could be very grave."

Now she was angry. "Enough of this! Stop the games, and just say whatever it is that you came here to tell me." Her chair gave a hostile squeak as she pushed it out to stand. "Spit it out, or I'm going to call security." She moved her hand in the direction of the phone on her desk, and I knew I had to get control of the situation.

I was over the desk, with her arm clenched tightly in my hand, before she even had the chance to blink. The space was so confined, our bodies were pressed tightly together, her face so close I could feel her warm breath. We were almost exactly the same height, and it was unsettling to be looking into a face so much like my own. Her breath hitched in her chest. "You're hurting my arm."

I was clenching her with such force, her hand was becoming an alarming shade of red. I let go, and she rubbed her injured arm. I leaped back over the desk and closed the door. I returned to my seat and decided on a more direct approach. "Now let's really talk." Her gaze flicked to the phone, so I reached over and ripped the line from the wall. "Without interruptions."

She lowered herself to the chair, nodding her agreement. "What do you want?"

"To talk; it's that simple, and after you've heard what I have to say, the rest will be up to you." I paused, trying to be careful in choosing my words. I wanted the story to unfold in way that would evoke the least amount of alarm or fear. "First of all, I'm sorry about your arm. It was not my intention to hurt you, and it wasn't my intention to hurt anyone twenty-five years ago either. It was simply the only way."

She settled back in her chair, relaxing her posture somewhat but still cradling her arm with her other hand. "I don't understand."

"Well, I met someone, someone I came to love very much, and to be together we had to leave everyone else in my life behind. Circumstances beyond my control made it so."

"I know about the man; well, we all did. Not his name or who he was, but we knew that there was a man."

That admission caught me off guard. "From Shannon?"

"Was she your roommate?"

I nodded.

"Then yes, from Shannon. After you disappeared, she called Grandma, um, your mother, and told her that she hadn't seen you in a while, and there was some talk about you acting strangely in the months leading up to your disappearance and the fact that you had gotten involved with someone."

"I figured it would have gone something like that. I didn't know if Shannon would put my disappearance and my meeting Giovanni together. She only saw us together the one time, and I tried to keep everything about our relationship to myself."

"Giovanni?" His name sounded strange in her childish voice.

Tears welled in my eyes as I met her face. "Yes, his name was Giovanni, and he was, is, the love of my life."

"Why did you have to leave?"

I let a little of the monster inside slip out, and Danica shuddered but did not look away. "Because of what he was and what I had to become to be with him."

The room was very quiet and warm. She was struggling to

accept what I revealed to her, and I felt the deepest sympathy. It was not an easy thing to understand or accept. As humans, it has been drilled into our heads that monsters do not exist, when in fact they do. For certain, there is much monstrosity that lies within humanity itself: killers, rapists, and warmongers, but vampires were the things of nightmares. I smiled, allowing a small glimpse of my sharp fangs.

"Are you going to kill me?" she asked.

"No," I answered.

"Then why are you here?"

I shook my head, saddened not to have a real answer for her question. "I'm not sure, really. I haven't thought much of the life I left behind, at least not until very recently, and then when I saw you at the club, I don't know. It was like something inside of me switched on, and I realised something was missing."

"I don't know if I understand. Didn't you leave for something that meant more to you than what you were leaving behind? What happened?"

"I lost Giovanni, and I don't want to get into the details of it right now, but suffice it to say his loss illuminated how everything I am was dominated by my love for him. And don't get the wrong idea, he was perfect for me, and I went with him willingly. If he were still with me, I'm sure that I would never have come to you like this. I guess I just wanted to know that you are okay."

Uncertainty strained her features. "Really? Well, I'm fine, I guess. I have a good job here. I'm working on a book. I have some great friends and colleagues...and my parents are still healthy."

I glimpsed an image of my brother and his wife, then my nephew, as seen in Danica's mind. My brother was pretty much the same, a little heavier, greyer, and wrinkled. Much like I should have been. "And are they still in Kingston, still working?" I was surprised at how much I really wanted to know.

"Yep, still in the same house. Dad's still at the ministry, and Mom is working for Queen's. I think she was at the Board of Education when you left."

"Yes, she was, and how's your brother?"

"Good, he got married last year. He's a social worker, and he and his wife just bought a house. He came down here for a visit about six months ago. As far as I know, things are good with him."

"And my mother?"

Tightness pulled at her jaw line as I asked, and I knew intuitively the answer was not going to be a happy one. "She died about three years ago, cancer."

"I see." I forced myself not to think about it. I'd had enough grief. "And what about you? Are you married? How did you end up in San Francisco?"

She regarded me silently, eyes narrowed. The anger seemed to be seeking a way back in. "Am I just supposed to believe all of it, that somehow you have become something that allows you to stay young forever? It is ridiculous! You come in here and flash obviously well-planned theatrics and start playing on my emotions over the loss of a family member! It is sick."

"What would it take to convince you that I really am Rachel?"

She shook her head.

"How about the last time you saw me? It was at Thanksgiving dinner at my mother's house. You were there with your parents and your brother. My mother's husband, John, was there and his son James and his wife. You and I snuck downstairs after dinner and watched *The Wizard of Oz*, which was always one of your favourite movies as a child. Your dog's name was Gypsy, and she was a black-and-white mutt, who once chewed up your favourite doll, and she died after being hit by a car. Um, we took a trip once as a family to Prince Edward Island; you were about four, and we went to this beach that was covered with washed-up, dead jellyfish. Do you remember that?"

Tears were streaming down her face by that time, but I ploughed on in my quiet, even voice. "Your dad used to call you 'Peanut,' and you used to love the Jackson Five. I gave you a jewelry box with a spinning ballerina in it for your seventh birthday, and your mom took you out later and got your ears pierced. What else can I say?"

"How can it be true?" Her words were heavy with emotion.

"It's true because I fell in love with a vampire, and he made me like himself. We left because there was no way to explain why we never aged or never ate or came out in the sunlight. We left to avoid hurting and frightening people like I am doing to you right now."

"Show me," she said. Her lips trembled.

I closed the space between us, leaning her back over one arm and twisting her neck to expose her smooth, white throat with movements too fast for her human eyes to process. I pressed my fangs into her flesh just hard enough to break the surface. She gasped at the pain, as I was not using any mind tricks to cloud her memory of the experience. I tasted her blood, bright and hot on my tongue, and struggled to keep myself under control. I pulled back with fangs exposed, continuing to hold her with a strength she had no chance of fighting against. She looked at me first with wild, fearful eyes, but then the expression softened, changing into something close to pity. "Rachel, I can't believe it's you. I thought I would never see you again."

I dropped my arms, and she reflexively touched the wound on her throat. Then she reached her hands toward my face, tentative, and I stood still under her touch, much more still than any human could have been. Her fingers were so warm against my own cold flesh.

"And now that you are seeing me again, how do you feel? Are you afraid?"

"Yes, but I'm also so happy to know that you're still alive." Her expression was strained, but her words and intent were sincere. Suddenly she threw her arms about my body, and I hugged her back. It was difficult to reconcile this grown woman with the child I left behind. I pulled back, and with genuine affection ran my hand over her loose waves of hair.

"Well, technically I'm not alive."

Those words washed the semi-smile from her face. "I supposed you aren't." She poked a finger at my arm then with a hand cupped under my chin moved my head slowly from one side to other, all the while scrutinising me from head to toe. "You're so cold, and your skin is so smooth and perfect, so beautiful."

"It's something that happens to all of us."

"And yet," she continued as though I hadn't spoken, "you're still the Rachel that I remember." Her eyes were intense, and I was touched in a way not experienced for many years.

I made my way around the side of the desk to my seat, rather than leaping over it. She finally sat again. "Can we finish our conversation?"

"Of course, I'm sorry. It is just so amazing to me. It must be fate, of all the places that either one of us could have ended up, here we both are in San Francisco." Her words poured out, and I could not help but be pulled along by her enthusiasm.

"Which brings me back to our earlier conversation. What brought you here?"

"School. I came here to do my PhD in Sociology." Then she paused and made a strange face, pursing her lips and crinkling up her nose. Embarrassment clouded her thoughts. "Well, that's not completely true. I met a guy on a six-week course in England, after completing my Master's. I was madly in love and ended up following him here to San Francisco, derailing my studies in the process. I had to do a year of part-time courses before being accepted into the PhD program for the next school year, and, of course, by that time, the relationship had fizzled out, but I had already settled here, and it was a good program, so I stayed, and it all worked out in the end."

"It's funny what you'll do for love, isn't it?" I let that comment sit between us, the heaviness of its meaning like a chaffing presence in the room.

"What about my dad or Chris? Are you going to contact them?"

I shook my head emphatically. "If you choose to go any further in this with me, you will have to do it alone. Too many people knowing brings too many chances for danger. There are more people who would like to see us dead than accept us as we are, despite what you might read or see at the movies."

She didn't laugh at my attempt at humour, and I understood why. "I see. That's sad, isn't it, to be this wonderful, powerful being, yet to always be fearful of your destruction."

"And just like that you're okay with it, with what I am?"

"What choice do I have? Being angry or rejecting you isn't going to change anything. It would only mean that I would have to lose you again, right? Because you're not going to stay around with a loose cannon on the horizon, and you've already said that you're not here to hurt me. How else should I react?" Her face was calm as she spoke, startlingly so.

"I don't know what I expected, screaming and running for your life maybe." I was only half joking, but her quick acceptance unsettled me, yet her mind held no traces of malice or attempts to be deceitful. There was only peace and acceptance.

"So, where do we go from here?"

"I'm not sure. I'm going to have to discuss this with my...my companions and see what they think." I started to get a familiar tickling at my brain, followed by a sudden, overwhelming compulsion to get out of there, immediately. Then as quickly as the feeling had come, it vanished. I had my suspicions as to why. "I know where to find you, and you can always try to get a hold of me at the club." I stood, and Danica rounded the desk as quickly as she could.

"I don't want you to go," she said sadly.

I gave her a quick hug then opened the door to leave. I felt her trailing along behind me and knew I could not stop the inevitable. Eli was waiting for me, leaning in the doorway to the hall. He appeared unperturbed on the outside, but his mind lashed out lividly. Danica watched without comment, yet with understanding in her eyes as I went to him and took his hand. I gave one last look over my shoulder before being led away from her office.

"What the hell are you doing?" Eli spat out between clenched teeth. His words would not have even been audible to the human ear, but to me his vehemence was rattling. His anger burnt across my skin.

"You don't know the whole story."

"You just exposed us without even a warning, let alone a discussion of any kind."

He stopped just before the end of the hallway, so suddenly I stepped on the back of his foot. "What are you thinking?

We've just gotten settled here, and I thought you were doing well with the club...and I just don't understand."

"How much of the conversation did you hear?"

"Enough to know that you told her what we are!"

"She's my niece," I said. There was nothing else to say.

Eli did a double take. "What? I thought your family was back in Ontario?"

"So did I; I was just as shocked as you are. I never imagined I would see my family again. I certainly had no intentions of it, but once the situation presented itself, I couldn't resist."

He looked back in the direction of Danica's office. "And you think she can handle it, honestly, and what about Charles? He's not going to like this."

"He knows already. Well, not that I've spoken with her, but that she's here. We ran into her one night at Carmilla's."

He squeezed my hand very roughly then. "What is going on with you, Rachel? You used to tell me everything. We used to be so close. Now I feel like I'm the last one you come to." His pained expression troubled me, filling me with shame.

"It's not like that, Eli. You are and will always be my best friend. You are the one I trust more than anyone."

He pulled his hand away and stepped out into the hallway. "It doesn't feel that way," he offered as a parting shot before disappearing from my sight.

I had barely enough time to process what just happened between Eli and me when I heard footsteps behind me. I turned to find Danica, briefcase in hand, about halfway up the hall to where I stopped. I knew I should bolt, but for some reason I didn't. "Your friend's gone?"

I nodded.

"He's like you." It wasn't a question.

I turned and met her open expression. I couldn't help but smile at her easiness. "Yes, he is. He is also my best friend."

"He's a student here, isn't he? I'm sure I've seen him around the campus."

"He is. It's easy to blend in here."

"I guess it would be." She looked out over the empty hallway, then back to my face again. "I know you said you would get in touch with me, but I'm here now. Why don't we go somewhere and talk?"

I shrugged. "Why not?"

I followed her to an exit I never used before, and we came out onto the far side of the lot where I parked.

"Did you drive?" She scanned the rows of cars.

I pointed out my car, and she mutely followed me to it. She seemed very trusting, considering the company she was keeping. I was proud to see what a strong and competent woman she turned out to be.

I was just backing out of the parking space when my cell phone rang, startling me. I stopped the car and retrieved it from my purse. "Hello," I answered sharply after seeing Eli's number on the caller ID.

"I'm sorry I stormed off," Eli offered, despite my not-so-friendly opening.

"Uh-huh." I continued to back out, not sure I wanted to talk with him or that spending time with Danica was a good idea.

"Where are you? Where are you headed?" His voice sounded tinny. I pulled out of the lot onto the road, not entirely sure where I was going.

"I guess I'm headed to the club." I paused and gave my niece a sideways glance. "And I have Danica with me."

If he was bothered by the fact, he didn't let on. "Fine. I'll see you in a few." The phone went silent.

We pulled into the lot behind the club, something I did a hundred times or more, but it was the first time that the experience came with unease. What was I doing? Could it end any way but badly?

Inside, the employee hallway was quiet. No live music was playing that night, so the dressing room was unoccupied, and Jared and the wait staff were all out front. I unlocked the office door and held it open for Danica. Our positions were now reversed as I took my chair behind the desk, and she pulled up another seat to face me across the superficial divider.

"So," I offered casually.

"So, indeed." She looked about the room, taking in the Frida Kahlo and Gustav Klimt prints adorning the wall, before her eyes returned to me. She scrutinised me intently, absorbing my fiery red hair, my porcelain skin, and my eternal youth. "You look exactly the same as I remember you. Well, you know what I mean. I always thought that you were so beautiful...I looked up to you so much." I was touched by her words, especially since I knew they were sincere. "And now here we are, and you are the same age as when you left, and I'm the older one." She laughed, like a soft tinkling of chimes. "It's funny, isn't it?"

"Funny is maybe not the word I would have chosen, but I know what you mean." Now that we were alone, I wasn't sure what to say.

She seemed to pick up on it, so she dived right in. "So, where did you go? Where have you been all these years?"

Then I let myself open up, my story spilling out honestly and without justification. I told her about Europe and finding Eli. I told her about Charles and the Desmarais, Asia, and our time in England. The only thing I didn't speak about was the night of Giovanni's destruction and the pain my life had been after it. It was brazenly apparent I was leaving out a major piece of my story, but she didn't pry. "And now we're here. We moved here about a year and a half ago, and I've had the club a little less than that. Things seem to be going well, but you just never know." I smiled sadly at that comment, knowing all too well how true that was.

"So, you raised Eli then, from a little boy?" Her words seemed cautious as she entered this stream of conversation.

"Yes. He's been like a son to me and now my best friend."

"But it's all he is?"

I didn't think I had a way to put my feelings for Eli into a satisfactory answer. As luck would have it, I didn't have to think too much about, as a knock on the door interrupted us. I knew it was Eli before I saw him. His anxiety over our earlier tiff lowered his ability to block me from his mind. He was very sorry and beating himself up over what he felt was another screw-up on his part. He bypassed Danica, coming around the side of the desk as though she wasn't even there, and pulled me up into his arms. He hugged me tightly and whispered his apologies in my ear.

"It's all right," I murmured.

He pulled back and acknowledged Danica's presence.

"I'm Eli," he said, coming to stand in front of her chair with his hand extended.

She took it without hesitation and shook it. "Danica."

He stared at her a moment and turned to me with a strange, wistful look on his handsome face. "She looks a lot like you, doesn't she?"

"Yes, she does." Danica shifted uncomfortably under both of our stares. "Well, let's not scare her off before we get a chance to know her."

"I'm not scared," she said defensively. "I just don't like being the center of attention, and with you both staring at me like that…"

"Well, Micah's out at a table waiting for us," Eli said. "Why don't we go join him?" The shield on Eli's mind shot up as he thought of Micah, and I found it to be a curious reaction on his part. "That would be Dr. Micah Lazenby," he added for Danica's benefit.

"From the university?" she was clearly surprised.

"Yes, we've become friends. I've taken some of his classes, and he plays in the house band here."

She pulled at her lips, her nervousness like perfume. Then realising what she was doing, dropped her hands back into her lap. "And does he *know*?"

"No."

"Okay then. Let's go have a drink." She stood up and went for the door. We trailed along behind her, when she stopped suddenly and turned back to regard us. "Can you drink, I mean…can you drink alcohol, water…"

Eli smiled, and I pressed my heel down on the bridge of his foot. "Yes, though it doesn't give a lot of physical pleasure. It's more the memory associated with the action or the smell," I said.

"I guess this is a whole new learning curve for me."

It struck me as funny. "It's one way of looking at it."

Micah was sitting alone when we joined him, a tall glass of ale untouched on the table in front of him. Eli took the spot next to him with me on his other side. We spent the next few hours listening to music and discussing safe topics. It was odd, and yet it seemed so natural. I noticed several times throughout the conversation that Micah affectionately touched Eli's arm and that Eli had a vibrant and warm reaction to the contact. Something was definitely going on between the two men. I just wasn't certain what it was. It made me wonder though, and I found to my surprise that it made me terribly jealous.

CHAPTER 5

"So, what's going on with you and Micah?" I asked a few hours later, while lying with Eli in a tight, post-coital embrace. Their casual intimacy bothered me the entire evening, to the point that I ended our gathering long before it was necessary.

His body stiffened, and I knew without a doubt he was keeping something from me. "I don't know what you mean. We're friends; we play in the band together. He's my professor."

"Well, there seemed to be more to it than that to me, with the way that he kept touching you." I tried to keep the jealousy out of my voice, and my words sounded twisted with hostility. It was strange to be the one on the other end of what Eli usually contended with. It was a marked difference from the relationship I had shared with Giovanni, where real resentment or worry had not existed.

A flash of panic shot from his thoughts to mine before his mind shut me out, and then he pulled me closer to him in an attempt to make the issue seem unimportant. His actions only made my suspicions burn brighter.

"He likes me, I guess. He likes men." He let that admission sit between us as though it meant nothing, when it meant everything.

I shouldn't have been surprised really. We were, after all, living in a city with a strong homosexual community. It made me even more envious somehow to know a man coveted my Eli, as there was no way to compete with that. *My Eli*, I thought, surprised by the conviction behind it. I knew he had caught my thought, because a smug and pleased expression slid across his face.

"Stop it," I snapped, "but he had a girlfriend once, he told me about that night he was here with Mary-Jane."

"So, lots of people who are gay have had heterosexual relationships, and stop trying to misdirect me! You're jealous," he needled excitedly. "After all the girls I've been with or could be with, it takes the interest of another man to make you aware of your feelings for me." Before I could say another word, he started touching my body in ways that made me abandon all coherent thoughts. He stayed that day with me, in my bed, holding me tightly until the night returned.

The next evening Eli scampered off to meet friends to "study," though he probably knew the subject matter better than the teacher running the course. Then he was going to some kind of house party, and I didn't expect to meet up with him again until the early morning hours. It was fine with me, as I needed some time to process not only my burgeoning feelings for him but also to contemplate the logic of pursuing a relationship with my niece.

I lingered about the house for a few hours, doing inconsequential things like reorganising my walk-in closet and skimming over a few articles I'd put off reading, but the harder I tried to clear my mind, the more jumbled and convoluted my thoughts became. Finally, I gave up in frustration and headed for the club.

I didn't expect anyone to be there yet, as it was more than an hour before the staff were supposed to start their shifts. It was a Friday night, and I anticipated a full house, a precedent set by the past few weeks. As I approached the back door, I was surprised to hear a steady heartbeat from within the building.

I found Jared inside, alone, busy unloading a shipment of beer. In worrying about everything else, I had completely forgotten it was the night Carmilla's main shipment of the month arrived. Of course, he hadn't let it slip his mind, and I inwardly chalked up another point in his favour. He was so absorbed in his work, he didn't even hear me approach, and remembering the last time I startled him, I made a small coughing noise.

He was still surprised but didn't drop anything this time. "You have got to stop doing that!"

"Sorry," I said, amused despite myself. My smile faltered

when I saw how haggard he looked. Deep bags showed under his eyes, and a few days' growth of stubble on his chin. His skin was sallow and he exuded an air of complete exhaustion. "Wow, you don't look so great."

"I had a rough week." He was trying not to think about something that had happened or perhaps someone he'd been with, but he slipped. I caught an image of the same woman I saw in his mind a few months before, a woman I assumed to be his mother. In this new memory, she was much older and extremely frail looking. Her skin was almost translucent, with blue spidery veins crisscrossing her exposed limbs.

He had told me his mother had died, so perhaps it was someone else from his past. I wished I could get him to speak to me, as it was obvious that he needed to release some of the pent-up anguish associated with this person.

"You want to talk about it?" I asked, gently nudging the crack in his defenses with my otherworldly influence.

He resisted, stubborn and desperate to block out the painful memories. He had a strong will, which surprised me. Glamouring, or influencing human thoughts and memory, was not my strength, though all vampires had the ability to some degree. It's how our existence managed to remain secret for millennia, it and the trail of bodies left behind. Human servants and allies were chosen most carefully. They could be incalculably strong resources to tap into, or they could be the harbingers of danger.

He was trembling, fist clenched at his sides. When it seemed I would not be able to capture his mind completely enough to force him to speak of the things he was trying to repress, he cracked.

His eyes clouded and the tension drained from his jaw and shoulders. The force of the sadness, shame, and anger that hit me when his emotional wall crumbled was staggering. I had never felt anything so forcefully before except from other vampires. When I picked up on human emotions or the emotional sensation attached to a particular thought or memory, the experience was always much more diluted. It was the emotional equivalent of being hit with the spray of a fire hose. He drenched me with his inner torment.

Keeping him under my influence, I walked him down the hall to my office and deposited him in the chair in front of my desk. I leaned on the edge of the desk, lightly touching his legs with my own. I didn't know if it was necessary to keep a physical contact for the mind control to remain, but I figured it couldn't hurt. I never attempted more than a passing influence over people I fed off of but not killed. Even then, I was certain they were left with more of a feeling of confusion, rather than a complete loss of time. I certainly didn't have strength over others like Eli or Charles.

"Why don't you tell me what it is you've been hiding? It's eating you up inside. I think you need to let some of it go." I spoke to him in a very soothing, almost monotonous tone.

He looked up at the sound of my voice, and I was struck again by how terrible he looked. "I don't know if you're who I should talk to. You remind me too much of..." His voice trailed off as his mind wandered back to a particular boyhood memory.

He was in his bed asleep, when the door was thrown open and his mother stumbled into his room. She was dressed only in a pair of panties and a faded t-shirt, her long hair loose and unkempt. Her face was very pale in the dim light spilling in from the hallway. She rushed to Jared's bedside, where he lay quivering under a cowboy-themed comforter. Her eyes were wild, and the boy, Jared, noticed blood on the edge of her shirt, a trail spilling down from a small wound on her neck.

"He was here again," she said in a husky, shaky voice. She was trembling, though not from being cold.

Jared hugged his mother with his arms. "You can't talk like that anymore, Mommy. Remember what Aunt Stella and Dr. Nelson told you; it's just dreams and stuff in your head. Maybe you forgot to take your medicine? Did you forget?" He got up and led his mother back to a room down the hall. The curtains billowed from the wind entering through an open window. The crumpled bedclothes looked as though they were thrown back in haste. As he sat her down on the edge of the bed, I noticed a large number of prescription bottles on the white bedside table.

He looked over a few of the names before finding what he needed. He shook a couple of pills out in his palm then handed them over to his mother with a half-full glass of water. As she dutifully took the medication, he went to the window to shut it and made sure the lock was secured. He gave a quick glance out into the night before drawing the curtains closed. His mother was already lying down when he returned. Her eyes were closed and her breathing ragged. After turning out the light, he lay on the carpet and attempted to go to sleep.

I felt his sadness as my own and understood the shame and defensiveness. The trauma and stigma of growing up with a parent with a mental illness, especially in the societal attitude of twenty years ago, was a heavy burden for any child. Yet something about the scene had a startling familiarity to it. There had been a time before Giovanni shared his secret with me, when I feared I was losing my mind. The parallel was eerie and begged the question whether there wasn't something more to the memory.

"Did your mother think someone was coming to her, someone who made her feel good, yet scared her at the same time?" I was almost afraid to hear the answer.

"Yes, a man, but I don't think she ever knew his name. All she ever talked about was how beautiful he was, with his pale skin, and how cold he felt when he touched her. Then when she started talking about him drinking her blood, my Aunt Stella couldn't ignore it anymore, and she called a doctor."

"And they didn't believe her, right? They thought she was imagining it, hurting herself?" I asked, though I already knew.

"Yes, and then she stopped sleeping. She stayed up all night waiting at the window for him to come, and she didn't bathe anymore, and she stopped doing the laundry and cooking dinner. Eventually Dr. Nelson took her away to the hospital, and she never came back. I stayed with my aunt for a while, before I ended up in foster care." Once the words started, they flooded out.

"But she's still alive, and you still see her sometimes?" I prodded, feeling his fight to pull the wall back up.

"She's still in the hospital," he relented. "She won't ever get out, I'm sure, but it was too embarrassing, you know, especially as a kid. So, I just pretended that she was dead, and then it was easier to go along with that than try to explain what really happened."

"And what do you think really happened?" I asked, trying to offer kindness with softness of my voice.

"I don't know," he said, but it was not the truth. Something hid in the hazy edges of his childhood memories. "Since I've met you and Eli, I've started to wonder if she wasn't telling the truth…. There's something about you that reminds me of things she used to say…"

"What really happened?" I asked again, with a little more pressure.

"One night, when I was sleeping, a strange noise woke me up. It almost sounded like people fighting, but as far as I knew there was only my mom and me at home. I got up and went to her room. The door was open a little bit, and I could hear two voices coming out of her room. At least I thought I did. As I pushed the door open a bit wider, I saw my mom on the bed, with a dark figure standing in front of her. The figure moved so quickly that I never got a good look; I just remember very white skin and bright blue eyes, and for all the years afterward I wondered if I saw anything at all. I went to my mom, who was acting really funny, and she had blood on her neck…and then she was so angry with me for coming into her room! She screamed at me to go back to bed, pushing me aside to go to the window, and, after that, she just went downhill…she could barely be spoken to anymore…" He was lost in thought, back to that night when he witnessed one of my kind feeding on his mother.

"And what does this have to do with me or Eli?"

"You remind me of what my mom described and even what I think I saw. You're so pale and yet so beautiful…and the time that our hands touched, your skin was icy cold, and a couple of times you seemed to move too fast, too perfectly…. When I'm around you I feel…so strange, not like I've ever felt around anyone else in my life. You make me want to touch you, and I think things that I shouldn't, but there are also times when you scare the crap out of me, and I don't know why…. Eli does the same." His honesty was so poignant I felt tears in my eyes.

"Do you think I'm going to hurt you?"

"No, but I think you could."

"Yes, I could," I agreed, "but I won't. I like you, Jared, and even more important than that, I trust you. I don't take it lightly, and now that I know your secret, there might be a way that I can help you, but I'll have to give it some thought." I did my best to slowly ease out of his mind, hoping to cause the least amount of stress and disorientation.

At first, he was still fuzzy, then the strength seemed to just snap back into place. He looked at me suspiciously but wasn't angry. I smiled at him, my feelings tender. "Are you feeling better?"

"What happened?"

"Well, you just about passed out back there. I helped you to the office, and you've been kind of woozy for the last few minutes." *I'm a friend. Believe me*, I thought.

He gave me an odd look but then recovered quickly. "I'm sorry. I guess I didn't get much sleep the last few days. I feel fine now, so maybe I should get back to work." That curious resistance to my peeks inside his mind returned. His wall was up, and I was only privy to what he wanted to let out.

"Sure," I answered casually. "Just take it easy, and if you're not feeling well, it's okay to go home. One of the servers can fill in for a night, and I can close up."

He stood and smiled, really smiled, for the first time in all the months I had known him. "No, I'm good. I feel much better." He walked to the door with the smooth confidence I was used to seeing. Then, without turning back to look at me he asked, "Did I say some stuff about my mother?"

"You mentioned her, yes."

"Anything else?"

"Not that I can recall."

"I can trust that anything that was said here will remain between us?" His words were cautious but not hostile.

"Of course. You can trust me, Jared."

"I know." He left to finish his chores before the club opened for the night.

I sat at my desk to process this new information. It was

obvious his mother had been visited by a vampire and, from the sounds of it, had been visited on a number of occasions. Why didn't he kill her? Perhaps he developed feelings for her; it certainly wasn't unheard of. What could I do to help the situation?

I was just beginning to turn over a plan in my mind, when I caught a touch of familiarity from out in the bar. Charles had just entered and was allowing me access to his mind, so I could pick up on his presence. He was warning me he was there, and he had someone with him.

Someone much stronger and older than he was, another vampire.

I waited until the knock sounded at my door, as I knew it would. "Come in," I called out, hoping I sounded calmer than I felt. One of the servers peeked in and told me I had visitors.

"Send them in."

Charles swept into the room with a beautiful and statuesque creature on his tail. He indicated the empty chair, and the woman came to sit, while he continued to stand. I remained where I was, alternating looks from Charles to the unfamiliar vampire.

She was very striking, even for one of our kind. Her long hair looked as soft as down. It was so pale, it was almost the exact same shade as her ivory skin. Her features were delicate but not childish. Eyes the blue of Siberian huskies stared at me, clear as a cloudless sky, and her lips were a very dark pink. She was quite thin, like a dancer, and very tall. Her hands were thin, too, but her fingers were almost too long to fit her body. The light blue dress she wore was made of a soft, shimmery fabric that clung to her in all the right places. She exuded strength and ancient power, and though I was certain she could overtake me with ease, I felt nothing but inquisitiveness from her. For some reason the word snowy came to mind when I looked at her.

"This is Alessandra," Charles offered. "We've known each other for quite some time now. She is one of the few with whom I try to remain in contact."

"It's nice to meet you, Rachel," she said in the sweetest voice I had ever heard. It was like a siren's call. She rose to her feet and offered her hand to me. I couldn't resist. I took it in my own, and instantly she was inside my head.

The event of her connecting with me was not like anything I had experienced before. With Giovanni it had been like a gentle caress, sometimes abrupt, but never painful. With Eli it was comfortable and non-intrusive. Sometimes with Charles the experience was intense, even bewildering, but with Alessandra it was something new entirely. For lack of a better explanation, it felt like a rape. I felt violated and exposed. Whether it was intentional or not, it wasn't a pleasant occurrence. She reached in with icy, phantom tendrils to rip my experiences and personal feelings away.

The expression on my face must have shown how painful it was for me, because her presence in my mind suddenly receded, and she dropped my hand. She smiled, and it was the most awful, frightening thing I had ever seen. It was like seeing death personified. Fear coursed through my veins. She came to me with her hand out, and I was sick with the thought of her touching me again, yet I could not move away. I saw the slightest flicker of something flash across Charles's face.

"Alessandra, enough," Charles said in a firm voice. She broke her gaze with me, and the feeling instantly evaporated. I was left weakened and tired. "She doesn't know her own strength sometimes."

"Yes, I do," she said, again with that wonderfully sweet voice. "I just like to test the water right up front."

I did my best to regain my composure. I tried to keep my mind blank and inaccessible, and I forced myself to meet her face again. "You're very old, aren't you?"

"Yes," she said. When she smiled this time, she showed me the face of an angel.

"Alessandra knew Giovanni, and she's agreed to help us. She has ties with several very old and very powerful vampires who could mean the difference between success or failure."

I looked to her, surprised that she knew Giovanni, as he never mentioned her name. "How did you know him?" I couldn't help but ask.

She smirked. "We crossed paths not long after he was made.

He was a mess, to say the least. He needed some guidance after being dumped by this one." She jerked her thumb in Charles's direction, but she seemed more amused than admonishing. "I took him under my wing, so to speak."

"And?" I asked quietly.

"And then we went our separate ways. I'm much too fickle to stay with one person or in one place for too long." It too seemed amusing to her, as though there was a joke that I didn't get, which she didn't wish to share. "Of course, we have crossed paths now and then over the years."

"I see," I said, though clearly I did not have all the information.

"I was glad to hear he had found someone at long last, of course. He was always such a silly romantic, so heartbroken and mournful. I never did get it, but you obviously did."

Her words sounded chiding, but I didn't take the bait. "Obviously."

"He was an excellent killer, though."

I didn't reply, as I wasn't sure what a proper response to that statement could be.

Charles had his blank mask in place again. It was disconcerting because I didn't know if he was agreeing with her or if it was simply his way to proceed with the meeting. Charles rarely showed emotion, but after more than a year of living with him, I was able to pick up on the subtle clues, and there seemed to be a bit of arrogance to the way he was holding himself. I had to wonder if Alessandra's antics weren't rubbing him the wrong way.

"Alessandra was most disturbed when I explained to her what has happened. She agrees that the Desmarais and their supporters need to be eradicated."

"And you think that others will feel as strongly about it?" I asked.

"Any threat to others of our kind should always be considered as a direct threat to ourselves," she answered. Even selfish motivations, like one's own protection, could be beneficial to a greater good.

"She will be staying with us for a few days and then will

take information and plans back to a group in Europe. When we are closer to the time of attack, we will meet up with them there. It seems the most prudent and acceptable course for all involved. All the sites we are targeting are in continental Europe or Great Britain."

"You know what's best," I agreed.

A brief silence filled the room before Charles abruptly ended the meeting. "I think that it's time for me to take Alessandra hunting. She arrived just last night, and unless I'm mistaken, she has not had the chance yet to feed." He turned to Alessandra. "I realise, of course, that one as old and strong as you does not need to feed often, but I would like to offer the opportunity."

Alessandra's smile was as sweet as apple pie, and I could tell the flattery delighted her. "Lovely. I have not been to this side of the world since before Prohibition. It will be interesting to take in the changes." She stood, hand held out for Charles to take. He did so graciously, reminding me of the difference in our respective ages. Alessandra and Charles represented a time when gallantry and manners were expected. She gave me a frighteningly innocent look, and I held my own, keeping my expression neutral.

"I can see why Giovanni picked you. You are very beautiful."

"Thank you," I said, because I wasn't sure what else to say. Her words didn't feel like a compliment. They felt like a warning. Alessandra would be a formidable ally, and God knew we needed all the help we could get, but I was still glad to see her leave.

When I went out into the club later that night, I made sure to make a connection with Jared. I smiled as he handed me my wine and was pleased to see his relief was still present. The warmth softened his usually serious face and made me bubble forth with laughter before I could help myself. He chuckled a bit, too, and I was certain he knew I had nothing but good intentions where he was concerned.

Back at the house, I discovered Charles and Alessandra had already returned from their expedition. They sat in the large entertainment room at the back, where weeks earlier Mary-Jane and Micah had been our guests. The doors were open to the unlit back patio. Charles looked even stiffer than he normally did, his neck craned away from where Alessandra sat at his side. He met my eyes when I entered the room and gave me a pained look. Alessandra positively glowed and seemed as pleased as a child on Christmas morning.

"Oh, wonderful. You're back," she purred. "Come join us."

I did as she asked, perplexed when she slid her chair from Charles's side to mine. She spoke quite intently with me, giving me her undivided attention, which wasn't at the top of my most favourite experiences. She was curious about every aspect of my relationship with Giovanni, how we had met, where we had gone, things we had seen. Charles remained silent during the entire hour-long exchange, appearing, by my estimation, bored and irritated. By the end of the conversation, I felt as though I had been through a vigorous interrogation, though she smiled throughout, and all of her inquiries were very carefully worded so as never to seem as though she were prying.

I was scrambling for some reason to excuse myself when I heard the front door open. A warm and comforting shift in the atmosphere took hold when Eli entered the house, and I tried to keep my relief from my face. Alessandra's attention was drawn away from me, and she appeared quite eager as she waited for Eli to appear. He came through the door with an easy smile on his face, eyes instantly locking onto me. He faltered just a fraction of a second when he realised it was not just Charles and me, then with confidence came to join me on the loveseat where I was waiting. He pressed a kiss to my cheek before acknowledging Alessandra's presence.

"Hello," he offered in her direction, before looking back to me.

Alessandra stood, with Charles instantly springing to his feet behind her as though he anticipated a problem. Eli pulled me to my feet with a gentle hand at my elbow as he rose. Alessandra had by then extended her long, ghostly hand, and dread seized my stomach as I relived my own vulgar experience at her touch. As their flesh met, Eli flinched, and his jaw tightened. Alessandra smiled without it being friendly in any way.

"You must be Eli. I have heard so much about you." Keeping

her grip on Eli's hand, she slid her other hand along his bare arm in a way that was much too intimate. She winked at me as she continued, "But you never told me what a beauty he was! You've been keeping things from me, you bad girl."

Eli's lip curled in a snarl, and I felt the revulsion for him. She was an ungodly, beautiful creature, yet there was something so vile about the way she made a person feel, it wiped away any attraction or lust one might feel for her, but she was also so powerful that we were all at her mercy. Eli pulled away from her, breaking her contact with both his hand and arm. Without hesitation, he wrapped his freed arm about my waist and clenched a tight fist with his other hand.

She never faltered in her smile nor her amusement for one second. "And a very lucky girl, by the looks of it. Always the most handsome men." Her comment was pointed and tormented me as it was supposed to. I was washed with shame, even though I knew I had done nothing wrong.

"Yes. I am very lucky to have the wonderful people in my life that I do." I answered as frankly as possible, hoping I held the biting tone at bay.

"People? You still refer to yourself that way? How sweet." Her look told me she thought it was anything but.

Charles stepped in smoothly, at that break in our exchange. "Eli, this is Alessandra. She has come to help with the Desmarais."

His fingers gripped my side painfully. "I see. Then things are proceeding, are they? I hadn't heard any talk of late."

"Well, we can't let these people get away with this, now can we? We are the superior beings here, and they must be reminded of it. Wiping any trace of that scum from the face of the earth is the only acceptable remedy."

"And you don't think that there will be any retaliation to these actions? You don't think it might inspire others to take up their cause?" Eli asked. I was yanked back down to the loveseat where Eli sat, like a puppet, with everyone else pulling my strings and controlling my actions.

Alessandra also sat, though Charles remained standing. "Alessandra has come a long way and is offering solidarity that she does not have to. We should all be thankful for it."

She cocked her head in Charles's direction. "Certain things are just not acceptable." Then she turned back to Eli. "And, to be truthful, squashing a pathetic group like the Desmarais would be most pleasurable."

Eli's face burnt with anger at her words. "I would not call them pathetic. After all, they did manage to kill an almost three-hundred-year-old vampire, someone whom we happened to love very much."

"Love." She spoke the word as though she had no idea of its meaning.

God, she was creepy, with her icy smile and her musical voice. I shuddered before I could stop myself.

"Of course, I meant no disrespect to Giovanni's name. They were excellently prepared to have accomplished such a feat, and they must not be allowed the opportunity ever again."

"I agree," Charles said harshly.

Alessandra's face softened, and she turned an almost friendly look in our direction. "Perhaps we have gotten off on the wrong foot. It's been a long time since I have interacted with other vampires as young as the two of you, and I must seem terribly abrupt. I have nothing but fond memories of Giovanni, and I am honoured to help in any way that I can to avenge his demise."

Charles nodded at me, and I understood the intention. "Of course, Alessandra, this is a very upsetting subject for us, as you can imagine. We are very thankful for your assistance in all of it." I did my best to appear reassuring, and it wasn't easy.

"Yes, thank you," Eli said, his body still rigid with anger. A cold silence enveloped us for a full minute before he spoke again. "I think that I'm going to retire now. Alessandra is welcome to use my room for the night. Charles, you know the code. Rachel, are you coming with me?" His point couldn't have been more obvious.

"Of course." Eli all but carried me out of the room in his hurry to leave. "Good night," I called over my shoulder. My last glance was of a disapproving Charles and a smug Alessandra, their white figures framed by the dark night.

Eli didn't say another word until we were in my room with the door closed and the locks securely in place. His voice, just above a whisper, was the only defense against ears that could hear as well, if not better than our own. "What is going on here? Who is that woman?"

"Eli, you were very rude. We can use her help. I know you can feel how old and powerful she is, and she has connections to others like her. It could be just what we need to get rid of these people once and for all."

He glared at me, eyes red with anger. "And just like that you're going to trust her? Didn't Giovanni tell us that most vampires are solitary creatures, concerned only with themselves? Did he ever mention her name before? Because I don't recall it. What if we count on her, and she fails us? One of us could get killed then. Have you thought about any of this?"

Eli was angrier than I had ever seen him. He seethed with disbelief and hostility.

"Charles trusts her."

"And that makes it so then? It wasn't so long ago that Charles himself would have been top of our list of vampires we can't trust!" His voice rose ever so slightly before he caught himself.

My anger flared in response to Eli's attack. "It may be so, but for the last year and a half, he has been nothing but a good friend to us."

"I know, I know. I'm a bit freaked out here."

"Me, too. I knew nothing about her until Charles showed up in my office tonight, but he trusts her, and it's good enough for me."

His outrage dropped a few levels before he spoke again. "And what's with her, anyway? What was she doing in my head? It was awful."

"I know; I experienced it myself earlier. She's very powerful."

He sat at the end of the bed, resting his head forward onto his hands. "You're scaring me, Rachel. It's like you've lost all perspective and reason. I am so afraid that you're going to get yourself killed with your recklessness or impulsivity. Have you though at all about what would happen to me if you were gone?"

His words hit right where they were supposed to. The sting was almost unbearable but was also getting old. "Stop, Eli, stop with your guilt. I can't take any more! I am doing the best that I can, and I'm not going to apologise for my feelings!" I snapped at him more harshly than I meant to, but I couldn't allow myself to be pushed any further. I had to draw the line.

He looked up, and his obvious hurt raked away at my fragile heart. "Why does it seem that all we do is fight anymore?"

I sat beside him, weariness a familiar companion. "I don't know. It seems like we're spinning our wheels, always coming back to this point. There will never be a chance for us if I have to deny my feelings for Giovanni or be pushed into being someone that I'm not."

"That's not what I'm trying to do. I love you for who you are, always have. It just seems like you're deliberately leaving me in the cold, like you don't trust me or care about my opinion. I mean you're leaving this whole thing with the Desmarais up to Charles, and I loved Giovanni, too. I want to help bring these people down. I need to be part of it, and then bringing strangers into our home, strangers who could crush us like bugs, and this whole thing with Danica…. I don't know."

I swallowed the lump in my throat, choking it down to where the rest of my pain resided. "I know you loved Giovanni, and you will be a part of it. I'm counting on you to be a huge part of it. The truth is simply that Charles is so much older and more experienced than we are. He has more resources and more influence, and it has to succeed. As for everything else, no matter how much I may love you or what direction our relationship may go in, I can't defend everything I do to you. You can't expect it of me, and I would never ask that of you."

"I'm so afraid of losing you." He threw his arms around me.

"You will never lose me no matter what happens. I love you too much for that." I hugged him back, feeling so right in his arms. "Let's get through it together, please."

We fell asleep in each other's arms that night, naked bodies pressed together. Eli was an unshakable part of my soul. I knew I couldn't live without him, any more than he could live without me. He gave me focus and comfort, and he pulled me back down to earth when I needed grounding. I loved his mind, his body, his empathy and loyalty. I needed his unwavering commitment to make it all worthwhile. Once Giovanni's loss had been avenged, the only person left to continue for would be Eli.

For the first time in many months I really rested, and I didn't dream.

CHAPTER 6

Eli was already gone by the time I decided to head out to the club. I spent an uncomfortable hour "socialising" with Charles and Alessandra before they decided to leave. Alessandra wanted to see a particular play currently being performed in Los Angeles, and Charles had no real choice but to accompany her. I chuckled at the thought of him sitting in an audience of intense, appreciative theater-goers, as much as it obviously pained him. She planned to depart the following night, so humoring her whims was the least he could do. What we would receive in return for placating her for a few days was well worth the inconvenience.

It was Saturday night, and as expected, Mary-Jane and the band were already there when I arrived. Surprisingly, so was Eli. He was hanging out in the small changing room with the others as they unloaded instruments, talked, and individually prepared for the night's performance. As I peeked in, Eli gave me a sly wink, and Mary-Jane greeted me with her usual quick hug. She was always so warm, her scent exhilarating. I tried not to let anyone, especially her, see how much her nearness aroused the hunger in me. I don't think anyone except for Eli, who was similarly affected, noticed any strange reaction on my part. It was all an essential component of being what we are—deflecting, hiding, and assimilating, but Eli was right, she smelled good enough to eat.

I perched on the edge of the sofa where Eli lounged. "What are you doing here?"

He pulled himself up closer to my side as he answered. "The

regular piano guy bailed. He apparently decided to take off for
New York a couple of days ago. They're stuck until they can find
a permanent replacement. I said I'd fill in for a while."

"He's our saviour," the guitarist offered half-jokingly.

Eli shrugged indifferently. Micah was watching our
exchange, looking almost longingly at Eli as he sat mere inches
from me. I could tell Eli noticed as well but was intent on
ignoring Micah's appreciative glances. We had always been very
careful about how our relationship with each other appeared to
those around us, even before Giovanni was killed. Outwardly
to the people we interacted with, Eli and I were close friends
and distant relatives. Anything else was solely between the two
of us.

I was caught off guard when he reached out and traced
his hand along the outside of my thigh. I raised an eyebrow in
his direction. Micah never wavered from his consideration of
the exchange between Eli and me, but he also didn't show any
outward reaction. He wasn't privy to the fact that both of us
could see his thoughts to a certain degree and were absorbing
the feelings he couldn't help but project. He was full of longing,
confusion, and jealousy. I wasn't sure whether Eli's action had
been for Micah, to entice a jealous reaction, or for me, to show I
could have competition.

Mary-Jane smirked, then turned back to finish her makeup.
I stood to leave, and as I bid my goodbye, Eli followed me from
the room.

"I want to talk to you before we head out," he whispered too
quietly for the others to hear.

We walked to my office, where he shut the door behind us. I
remained standing, somehow uneasy without knowing why. "I
overheard Charles and Alessandra talking before I left tonight.
I think that some type of problem has come up."

"What kind of problem?" I asked, concern started to buzz
at my senses.

"I'm not sure exactly, but it sounded like the Desmarais
may have turned one of Charles's accomplices and let some
information slip, something that might have indicated where we
are currently." He was delivering the words so unemotionally

that it was even more unnerving than if he had been angry or upset.

"Did you get a sense of whether or not it has been resolved?"

A slight shake of his head indicated not. "All I heard was that the breach has been eliminated, and I think we both know what it means. Then they both clammed up once they figured out I was listening. I just have a feeling that all is not going as smoothly as Charles might want you to believe." He took my hand and squeezed it softly. "I think you should talk to him."

"I will." I was worried but more unsettled by Eli's seemingly detached reaction. "I haven't really spoken with him about it at all since that night he approached me with the plan, and it was months ago."

"Maybe we need to start being more involved. After all, we will be putting ourselves in the line of fire, and the outcome of it is going to have the most meaning for us. To the others, it will simply be about financial reward or, in the case of the other vampires, dominance. It's not personal for them, but it is for us."

I leaned into his chest, so firm and strong under my cheek. How could loving him give me so much conflict? It didn't make sense in moments like that, where it was just us and the way we made each other feel.

A knock at the door interrupted the moment, and with regret I pulled myself out of his embrace. When he looked at me this time, his face showed his concern and affection.

"Come on, Eli," Mary-Jane called from the hallway. "We're going to the stage now."

"I'm coming." He placed a quick kiss on my hand. I remained rooted in place as he pulled the door open and moved away from me to meet the band. Once he was out of sight, I was overcome with the most violent chill and an irrational fear I would never see him again. I raced out into the hallway after him, and he turned when he heard my approach.

He frowned as I neared, picking up on my anxiety. "What's the matter?"

"Eli…" I began, but sufficient words did not exist to express what I felt. I launched myself into his arms and kissed him with unabashed passion, while the members of the band watched in surprise. His hands were in my hair and, with our bodies pressed together, I lost myself to the feeling of his lips against mine.

Sounds of laughter and catcalls erupted, bringing our moment of intimacy to an unceremonious end. I was never demonstrative in my physical affection for him, and my sudden outburst had caught him off guard.

He hugged me quickly and kissed my cheek before swaggering off to join the others, who were waiting at the mouth of the stage hallway. "All right, show's over. Nothing more to see, people." He was met with laughter and a high five from the new acoustic guitar player.

Mary-Jane was smiling and gave me a sly wink. Only Micah seemed less than amused.

I wasn't sure what possessed me, but I felt a tremendous sense of relief, as though a kiss could change anything, but somehow I knew it had. Perhaps it was the step I had needed to take and the reassurance Eli had been silently craving.

When I came around the bar from the back, Jared was joking with a few female patrons, and I was pleased to see him so open and happy. Our conversation seemed to have let something loose inside of him. He was emotionally freed, available to connections, which for so long had been shut off from him. I hoped things would be easier for him, and these new experiences would fulfill him in ways he had never imagined. A little flirting from some attractive and attentive women never hurt anyone.

I took my glass of wine with a knowing look, which Jared returned with a self-satisfied smirk. The band started to play as I settled at my usual table. I was enjoying a new number Mary-Jane and the band hadn't performed before when I caught a figure approaching my table in my peripheral vision. Danica's distinctive musky scent touched me before she was closer than ten feet. She stopped at my side, hesitating, and I turned to look up into her fretful face. I tipped my head in the direction of the empty chair, and with an air of relief she sat.

"What are you doing here?" I asked, as pleased to see her as I was apprehensive.

She strained her voice above the music to respond. "I haven't heard from you in a few weeks, so I thought I would take my chances. I figured the worst that could happen would be that you weren't here or you would ask me to leave." She looked at me expectantly, waiting to see if that was indeed what would happen.

"You don't need to leave. I'm just listening to the band, and you're more than welcome to join me."

She stopped herself just before a huge smile crossed her face, and with a flick of her long, dark hair settled back into her seat. I gave her a cursory once over, surprised to find her in skinny, dark jeans, slouchy boots, and a shimmery capped sleeved shirt in a bright aqua. She even wore a bit of makeup. It was a big departure from her usual blouses and long skirts. Catching my appraisal, she looked nervously down onto her outfit.

"You look nice," I confirmed. She was out of her comfort zone, something I could relate to.

One of the servers passed by our table, and I raised a hand to get her attention. I asked for a replacement for the wine I barely touched, and Danica ordered a rye and ginger. We sat together in a comfortable silence for the nearly two hours the band played. Every so often she made a half-hearted attempt at conversation, and even then, it was light and inconsequential.

As the band retreated from the stage, she turned to me. I studied her face, so much like my own and yet very attractive in its own way. Her cheeks were slightly rosy and her lips much fuller than mine. With the makeup, her eyes seemed enormous and electrically blue. I thought of what time would ultimately do to that face and felt a sharp stab of regret.

"So, I've seen Eli around the campus a few times. He has classes in the same area where I teach on Tuesdays and Wednesdays. I've seen him leaving with Micah a number of times."

I was curious why she felt compelled to mention that particular fact to me. Had my resentment at Micah's repeated physical contact with Eli during the last time we were together been that obvious, or were there things going on outside of my knowledge that had drawn her curiosity?

Just as I was about to answer, Micah, Eli, and Mary-Jane joined us. Eli came immediately to the empty seat at my side. Mary-Jane took the one on the other side of Eli, and Micah pulled up a chair from another table to sit between her and Danica. Mary-Jane was obviously pumped up from the set as her eyes were bright, her movements quick. She was like an excited little sprite, bestowing her infectious enthusiasm on our group. I couldn't help but return her smile, and I vicariously enjoyed the unselfconscious way she rocked to the music from her seat. Someone grabbed her attention, and she raised her hand in a vigorous wave. After whispering in Eli's ear, she bounded off to join a friend at the area near the stage to dance.

Within thirty minutes or so, the club had thinned noticeably. The four of us remained at the table, talking about activities at the university. Mary-Jane popped over every now and again for a quick drink before returning to her friends. By last call, there were only about fifty people left, and we waited it out until the last of the patrons cleared. Mary-Jane, Danica, Micah, Eli, and I stayed after the club closed for the night, even after all the staff except for Jared had left.

The overhead lights had been turned on, washing the space with an overly bright, yellowish light. Eli and Micah jumped back up on the stage to play along with the music from the sound system the staff left on while they had cleaned and closed up. Eventually Mary-Jane joined them, her apparent intoxication not diminishing the quality of her voice in the slightest.

Jared soon joined Danica and me at the table with a tray of shots and a large glass of beer for himself. Danica grabbed one of the shots and tossed it back with a "What the Hell." She grimaced at the aftertaste, and Jared and I both laughed at her reaction. Micah returned, downing three in fast succession, while Mary-Jane wisely refused. Under normal circumstances, it would have been just a fun, relaxed time among friends, but with us, it was never normal circumstances, and too many overlapping pasts, feelings, and uncertainties existed.

The alarm shrieked, and before anyone had a chance to react, Charles, with Alessandra in tow, appeared from the door behind the bar. He would never have drawn attention to himself that way without just provocation. I knew instantly that something very bad had happened.

"We need to get everyone out of here," he ordered, as he came with quick, long strides to where we sat.

I saw the understanding in Danica's eyes as she looked first to Charles then to Alessandra. Eli jumped from the stage, moving a little too quickly. A cold look of shock flashed across Jared's face, and his body tensed, but he did not make a sound.

"What happened?" Eli's voice was heavy and nervous.

"The Desmarais have men here in San Francisco. They could be on their way."

Charles's eyes were pits of anger.

"How could this have happened?" I stood, and my chair fell away from me with sharp smash against the floor.

Danica jumped.

"There was a leak. One of my contacts had a man who thought it might be more profitable for him to play both sides of the fence. Unfortunately for him, it only got him and his family a trip to the bottom a very deep lake, but the breach has been made nonetheless, and the Desmarais have sent some men to check out the tip."

Fiery panic erupted within my body, but my mind was curiously calm. *Get everyone out*, I thought. Micah and Mary-Jane had joined us by that time, and I looked over the innocent and frightened faces before me.

"Rachel, we need to leave, now." Eli sounded pissed.

I grabbed Danica's hand. "You're coming with me." I was compelled to protect my niece, no matter what. We had barely taken a few steps from the table when the distinctive sound of gunshots rang out in the hollow space. "Jesus, get down!"

The door from the back hallway burst open at just about the same time as a small group of men spilled in from the front doors. Men shouted out excited, hurried instructions in French. More shots rang out, piercing the startled silence. One of the glasses on the table burst apart in a shower of glass and liquor. Eli reacted immediately, racing forward to grab the first two men from the front-entrance group. He reached the men in the blink of an eye, snapping the neck of the first without effort and breaking the back of the second over his leg like a twig. The second man's body was tossed back into their numbers, causing a momentary distraction.

It was just enough time for me to grab my niece and Jared and race them back toward the stage end of the club. I lifted them over the wall of the DJ booth, instructing them to stay down. They both complied without resistance. Micah and Mary-Jane still stood near the table, confused and alarmed. A shot exploded from the back of the club, and there was no chance I would get there in time. I watched as the bullet slammed through Micah's shoulder and Mary-Jane shrieked. Charles grabbed the gunman. In his cold and deliberate way, he twisted the man's head from his body. A shower of blood sprayed across his light tan jacket.

Micah grabbed his shoulder, stumbled, but didn't go down. "Mary-Jane move!" he screamed. He grabbed a rifle from the ground that had fallen from the hands of Eli's first victim and, setting his sights on the intruders, opened fire. He took down two before the shock of being shot wore off, and the first wave of pain seized him.

Looking back, I saw Alessandra had made short order of at least three men, and her fangs were sunk into the throat of another. The man thrashed helplessly in her arms, squealing, "No vampire! No vampire!" in English thick with a foreign accent. I could only assume he was begging to not be made into one of us.

Charles eliminated all the others who came through the back way. "I'm checking outside," he called out before disappearing around the end of the bar.

Everything was happening at a dizzying pace, but my focus remained solid. I joined Eli, who was still contending with several of the Desmarais attackers. As I neared, I realised he had been shot several times, and I could smell the distinctive scent of his blood in the air amid the sweat and firepower.

Then I caught sight of one of the prod-like instruments the Desmarais used in Giovanni's murder, and my mind snapped. It was clutched in the hand of a dead man on the floor. Uncontrollable anger and hatred boiled to the surface. I kicked at it with fury, knocking away not only the prod but also the hand that held it. It flew across the room, connecting solidly with the wall. The prod made a sharp twangy sound as it fell to the floor, and the hand left a long splat against the wall before joining the vile device it had been holding. The wet and heavy sound it made as it landed on the floor was pure satisfaction.

Next, I grabbed the man closest to me and punched through his chest, the ribcage offering little resistance against my supernatural strength. My hand closed around his heart and I ripped it from his body. His blood was hot and thick, soaking my skin and calling my thirst. I squashed the organ under my shoe and dropped the body to the floor. I licked the fresh blood from the fingers of my right hand.

Seeing it, the man behind him bolted, but I caught the strap of his rifle as he attempted to flee. His comrade's blood was smeared across my lips as I pulled him back to me. I smelled urine as I grasped him in my arms. He was so young, barely out of his teens, but I felt nothing but righteousness as I forced the life from his body with my bare hands. When I was done, he wouldn't be easy to identify. I heard a body drop, and as I turned, Eli wiped a hand across his mouth. I dropped my line of sight to the corpse at his feet, taking in the jagged wound where Eli's fangs had pierced the man's flesh. All was suddenly so quiet and still.

Alessandra made her way toward the center of the room with deliberate movements, eyeing all the motionless bodies littering the room with unconcealed delight. Her face was so lovely I ached looking at her, but the blood soaking the front of her soft blue dress spoiled her perfection and belied the reason for her euphoria.

Dimly I became aware of someone crying. I turned to Eli and pressed my hand to his shirt, damp with blood. He shook his head to indicate he was fine and pulled me close. Nowhere else could I feel as wonderful and as safe as I did when in his arms. "I need to check out front," he said.

Wild panic seized me. I clutched onto him with all my strength.

"Rachel, please, I'm fine. I have to be sure that no one got away."

It was agony to let go. Without another sound, he disappeared around the wall leading to the front door. I felt a powerful tingle along my skin and turned to find Alessandra at my side. "Well, that was fun." She smirked, but I experienced nothing but cold dread. It was too much like the night Giovanni had been taken from me.

"Rachel," my niece called out with a surprisingly steady voice. "I need some help here."

I followed the sound of her voice to find her bent over Micah, who was leaning back against the side of the stage. She pressed her hand to his damaged shoulder. His shirt was soaked with blood, and my inner beast threatened to spill out as I caught the scent. Mary-Jane was crying softly, crouched at his side.

I scanned the area until I located Jared. His face was very white, his eyes blank. He remained in the DJ booth, visible through the open doors. I tried to reach out to him with my mind, but he was completely shut down. His heart was pounding, but outwardly he showed no signs of distress. He was processing what happened, most likely trapped in an internal struggle to reconcile the events against certain childhood memories.

"Rachel!" This time Danica sounded more urgent.

I rushed to her, pushing aside all other thoughts. I gently pulled back her hand and surveyed the wound. "It went right through," I commented softly.

Mary-Jane cringed as I touched Micah's shoulder. Danica put an arm around the frightened girl and led her away to a nearby table.

"I'm okay," he said through clenched teeth. "I can feel my arm, and my hand still works." To prove his point he squeezed my hand, meeting my eyes with a knowing look. "I think you can stop the bleeding."

I rocked back on my heels, stunned by his frank demeanor. "Yes, I can." He nodded. I ripped the shirt away from his body and slowly lowered my mouth to the injury. The blood was sweet and warm, but I did not allow myself to linger. Vampires have healing qualities in their saliva, allowing them to leave neat, barely noticeable marks from feeding, when the blood lust is controlled and when they choose to. I used it to stop the flow of blood.

"You should still clean this thoroughly and use a sling for a few days to allow the damage to heal properly." I felt like a nurse giving after care advice, instead of the monster I had just revealed myself to be.

Eli reappeared at my side. I leaned into him as he bent down beside me then turned back to survey the carnage. Bodies were splayed everywhere, their blood impossibly red in the harsh light. I counted fifteen men altogether and was sickened at the vicious recklessness that caused their demise.

I eyed Jared, still seated awkwardly in the DJ booth, Danica, and Mary-Jane, huddled together at a nearby table. Then I turned back to Micah, who was regarding me with a look of uncomfortable awe. He then looked to Eli, and I absorbed the accompanying rush of attraction, fear, and wonder.

Reality dragged me back as Charles rushed in through the rear entrance. He stopped at Alessandra's side, taking his own time to peruse the mess. He looked to the four human witnesses, and I stiffened as the next thought passed through his mind. *This is not good. Too many witnesses.*

I returned my gaze to Eli's face, and his painful agreement with Charles's assessment washed through me. I jumped to my feet, quickly closing the distance to where Charles was standing.

"There's no way," I said, my anger riled up once again.

"Then what do you suggest? That we allow them all to leave and hope that they won't disclose what they have seen to others? Or wait for them to turn and bring destruction to us themselves?" His voice was quiet but seething with hostility.

"They've done nothing wrong here, Charles," I countered. I flicked my gaze about the room, taking in the undisguised nervousness of the four.

"I agree." Eli joined us, weariness evident in the way he held his body. I looked at Charles then to Alessandra, who remained silent the entire time. Her small, satisfied smile was terrifying. "I think the only one who might be a problem is Jared. The others seem to be coping well, and I don't get any thoughts of retaliation or animosity from any of them. They are simply afraid."

Four pairs of vampire eyes fell onto the shaken humans before them. I could taste Danica's quiet fear but also acceptance. Mary-Jane was scared, confused, but also, in her own way, tolerant. Micah was physically affected but was strangely curious and pleased. Jared was the only hold-out. His mind was protected with an iron wall against all my attempts to penetrate it. He solidly met our collective gaze, and I thought I felt an uneasy resignation wash out from his direction.

"Let me talk to him."

As I started my approach, Jared's eyes widened, and I did my best to reach out to him soothingly. His mind was held tightly shut, but his pale, blank face betrayed the extent of his shock. He was still seated, with his back pressed against the back of the DJ booth. I entered the small space and sat next to him on the floor. There was just enough space between us that our bodies did not touch. He turned to me.

"You're a vampire, aren't you?" His hands were trembling.

"Yes," I answered and gently placed one of my hands over his.

"And my mother really saw what she said she did?"

"Yes," I responded.

He shook his head, the ramifications of that truth sinking in. "And no one believed her, not even me. What she must have gone through…"

"It's not your fault, Jared. We go to great effort to make sure that as few people know about us as possible. Even most of the people that we interact with on a regular basis don't know our true nature. If you hadn't seen what you did here tonight, our existence would have been all but impossible for you to believe."

"Are you going to kill us?" His strangely-coloured eyes were luminous and touched me with their intensity. It was the second time in the past few months I was asked that question by someone toward whom I had no ill intentions.

"No, I'm not going to kill you, but I am going to ask if you can handle this knowledge and keep it to yourself." I waited patiently for his reply.

He sat silent for a few minutes, clearly thinking about the request made of him. His inner shield began to slip, and I understood the turmoil and conflict he was experiencing about his feelings toward me. "Do I have a choice?"

"Of course. If you are afraid, or if what you witnessed has turned you against me and by extension against all of us, then we will have to do something about it. There are several strong vampires here who can take this night's memory from you, and you can go back to the way things were before."

"But it also means that I won't know that my mother has been telling the truth all these years."

"It's true. Only you can decide what you can live with."

He was briefly silent, lips pursed in contemplation. "I need to tell my mother I believe her. She needs to know that someone does."

"I think we can do better than that." I smiled with as much reassurance as I could and was glad to see him relax somewhat.

I stood and offered him my hand. He took it after a brief hesitation, and I easily helped him to his feet. We walked over to the table where the others sat together. No one was speaking, and the quiet was unnerving. Mary-Jane kept darting furtive glances back at the pile of dead bodies on the floor. She appeared queasy, and I wouldn't have been at all surprised if she threw up, considering the amount of alcohol she had consumed. I sat next to Eli and gave him a nod to start the conversation.

"Well, I guess we all need to decide how we're going to proceed from here." He looked around the table, meeting each set of human eyes before continuing. "Our secret is out in the open now, and there's no going back to the way it was before, and I want to assure all of you as well as I can that no matter what happened here tonight, we have no intention of harming any of you."

"I can't believe it," Micah suddenly interjected. "After all the years of studying and lecturing, I've actually met a real vampire, vampires. You really exist." His astonishment was evident, undercut with exhilaration.

"We really exist," I agreed in a quiet voice, "but it is not something that can leave this room. The continuation of our existence depends on it. You can understand it, I'm sure, especially after what happened tonight."

"What did happen tonight?" Danica's question was directed at me, but it was Charles who jumped in with an answer.

"An old enemy has resurfaced." His voice was icy, and his haughty accent made his words seem even more antagonistic.

"An old enemy? I don't understand. They were men, not vampires, and some of them weren't much older than boys," Danica stated.

"Yes, they were, but they come from a family that holds on to a terrible vendetta, and they pass on this vendetta from one generation to the next, always with the same driving intent."

"Well, it's not completely true," I interrupted.

Charles's green eyes flashed in my direction. "I suppose you're right. Their mission has veered off course somewhat since their last attack."

I winced at the horrible image his words invoked.

Danica caught my reaction and said, "They are the men who killed Giovanni?"

I nodded, and Eli's hand clamped onto my leg. "Yes, the same group, anyway. They killed Giovanni, and now they are intent on killing any he was associated with or any vampires in general."

"But instead we're going to kill them," Eli cut in.

Danica looked alarmed at Eli's statement, and Charles's face became tight with barely concealed annoyance. Only Alessandra's demeanor remained unchanged. She sat as still as a statue, with that same awful smile pulling at her lips.

"Eli, we don't need to go into it now." Charles's words were a warning, and Eli wisely heeded them.

"We need to worry about cleaning up," said Mary-Jane, and there was a collective feeling of surprise from all of the vampires. "The rest we can figure out tomorrow." Everyone turned at the sound of her voice, and then we looked out to the litter of corpses.

Charles whipped out his cell phone and walked away from the group as he started dialing. His call was answered almost as soon as he punched in the last number. "Nomo, we need disposal and cleaning right now." He paused momentarily as the voice on the other end countered. "Fifteen." Another pause, followed by a loud response in rapid Spanish. "The cost doesn't matter; the quality and speed of the job is all I am concerned with. I want a crew here within thirty minutes." More fast talking. "No excuses." He ended the call after giving the address and returned the phone to his pocket.

He returned to the table, facing several anxious expressions. "I think Alessandra, and I can handle things on this end." She nodded once, without losing her smile. "Rachel, Eli, you take the others back to the house. We should all remain together until things are settled. We'll join you when we're done here." He looked around the table but was not met with any argument. I felt a swarm of powerful feelings: fear, apprehension, and confusion. Danica smiled bravely, and even Jared managed an agreeable expression.

I took the lead, and we all filed out to the back parking lot, with Eli bringing up the rear. I took Danica and Mary-Jane with me, and the rest followed in Jared's car. It was a short but silent trip to the house. I punched in the code, moving ahead to allow Jared's car to also pass through the open gates.

Eli jumped out and, in a blur of movement, punched in the code to close the gates securely behind us. He came to my window, leaning down to speak with me. "I'm going to take a look around. Take everyone in and contact the security company to ask that they do some extra patrols tonight and tomorrow. Make sure you set the alarm." He looked at me with hard eyes, and I didn't take offense at him stating the obvious. He was deeply concerned for my safety, as well as the safety of our unexpected guests.

Rushing everyone inside, I entered the code as soon as the doors shut. I settled them in the large entertainment room, where I made the call to the security company. I arranged for an hourly patrol for the next twenty-four hours, with a reassessment to follow. Micah took a seat by himself, while the other three sat on the leather couch, looking equally shaken and anxious. I sat in the chair next to Micah, trying to project a confidence I didn't feel.

"Well, it was quite a night," Micah offered.

Danica gave a nervous laugh and looked to Mary-Jane, who

smiled thinly. "Yes," she agreed. "Definitely more than the few drinks I bargained for."

"Did you know?" Mary-Jane asked with sudden vigor. "I mean, did you know that Rachel was a vampire? You seem so calm, like you weren't surprised at the club." Her eyes darted back and forth between the two of us as she waited for an answer.

"Yes, I did know. I found out a few weeks ago." Her honesty was a relief.

"And you're still coming around? I mean, aren't you scared, you know, that she might hurt you?" Her eyes were huge with confusion and doubt.

Danica looked straight at me when she answered. "Rachel won't hurt me. She's my aunt. She won't hurt any of us here."

Even Micah and Jared looked surprised at Danica's words. "You do kinda look alike," Jared agreed.

"Is it why you were asking me about her a couple of months ago?" Micah asked me, leaning forward from his chair.

"Yes, I saw her one night at the club, and I followed her home. I was suspicious because she looked so familiar, but I wasn't sure because I haven't seen her since she was a little girl." I heard Eli entering and reengaging the security system. "When I was certain who she was, I approached her. I must say she took the news pretty well, all things considered."

She gave a sheepish grin, and I smiled in return.

Eli was at the back of my chair, his strong hands on my shoulders. "Everyone okay?" His voice was even and light.

"I think so." There were a few nods in agreement to my answer.

"So, you haven't been a vampire for that long then?" Micah asked.

Eli sat on the arm of the chair, and I leaned into his body before answering. "A little less than twenty-five years."

Micah looked up at Eli. "And what about you?"

"Almost two years, but I've been with Rachel for about twelve now. She took me in as a child."

Micah shook his head but didn't look upset. If anything, he seemed puzzled, as if he was mulling the information over.

"And did you wait until he was an adult to change him? Did he know you were a vampire as a child?"

Micah's interest unnerved me, but Eli cut in before I could answer. "It didn't happen exactly like that. It wasn't planned, and I knew on some level as a child, eventually figuring it out, but she never confirmed it to me until I was eighteen. Rachel and Giovanni were always good to me, they were both wonderful parents."

The use of the word "parent" made me squirm, especially considering the current nature of our relationship.

"What happened to Giovanni? You mentioned that he was killed, but considering what happened tonight, I imagine that there's quite a story behind his death." Micah looked at us both, waiting for an answer.

"Aren't you already dead?" Jared ventured.

Eli and I both turned at the sound of his voice. "Yes. We are, and we aren't. We don't breathe, and we don't have a heartbeat, but we still move about, think, and feel. We're sort of trapped between the two," I said. I looked back to Micah before I continued. "As for Giovanni, there is quite a story, but I think the condensed version should suffice. Those men who attacked tonight are led by a family that pursued Giovanni for three centuries. He killed two of their family members, and the rest have committed themselves to his destruction, as well as the destruction of all vampires. Over the years, they have amassed quite a network of associates and resources. We had a big showdown about two years ago. Giovanni was killed, and I changed Eli. Then we came here." I skirted around a lot of the details, but my point was clear.

"And what's it like?" Micah questioned with undisguised curiosity.

"Being a vampire?" I asked.

"Yes." He nodded.

"Well, in some ways it's wonderful, and in others it's not. I mean we are powerful, we never age or get sick and could possibly live forever, but we also have to be secretive, move frequently, and be on the alert for people like the Desmarais."

"And the two of you, you're a couple now?"

"We're very close." It was all I offered, and Eli took my lead by remaining silent.

"And so now what does this mean for all of us here?" Micah's tone was becoming antagonistic.

"That's what we're here to work out."

"I think we should wait until Charles and Alessandra get back before deciding anything," Eli stated firmly. I had no argument with him.

"Why don't we take our guests upstairs and get them settled in the guest bedrooms?" We stood, then I looked back to the group who remained seated. "Is everyone okay with it?"

"I don't know if I'll ever be able to sleep again." Mary-Jane had a slight tremor in her voice.

"I understand how scared and confused you are; I really do. I have been through terrible things in my life also, things I never thought I would recover from, but the human mind is an amazing thing, and I have also discovered that love and friendship come in many forms, sometimes from the least likely of places."

She looked at me, eyes shimmering with tears. "And if we want no part of it, will you really just let us go?"

"Of course, but for tonight I think we all need to remain here. Tomorrow we will have no choice but to move on as word of what happened will get back to the Desmarais. You can decide then what to do."

"Okay," she agreed before following me out of the room. I directed her and Danica to a large room on the second floor with a huge four-poster bed and a smaller day bed underneath the room's south-facing window. They could decide among themselves whether they wanted to share the bed or sleep separately. I imagined Mary-Jane was going to need some comfort to be able to settle enough to sleep.

Eli led the men to two separate rooms at the other end of the upstairs hallway. They were informed to help themselves to food or drink as they wanted and to take advantage of any of the amenities the house offered. Eli wisely removed all phones and turned off the internet in case anyone got any ideas of sending out a request for help. As for getting out of the house, there was no way to disengage the security system without the correct codes. They were our prisoners for the upcoming day, though I liked to think of it more as them being under our protection.

A little less than an hour remained until sunrise when Charles and Alessandra finally appeared at the house. Eli and I were waiting with growing anxiety in the smaller sitting room. We'd been passing the time talking about anything but what happened that night. At the first sound of their approach, we both jumped to our feet. Charles appeared in the doorway after less than a minute, Alessandra following right behind.

He swept into the room like a powerful wind to perch himself on the edge of an antique straight-backed chair. Eli and I sat close together, hands clutched between us.

"The clean-up is going well." His green eyes blazed. "The bodies have already been removed and are currently in transport out of the state to be incinerated. The club has been thoroughly sterilised, and all signs of violence have been eradicated. Tomorrow the whole space will receive a new coat of paint, and the floors will be refinished. It will simply look as though the place had a bit of a renovation."

"And what about the Desmarais? Surely they were expecting some type of communication from the team they sent?" Eli spoke before I had a chance, though I was thankful for his command of the situation.

"I have contacted my man, who let me in on the breach in the first place. He has someone on the inside of the Desmarais group. They were to make contact by sunrise our time, and failure to do so will trigger a second group to follow up. The second group arrived tonight and is assembled just over the border in Nevada. I'm suggesting that we leave first thing tomorrow, and I have arranged for people to intercept these men. We should then continue to a safe house I have up north. From there we can decide our next steps."

"And the plan for the attack on the Desmarais compounds is still to go ahead?" I asked with unconcealed concern.

Charles looked right at me, and for the first time, I saw the powerful determination he had been keeping in check. "Yes, the sooner the better. We have all the recon information that we need. Alessandra is going to return to Europe as planned and assemble as many allies as she is able. She will give us word in the next few days where we can meet up, and then we will strike from there."

"And you're not concerned at all about the plan being blown?" Eli asked.

"Our plans are tight. The man who let our location slip has been eliminated, and he did not have access to the final steps of the plan, anyway. He was a grunt who got too greedy. It has thrown but a small wrench into the larger picture. All three sites have been staked out, every detail of their operation recorded. All associates, however minor, have been documented. We will have three main teams at all of the sites, with both vampires and humans to carry out the attack. Smaller groups will attack the other smaller sites, individual homes and businesses. By sunrise on that night, there will be no one left."

"And by everyone, do you mean families and children?" I squirmed as Eli asked the question that was also on my mind.

"Everyone." His words were as cold as the sentiment with which they were expressed, shooting straight to my core.

Eli turned slightly to gauge my reaction, but I didn't indicate an opinion of any type. If any of the other three wanted to know how I felt, they simply could have obtained the information with their minds. I was the weakest in the ability not only to assert my own will over others, but especially to block other vampires from my mind. It took great stores of energy to raise my inner shield up high enough to block unwanted intrusions, but the three with me were either too strong or, in Eli's case, simply naturally inclined to that ability.

It made me wonder again about my connection with Giovanni. With us, the ability to communicate silently was there even when I was still human, and we were always intensely aware of the other's feelings. The thought crossed my mind again that violent or negative emotions were somehow easier to read or project onto others. Dark intentions and reactions often erupted rapidly, especially when close to one another. Perhaps my connection with Giovanni was unique, even in the world of other undead.

"Understood. Please make sure Eli and I are involved in every step of the way from now on. I think we both feel like we haven't been involved enough."

Eli nodded his agreement as I turned to Alessandra. I reached out with my hand, trying not to let it tremble, placing it on her arm. Her power instantly shot through me like an electric current. She didn't react. "And Alessandra, I want to extend my most heartfelt thanks for your help and support. I know that this is something that you do not need to involve yourself in, but I appreciate your actions more than I could ever say. I know your assistance, and the assistance of your allies, will make all the difference."

She leaned in very closely to me, so close that if she had been breathing, I would have felt the warmth against my skin. "Giovanni will be avenged, and this Desmarais scum will be wiped from the earth. I will have it no other way."

I nodded in agreement and removed my hand as quickly as I could without seeming rude. I suddenly felt so drained, wanting nothing more than to retreat to my bedroom and fall asleep in Eli's arms. As if in response, he pulled me to his body and kissed my cheek.

Charles stood. "I think we have accomplished all that we can tonight. What about our guests upstairs?"

"Micah and Danica are fine; I have no worries there. I'm ninety-nine percent sure that Jared can be trusted. There are some issues there that I'd like to discuss with you at some point. Mary-Jane's the only one who's waffling. She could go either way."

"I thought Jared was the one to be worried about?"

"Well, he has a past the rest of you aren't aware of. A vampire fed on his mother when he was a child. No one believed the woman, and she was committed to a psychiatric facility. This episode tonight has, in a strange way, brought him some closure and has also opened up some new guilt for not believing her himself. I don't think he will expose us. In fact, I think he may come to me for help with his mother when it is all over."

Charles pursed his lips as if he had just tasted something sour. "Well, it's an interesting twist to things. He's an odd one, though, very tightly closed off and hard to read."

"I agree. Even I have had trouble reading him," Alessandra added.

I found it surprising but somehow comforting. It was good to know she wasn't omnipotent or infallible. It gave me hope that my own strength and abilities would increase with the passing years. Charles gave us a cheerless "Good night" then retired to his room. Alessandra followed him to rest in Eli's room.

When we were alone, Eli pulled me into his embrace, placing his lips firmly on mine. He kissed me deeply and wantonly, making the horrors of the night melt away. He had just slipped a hand inside the back on my shirt when a timid knock sounded at the door. Eli stopped but didn't pull away. "Come in."

The door was slightly open, and the person on the other side pushed it even wider. I was expecting Danica and was surprised to see Mary-Jane standing hesitantly before us. Her face was blotchy from crying.

She took another few steps into the room and stopped, her hand resting on the doorknob. It trembled. "I just wanted you to know that I'm okay now. You don't have to worry about me. I'm on your side."

Even I had no trouble ascertaining that her words were true. It was also apparent that she was completely terrified. Her mind was swimming with an internal argument about fear versus loyalty. I approached to hug her gently. "You were always okay, and you will always be our friend."

She hugged me back with all the force she could muster. "And you will always be mine. You both believed in me when no one else did, and I will never forget that."

Eli came to give her a quick hug as well before she slipped out of the room and back to her borrowed bed. We left right after her departure to my bedroom.

As soon as he engaged the security system, Eli scooped me up in his arms and carried me to the bed. We undressed each other with desperate hunger and fell naked onto the cool sheets. Our lovemaking was fierce and intense, stripping away the lingering seediness of the night's events.

As I lay with my head resting on his firm chest, I was

overcome with a rush of feelings so intense I could barely process them. I filled with love, guilt, anger, triumph, and hope. Tears trailed down my cheeks to spill onto Eli's cool flesh. He flinched as they made contact, but I had already turned to meet him face to face. "I love you, Eli."

"And I will always love you."

CHAPTER 7

TABLES TURNED

The others were already awake when Eli and I emerged from my bedroom the following night. Mary-Jane, Danica, and Jared were seated at the small round table in the kitchen, lingering over plates of Chinese food. They all looked up as we entered. Danica appeared as though she hadn't slept a wink, and Mary-Jane had the wide-eyed look of a startled deer. Jared managed a disheartened smile as he pushed around the remains of his meal with a plastic fork.

I took a seat on one of the stools at the kitchen's immense island. Eli remained standing, leaning on the brown granite countertop. He eyed the assembled guests, apathy knitting his dark brows together. His mind was fuzzy, but I picked up on his unease. Mary-Jane's mind swirled in a frantic loop of uncontrollable thoughts: fear, guilt, and conviction, over and over again. Jared was a blank wall, as usual, but his stony expression said it all. He was angry but solid in his acceptance of his role in the situation.

I turned to Danica, who looked so tired and wan. Her thoughts were also dim, like the effect of a few drinks to take the edge off. The plate before her was full, as though she hadn't touched a bite.

"You should eat something, even if you don't really feel like it," I encouraged.

She looked to me and I saw, with a pang of guilt, the bruise-like bags under her eyes. She forced a small forkful of rice into her mouth, more to appease me than to satisfy any need of her own.

"Are we going to be allowed to go home soon? My roommate is probably wondering what's happened to me by now." Mary-Jane's voice was much steadier than it was the night before, and I was glad to see that the girl I came to be so fond of was returning.

"Yes, of course. I just want to speak with Charles, and then I don't see any reason why you all can't head home."

"He's in the back room with Micah and Alessandra," Jared offered in a calm voice. I noticed the slightest inflection on uttering Alessandra's name and could understand his reticence. She was a terrifying creature.

"Please excuse me then." I left silently, trying not to appear as uncertain as I felt.

Alessandra's cold, ancient power poured down the hall as I approached the room. Her presence seeped out like ghostly tendrils of seductive malice. Her power beckoned me, warming me with need yet chilling me with fear. She would be difficult for a vampire to resist and all but impossible for a human. I braced myself to be before her, shielding as best I could. Still, she reached out to me, and the sound of my name in her sweet voice gouged itself into my brain, *Rachel*.

As I rounded the corner, I collided with her icy smile, Charles's grimace, and Micah's strangely smug look. The oddness of the grouping wasn't lost on me. I did my best to return Alessandra's grin before joining Micah on the couch.

"Good evening, Rachel," he offered in a pleasant tone.

I had mixed feelings about Micah's presence, so the best I could do was nod, before plunging right in, "So, Charles, how do you suggest we proceed from here?"

"Well, as far as I'm concerned, our dear friend Micah is free to go. He was most willing to allow me to peruse his thoughts, and I have found no indication of ill will. In fact, I would say that he is a strong supporter and will be an ally for the future." Micah smiled slightly but was wise enough not to comment. "I think we're both in agreement that there is no problem with Danica, so that just leaves Mary-Jane and Jared. I would like the opportunity to address them each in private to assess their position. I mean no disrespect, Rachel, but your ability to penetrate the human mind is not as encompassing as mine. I can access even the most well-hidden of thoughts. I realise that

Jared has some natural ability to shield, but I think that with enough time and focus I can break past it." His gaze slid to Alessandra, who sat in satisfied silence at his side. "Failing that, I'm sure Alessandra could get to the truth."

I inwardly shuddered at the thought of her forcefully trying to delve inside any human mind. I fully understood the legends of vampires being minions of the Devil, with what her power could do. Even to her own kind, she was terrifying and humbling. I had long thought of myself as strong, but I was a child when compared to her.

I knew she understood my thoughts when she turned her icy smile in my direction. Her eyes were as cold as the barren Arctic landscape and as predatory as a wolf's. I could see how easy it would be to lose one's sanity, drowning in the seductive pools of those wintry blue eyes. *So lovely,* she thought, and the sentiment chilled rather than flattered.

"Don't worry," she said in that sickly-sweet voice of hers. "I take no offense at your thoughts. I have been told on many occasions, and by vampires much older and stronger than you, how unsettling my presence can be."

I did my best to streamline my thoughts and force my resolve to hold. "Yes, your power is quite incredible. I must confess that your abilities dazzle and sometimes frighten me."

She smiled, and that time it seemed genuine. "I am such a sap for flattery. I do appreciate the honesty and the respect. I quite like you, *mia bella ragazza*. Ahh, see, I even slipped into my more comfortable tongue. I do it sometimes when distracted by great beauty."

"I thank you in return for your flattery."

"I understand that my insertion into other's minds is quite intense and disorienting, even painful, depending on the mind and, of course, on the pressure that I exert. I have been known to overdo it on occasion."

"Your power has obviously grown over the years." Charles chose his words carefully.

"It's true, but not all as old as I have the same abilities. Not all have the complete and unstoppable access to the minds of humans like I do. Some of it is an inherent talent. Even as a young human girl, I had the ability to see thoughts and know others' feelings. Becoming a vampire only intensified this talent."

I found the remark very telling, and she was being so honest, I took my chance to learn more. "So, you're saying that not all vampires can read minds like you do? Not even the very old ones?"

"Well, I think we all can, on some level, just not as clearly as I can. What may appear to be mind-reading in some cases is nothing more than reading body language and interpreting feelings and imagery, something that one becomes very good at with years of practice. You understand, I'm sure. It's like some of us are better at influence over others, like your Eli. Some of us are stronger and faster, despite age. I think we all carry over a bit of our human selves into our vampiric existences."

Her statement was rather cryptic, but I let it go. "And may I ask, Alessandra, how old you are?"

"I remember when Dante Alighieri came to the public's attention. I even had the occasion to speak with him once."

So, she was several hundred years older than Charles, I surmised. If she was telling the truth, that was. For as open as my mind was to her, hers was like a wall to me. I turned to Micah, who had remained silent through the entire exchange. "Is it what you always dreamed it would be?"

"Even better." He was settled, content. There was no controversy, not a hint of deception or uncertainty, a real friend and a solid ally.

"Well, I'm glad some good has come out of all of this."

"And more to come, certainly, some retribution for a terrible wrong." Alessandra spoke coolly but not without feeling.

"Yes. Hopefully avenging Giovanni's death will give me some peace at last. Removing the Desmarais as a threat can only be beneficial for us all."

"I think we all agree with that sentiment." I locked eyes with Charles as he spoke, but his face revealed nothing. The mask was back.

"Then I can tell Danica she can go?"

"Yes, and send Jared and Mary-Jane in here to speak with us." He turned to Micah, his expression never changing. "You can go with Rachel." It wasn't a suggestion.

He got up immediately, stopping briefly before Alessandra. She met his height inch for inch, every bit the terrible, icy goddess. "It has been an honour to meet you, Alessandra. Perhaps our paths will cross again one day."

She smiled and traced a long finger down his jaw line. "Perhaps. I'm sure we both would enjoy it."

Back in the kitchen, I informed Danica she was free to go and let the other two know they were wanted in the other room. Mary-Jane's eyes immediately flooded with tears. "She's not going to hurt us, is she?" she asked, her hands tightly gripped about my arm.

"No, they won't hurt you. It is about making sure we won't find ourselves in any more danger in the future."

"I already told you that I was on your side."

"I know, and I believe you. They just want to be certain for themselves."

Jared left without a word. He was a tough cookie, that one. Mary-Jane followed him, trailing slightly behind. I understood her apprehension and didn't envy her having to be alone with those two under the circumstances. Danica remained at the table, though the plates had been removed. I could still smell the garlic and grease in the air. I offered her my hand, which she took without hesitation. "Let's get your things, and then I'll drive you home myself."

"Okay."

As we made our way from the room, I noticed Micah had come to stand at Eli's side. He was so close, his arm brushed against Eli's, who gave no indication he either noticed or cared, which seemed odd. I felt another uncontrollable stab of jealousy, exacerbated by the visuals I was picking up from Micah. Whether the images were from fantasy or memory I wasn't sure, but I made a silent promise to find out.

"You'll make sure that the others get home?" I offered in Eli's direction as we passed.

"Of course." His eyes flickered to his side, and I wondered

if he was picking up on what I saw. "I'll meet up with you later at the club?"

"Yes, I'll see you later."

Danica was very quiet on the ride home. Her thoughts were jumbled, her feelings dark. Her mood washed over me like gritty rain. I had a hard time discerning anything coherent but understood that her mood was rooted in worry. I gave her a sideways glance as we pulled onto her street, but she was looking out the window at the passing scenery. When the car came to a stop, she finally looked at me.

"It is very serious, isn't it?"

"Yes," I answered.

"Like a war, with one side's destruction the only way to end it?" She looked down at her hands, clenched in her lap, as she waited for my response.

It was a poignant moment. I couldn't lie to her. We had come too far, and she was too smart to believe me anyway. "Yes, the only way it will stop is if we wipe these people from the face of the earth. It's the only way that Eli, Charles, and I will be safe."

"Then I won't hold anything you have to do against you." Our eyes locked, and her gaze was steady. I touched her hand, and her skin was so warm. She leaned into my shoulder, and I could smell her perfume and the leftover scents from the club the night before. "I want the chance to know you better. For however long I may have on this earth, I would like the chance to be a part of your life."

I was so touched, I ached. "I want the same thing, but I also want you as far from this danger as you can be. You understand me?"

"Of course."

"Then don't be angry, or think I've disappeared, if you don't hear from me for a while. I'll make sure to get in touch when it is all over."

The door clicked loudly when she opened it, and I felt a sudden loss as she pulled away from my side. With her legs out over the road, she paused. "I'm here and always willing to do whatever I can to help."

"I know, and I may take you up on it."

The door shut, and she walked away without looking back. I watched with a painful lump in my throat as she made her way up the stairs into her building. I sincerely hoped I could be true to my word and see her again. I prayed our side would be the triumphant one. I swallowed hard and pulled away from the curb.

It was the first night I could ever remember feeling uncomfortable at Carmilla's. For as long as I owned and operated it, the club had been like a second home. After a quick sweep through the outer area to check on the clean-up, I returned to the office, forcing myself to get caught up in all the paperwork. In truth, I was hiding. I was trying to divorce myself from reality by avoiding any uncomfortable interactions. All my attempts were in vain, as I knew I would not even be returning home that night, it was too dangerous. When Eli caught up with me, it would most likely be with news of where we would be relocating to.

All too soon that familiar tingle touched me, followed by a quick knock at my office door. He opened it without waiting for an answer. Eli's face was tight with the strain of the situation. He sighed as he lowered his lanky frame into the chair before my desk, and a heaviness rested between us that had never been there before.

"Everything's set." His voice was tight, and the sound of it tugged painfully at my heart.

"What's going on?"

He shifted in his seat. "Alessandra has set off on her return to Europe. Mary-Jane and Jared moved to a safe place in another part of California, where they will stay until they get word from either you or me. We thought it best since their association with us could be traced through the club. Danica should be fine, because no one outside of our circle is aware that she has any connection to you."

It all seemed so final and dismal. "And what about us?"

"As soon as you're ready, we're heading to a house Charles has up north. Alessandra will make arrangements with her contacts in Europe, and Charles has set the final stages of his plan into motion. We will all gather in about one week, and the ambush will take place. Then, hopefully, we will all be free of them." He tried to smile reassuringly, but his worry touched me. Fear chilled me to the core.

"I'm ready now. I've just been wasting time really." As I glanced at my watch, I realised it had been less than two hours since sunset, though it felt like an eternity.

"I guess you should inform your staff that you and Jared will be away for a while and make arrangements to cover for him?"

Always practical. "Yes, I'll ask Sonia to take over his duties and make sure the staff cover where they can."

The task took me but a few minutes, and I felt sick about the real reason for Jared's absence. As far as the other staff were concerned, they were told he needed to take care of a family crisis. Leaving the club that night felt like taking a walk to the gallows. I hoped to return, to see the club and my home again. Eli's car was waiting in the back lot with my clothing already packed. I was confident he knew me well enough to have brought the right things, but leaving like we were felt so dirty and cowardly.

Eli's cell phone rang, shrill in the quiet of the parking lot, and I jumped despite myself. My reaction obviously amused Eli, and a smile spread across his face as he snapped the phone open.

"Hello." There was a short reply, then Eli dropped the phone into the space between the front seats. "It was Charles. He's gone ahead, and we'll meet up with him. He already gave me the directions. Should take a couple of hours."

I expected us to be heading out toward the highway, but instead he drove in the direction of the university. I watched as the streets became more residential in nature, until we were in one of the nicer neighbourhoods in proximity to the school. We pulled up in front of a small, neatly kept house with a new four-door sedan in the driveway. The lawn was immaculate, and the beds surrounding the house were thriving and vibrant with colour. I lowered my window, catching the sweet scent as the wind rustled through the foliage.

"Where are we?"

Eli turned to me, and I couldn't read his expression. "Micah's house. He's coming with us."

I couldn't have been more surprised, but I barely had time to recover as Micah came around from the back of the house, a small suitcase in hand. His other arm was in a sling, just as I had instructed. He put his bag in the trunk before sliding into the backseat. He smelled of lemony shampoo, toothpaste, and the barest hint of cologne. "Hi, Eli, Rachel."

Eli was looking straight out over the road, and his reaction read like guilt.

"Hi, Micah. Are you sure you want to be coming with us? It is going to be very dangerous." My words didn't seem to faze him, nor did he seem to take any offense.

"I'm going to do what I can. I grew up around guns and did a brief stint in the military before university. I like to think I can hold my own, against my human counterparts, that is." He didn't smile but seemed somehow pleased to be where he was, or with whom he was, perhaps.

We took the highway, following it all the way out of California and into Oregon. Little conversation occurred as the miles of darkened landscape passed us by. Every once in a while, I felt Eli's hand touch my own or felt his attempts to connect with my mind. I heard my name whispered inside my head and his flood of reassurance, but I was so unsettled, I couldn't reciprocate. Micah seemed to be taking our lead, and he remained silent unless spoken to directly. Eli drove much faster than was legal, but with his preternatural reflexes and sight, I knew we were never in danger.

About eight hours later, we pulled off the highway toward the sleeping city of Portland. Charles apparently owned some property there, which he readied for us over the past few weeks. He was evidently concerned something might happen that would cause us to flee our present location. Like Giovanni, he preferred to be safe rather than sorry, and I was also sure that, like the house waiting for us there, many similar ones waited throughout the world.

We made our way through the town, Eli following Charles's directions from memory. Soon we were in an area where the homes were few and far between, and everything was deathly quiet. I could feel the approach of sunrise, pushing at my already high level of fear and uncertainty. The car turned onto a long drive, where we met a locked gate about a half a mile in. The car stopped, and Eli lowered his window to buzz at the almost hidden intercom. The call was answered immediately. "Yes."

"England, April, two thousand and seven."

The gate swung open, as the implication of the passwords became clear. It was the when and where of how Giovanni died. Eli deliberately didn't look at me after he spoke, and Micah had no reason to understand its effect on me. The gate swung shut behind us with a sharp clang.

We continued up the road, the fading darkness close and ominous about us. I could just discern the outline of a house farther up ahead, but like the majority of the houses we passed on this stretch of road, it was dark and still. Just as we reached the top of the drive, a garage door opened. A soft light spilled out of the opening, and Eli directed the car inside. The door closed behind us. Without a sound, Charles appeared at the head of the car, approaching quickly to the passenger side.

I stepped out into the hazily-lit space, feeling anxious. Charles leaned in and briefly embraced me. I was so surprised, I didn't reciprocate, but as he pulled back, I gave him a look he understood. Eli went to the trunk to remove our luggage, and I noticed Micah also emerged and joined him. As I caught sight of the two of them together, I felt a sense of rightness, and was disturbed at how good they looked with each other. They were both handsome men in their own way, and their easy familiarity with one another was apparent and appealing. I wondered again just how far their relationship went.

A door from the garage led us into the main house, where Charles punched in an alarm code as the door closed. The house was dark, with all windows covered, but a faint light shone from a back room on the ground floor. Charles motioned for us to follow, which we did in single file. The light came from a large, obviously unused kitchen. Though the space was clean, there were no table and chairs and no indication that the room was ever used for its intended purpose. Charles continued through to the far side of the space, where what looked like a piece of the paneling stood ajar. I supposed that when it was closed, it would appear there was no opening at all, and, of course, it was the intention. The light was off behind us as we all made our way through the makeshift doorway.

A long flight of stairs ended at a damp hallway with a cold stone floor. I remembered the night we spent in a similar space beneath the old servants' house of Charlotte's estate, the place where I took Eli's mortal life, bringing him over into the world of darkness. He took my hand, and I knew he was thinking the same, though for him it was the night his dreams for me came true. I, of course, could not completely share the sentiment.

The hallway ended at a steel door. Nearby was an alarm panel, which Charles used to open the door for us. The space inside was divided into several separate rooms, with the front part serving as a foyer or common area. He led Eli and me to one of the rooms without asking if we would share a space together, then took Micah to the one beside it.

Inside were a bed and a single, uncovered bulb hanging from a low ceiling that almost grazed the top of Eli's head. The room smelled of mildew and was dank and uninviting. Eli dropped the bags to the floor and quickly surveyed the space. "Solid rock," he said, meaning the walls. "We should be more than safe here. No way a fire could get through, and the alarm is in place. I'm sure that Charles has everything covered."

I sat tentatively on the bed's edge and wasn't surprised to find the mattress as hard as stone. Eli draped an arm about my shoulder as I asked him, "Do you want to tell me what Micah's really doing here now that we're alone?"

Eli struggled to keep his expression neutral. "It's just like he said in the car. He wants to help, and I suppose he doesn't want to give up the chance to meet more vampires if he can." I could tell by the sound of his voice he wasn't being completely honest with me. His mind was shut down tighter than a steel drum.

"And there's nothing else to it?" I didn't try to hide my disbelief.

"What else would there be?" His blank expression rivalled Charles's.

"Just be honest with me. I can take it. I know about the other women, and, until recently, there has been no real commitment between the two of us. If something's gone on between the two of you, just tell me." My voice betrayed me near the end of my words, quavering just the slightest bit.

Under the harsh light, his eyes were shards of sapphire. A slight crease appeared between his brows as he thought over what he would say next. "Okay, yes, there was something between Micah and me a while ago. It happened over the past summer. We met when I was in one of his classes the previous semester, I told you about that. We happened to meet up one night and ended up having a drink together, and then we went out a few more times, just out for a drink or to see a band. Then one night he asked me back to his place after we had been out, and I don't know why, but I agreed." He looked away from me as though he were embarrassed.

"Go on," I urged gently.

"So, we went back to his place, and we were listening to music, and then he leaned in and kissed me, and I couldn't deny to myself any longer that I was also attracted to him. I can't explain it; I have never thought of another man that way before, but with him it wasn't about us being two men; it was about the feeling he stirred inside me. I don't know if it makes any sense." He was struggling to let himself speak about it.

"And you were lovers?"

He met my eyes full on then. "Yes, we were, for a few months anyway. Then I pulled away, and more importantly, you started to open up to me, started to let yourself be close to me, and that was it. It's always only been you. You have to know it." The urgent desperation in his words startled me.

"I know how you feel about me, Eli, and you don't have to justify anything to me. You were and are free to do whatever you choose."

It seemed to hurt him, and I was sorry I didn't word it another way. "You're still only letting me in so far, aren't you?" The sadness on his face was almost more than I could bear.

"I'm doing the best I can, Eli. I do love you, have told you that I love you, but it hasn't quite been two years yet. He was the man I expected to share eternity with. It's not something I can just make myself get over. Believe me, at times I wish I could." Bitterness had crept into my voice, and I felt unjustly hostile. I asked for honesty, didn't I?

"But it changed how you feel about me, didn't it? How you see me, because I've been with a man?" Now Eli was on the defensive. A simple question somehow escalated into a rift between us.

"No, no. It's not true at all. It's not something that would change how I feel about you. You know me better. Attraction and love are powerful things."

It seemed to diffuse Eli's brewing anger somewhat. I would never judge him, and deep down he knew it. "Well, it actually feels good to have gotten it off my chest. I hate keeping things from you or feeling like I have to."

"And do you think that any of it has to do with Micah's reasons for wanting to come along? It seems obvious to me that he still has feelings for you. I've seen the way he looks at you…"

"I know. I've tried to talk to him about it, but he just tells me he understands and brushes it aside. I still pick up some wayward thoughts, and I know you have, too. I've seen your face." He leaned in to embrace me, and I melted into his arms. My head fit perfectly in the hollow at his shoulder, and his chin rested on the top of my head. It always felt so good and safe in his arms, one of the many reasons I could never pull away.

"Well, whatever the reasons, his intentions are good, and as he proved last night, he has the nerve and the shooting skills. The greater the numbers on our side, the better our chances."

"Did you realise that Valentine's Day is just a few days away?" His voice was husky as he changed the subject completely.

"I hadn't given it much thought, actually."

"Well, maybe this year you'll do me the honour of being my Valentine?"

"There is no one else I would even consider."

Sleep crept in like a silent thief. I was exhausted yet anxious and glad not to have to process all the what-ifs any longer that night.

A strange, dry sound filtered in. It was so pathetically soft that at first I was unable to recognise it as a voice. I strained to hear the words clearly, moving closer to the source with each utterance of sound. The space was so completely devoid of light, I could not make out any distinct shapes; there was only this scratchy, eerie voice compelling me forward.

My lower body made abrupt contact with something solid, and I reached out to feel what blocked my way. My hands traced along a hard, rectangular-shaped object, which seemed to rise from the floor to about waist height. The surface was cold and slightly irregular. Then the sound came again, and, for the first time, I realised it was someone saying my name.

"Rachel."

Terrible, burning pain engulfed my body, and I slipped down to my knees from the ferocious onslaught. The side of my head sharply smashed against the object in front of me, but it was nothing compared to the agony that wracked me. My body felt as if it were drying out and emaciating, like a forcefully rapid desiccation of my body while I still moved.

Horrible, violent images filled my mind, scenes of torture so disgusting I fought as best I could not to process them, but the harder I fought, the more overpowering the images became, until they slowed down to four specific scenes showing over and over again. They throbbed in my brain like a psychotic slideshow. I witnessed a man being electrocuted, being trapped in complete darkness and silence, being injected with something that incapacitated him to allow terrible damage to his body, and a male body so starved for nourishment, it was little more than a skin-covered skeleton.

The more vibrant and insistent the images became, the more detail was offered to me. I clearly saw the instruments of torture, the room where the events took place, faces of the monsters inflicting the pain, then finally the face of the recipient.

It was a scene so vile, a comprehension so intense, I felt I would be crushed under the burden of it. It was my beloved Giovanni's face I was seeing in all the horrendous scenes. His features were so marred by physical damage and deformed by pain and malnourishment, he was all but unrecognisable.

With a sudden burst of inhuman strength, I pushed against

the object before me and felt something give. It seemed to split in two, or perhaps there was a top that had been dislodged. In either case, the top slab moved aside, and, at the same moment, a sickly light appeared. I stood on trembling legs and looked down with horror onto the ghastly face of the man I loved. I screamed.

Reality came to me like ripping my way out of a wet paper bag. I was frightened, disoriented, and sickened. Screams shredded my throat. Cool hands grasped my arms, shaking me, but all I could see was blackness. Then a solid smack rocked my head to the side, and a bright stinging in my cheek pulled me back to reality. Eli's face swam into clarity before my eyes, and I all but leaped into his arms.

"Oh God, Eli! It was so awful...what they did to him, please! Make it stop!" My voice was harsh and desperate.

He crushed me against his chest before pulling back. His eyes traced their way from my face down and over my exposed body. He grimaced, and his reaction brought a thump of adrenaline to life in my body. I also looked down, confused and horrified by what I discovered.

I was noticeably thinner and almost completely covered with purplish bruising. I jumped from the bed, taking in the marks covering all the parts of my body I could see. Eli came to my side and forced my chin up with his hand. He used the other to pull back my lips, and what he saw forced a scowl onto his beautiful face. My tongue snaked out and touched my fangs, which were protruding painfully from my gums.

"I'm so hungry," I begged in an alien voice.

"It's still daytime, Rachel." His voice was quiet and thoughtful.

"I need to feed," I pleaded.

He pressed one of my sharp nails to the spot just above his heart, slicing open the flesh in a thin, neat line. Spots of blood burst to the surface, and the meaning was obvious. I pressed my mouth to the wound and sucked. It was wonderfully sweet and satisfying, and I lost all sense of anything but the taste of it. Soon, I felt his hands pulling my head away from his body. His expression was indiscernible. "What is going on?"

I was trying to form a comprehensive answer, when the way he was looking at me forced me to once again look down onto my body. Though the bruises were still evident, they were much faded, as if I'd had a day of recovery. Vampires healed quickly, as I well knew, even without the confirmation of the wound on Eli's chest closing. Yet, even vampires could be hurt and damaged, sometimes permanently. Sometimes we needed generous time to heal, depending on the severity of the injury.

He led me back to the bed and wrapped us both in the covers. We clung to each other there in the silence, both contemplating what just happened. "You had another nightmare?"

"Yes, but different this time."

"And it was about Giovanni?"

"Yes, it was terrible. It was about him being tortured and starved…. I can't, I don't want to think about it."

"You were screaming his name and thrashing about." He was quiet for a few moments, his voice stronger when he continued. "It's like you're having a physical reaction to what you see in your dreams."

"How can that be?"

"I don't know." He pulled at his upper lip, as he often did when thinking deeply about something. "When did these dreams start?"

"It's more like they've started again. I had nightmares almost constantly in the first few months after Giovanni was killed. Then, with time, they came with less and less frequency, losing their intensity. Then for a few months, I didn't have them at all. I guess they started again a few weeks before the incident where I woke with all the cuts. You were with me that night…"

"I remember. You scared the shit out of me."

"What are you thinking?"

"I don't know. It seems coincidental that they've started again since we've become closer and since this whole plan against the Desmarais has come together. Maybe it's guilt and fear and remembering what you saw the night he was killed. He was being tortured then with the prods and the net…. I don't know, Rachel."

"But they're not like they were after he died. Then it was

seeing what actually happened, played over and over again. These dreams are things that I never witnessed personally, but they feel like memories. I wish I could make you understand; they're so real and horrible…. It's like I'm feeling the pain, the fear…" I shuddered uncontrollably. Eli's lips pressed against the top of my head.

"I wish I could experience them, too, so I could understand, and so you wouldn't have to go through it alone."

"I'm so lucky to have you in my life. I don't know what I would do without you."

"Don't even think about it, 'cause it will never happen. I'll always be here for you."

I turned to him for a comfort I didn't believe even existed. I used his body and the ecstasy it gave me to pull me away from the horrors in my mind. I drank in every kiss, every caress as though it might be my last. I met his eagerness equally, pleasuring him with my mouth, my hands, and my body. Afterward we lay in the artificial darkness, waiting for night to come.

I don't know how to explain how vampires can be aware of when daytime turns to night, except to offer that it's a feeling comparable to an outside pressure lifting. The night is where vampires belong, and it offers protection and comfort.

We dressed and moved out into the main room, where we found Micah waiting, seated on the cold floor, with his back to the wall. The door to the main hallway was open, and I surmised Charles had already risen. He was much older and had some resistance to sunlight and the ability to move about during the daytime hours. I imagined he was double-checking plans and finalising details.

"Good evening," Micah offered amiably, as he stood from the floor.

Eli's hand stiffened slightly in my own. "Sleep well?"

"Well enough." He made eye contact with first Eli, then me.

"I guess Charles is already up. We should join him." I moved forward, with Eli forced to trail along behind. Micah fell in step at the rear of our procession.

"Time to get this show on the road," Eli muttered as we hit the stairs.

The house was just as dark and silent as it was the evening before. The light was off in the kitchen, but I detected some movement, then a voice from somewhere overhead.

"I'm upstairs," Charles called out just as I was about to suggest that's where we should head.

We trudged through the house, and as we found the staircase to the upper level, I realised Micah could not see as well as we could. He must have been following right at Eli's heels, because he didn't seem to falter. "Are you okay, Micah? I forget that you don't see in the dark like we do."

"I'm doing all right, but a little light couldn't hurt," he replied somewhat sheepishly.

I slid my hand along the wall at the bottom of the stair until I made contact with a switch. I flipped it and illuminated the second floor with a soft light. The bottom was still murky, but it provided enough light to help guide our ascent.

We found Charles in the last room at the end of the hallway. It was one of the few that seemed to hold any furnishings or indicate recent use. He was seated before a computer screen, with both a landline telephone and several cell phones within his reach. He was speaking with rapid-fire speed into a phone in a language I was not familiar with, but he nodded in the direction of a sofa on the far side of the room. We all took a seat and waited for his conversation to finish.

He abruptly snapped the phone shut, and in a blur joined us in the makeshift conversational grouping of furniture, which consisted of a lumpy sofa and a large chair covered with an alarming yellow-and-orange floral pattern reminiscent of the 1970s. There was also a cheap-looking coffee table, its top scarred with cigarette burns and water rings.

"I was just speaking with a contact in Norway. Everything is ready there for them to move out. We will drive up to Vancouver tonight and fly out to Toronto. From there we will make our way to the house I have set up. The plan is still to convene with Alessandra and the other vampires in England and proceed with our attack from there." Charles spoke quickly and matter-of-factly, leaving no room for argument.

"And all of the sites for attack are in France?" Eli asked.

"One in Belgium, two in France. Then there are several smaller storage facilities and personal properties in nearby Germany, England, and the Netherlands. The plan will be to go for all sites at once. The primary focus, of course, is the three main meeting and research sites, but every known home, facility, business, whatever, will be raided, all persons eliminated and all property burned to the ground. There will be nothing left when we are through. All numbered accounts will be seized and transferred to us. The ones that can't be reached will come to the attention of the correct authorities to take as profits of crime." His eyes burned like emerald fire. I was glad he was on our side.

"I think we should feed before we head out. I didn't last night, and I don't think Rachel did either," Eli said. I was glad he made no mention of the strange effects of my dream and my need for blood to finish the healing.

"I think we should, as well, and Micah should get something to eat himself and perhaps stock up for the trip." All three pairs of preternatural eyes turned on Micah, but he did not falter.

"Sounds good to me. Lead the way."

"I think we should hit downtown. There are lots of transients there or bars if you intend to go that way." Then to Micah, "And there's also a number of restaurants in the vicinity." Back to us, "Do we all have each other's current cell numbers?"

After confirming our contact numbers, we all set out. Charles had purchased a newish minivan for the last leg of our journey. We took it on our prowl into town, as the vehicle was unlikely to draw any attention. We parked on a side street, just outside the center of town. The air was bitterly cold, and a soft blanket of snow had fallen during the day. Charles gave us directions, and we agreed upon a time to meet back at the van. He left on his own, as did Micah, and Eli and I headed out together.

As we made our way into the heart of the downtown district, I caught sight of a couple of raggedy-looking kids ducking into an alleyway a few blocks ahead. I looked to Eli, who nodded that he also saw them. We quickly made our way up the street and ducked into the same space we had seen the kids enter. I picked up on their conversation as we neared. "...fuck that man was disgusting! He was like forty or something!" a young-sounding male exclaimed.

"Yeah, but at least we got enough to score," his female partner said.

We silently rounded the corner, surprising the pair as they were rolling a fat joint from the bag of pot the male held on his lap. They were both very young, no more than fifteen, thin and dirty. Runaways. I had a hard time continuing after I saw how young they were, but I pushed on, knowing we would not take their lives.

The girl scowled as we approached, trying to take a tough stance as she lit a cigarette. The boy stopped in mid roll, giving us both a deliberate once over. "You're dressed too nice to be cops. So, what are you? You like to slum for some kinky sex, that it?"

Eli ignored his crudeness and took a few steps closer. Though the girl tried not to show it, fear crept in. She looked nervously to her partner but took his lead in outwardly showing bravado. "Don't you know that it's dangerous to hang out in dark alleys? You never know who might come along."

"And didn't anyone ever tell you smoking will kill you?"

Despite myself, I smiled at Eli's sarcasm.

The boy's eyes narrowed to slits. He knew he was the butt of some kind of joke but one that he didn't get. "So whaddya want then?"

Eli caught his gaze, and even I felt the effect when he pushed his influence out over him. It tickled along my skin, whispering sweetly in my brain. The boy's eyes widened, and his mouth opened slightly. A soft blush spread across his thin cheeks.

"Come here."

The boy rose to his feet, the ragged jacket he was wearing falling to the damp pavement. He started walking forward toward Eli's waiting arms, his prominent Adam's apple working overtime.

"What are you doing to him?" The girl asked, though there was no force behind her words.

I stepped around the boy too quickly for the girl to discern and came at her. I was down at her side with my hand about her throat before she knew what was happening. I used enough force to prevent her from screaming and restricted her airway to the point that she passed out. Then I sank my sharp fangs into her tender flesh and drank. I felt the effects instantly. My skin was less sensitive, my mind more sharply focused.

I stopped long before the point of no return, though the girl would be weak and sore when she awoke. I pulled a wad of cash from my jacket and stuffed it in the front pocket of her worn jeans. I hoped she would use it to get some food and a clean bed to sleep in.

When I turned, I found the boy in a similar position and Eli waiting for me at the mouth of the alleyway. I flew into his arms.

"Feeling better?" he whispered against my ear.

"Much."

We spent the next hour or so wandering the streets, taking in the town that we had both never seen before. We ran into Micah as he exited a small diner, and together the three of us made our way back to the van. The snow crunched under our feet.

Charles was already there, waiting in the dark vehicle. The cold did not affect him, so he didn't bother to turn on the engine. Micah moved ahead to join him.

I was amazed at how well Micah seemed to adjust to things. He was taking it all in stride. He knew when to ask questions and when to keep his mouth shut. Even his thoughts were somewhat controlled, though every so often a fond memory of Eli slipped out.

We hit the road with Micah sitting up front with Charles, who drove. Eli and I took the middle seats, and we all settled back for the long drive to Vancouver. We had no problem at the border, as we all presented the proper documentation. I suspected that Charles left a parting suggestion with the guards to forget our passing, but I didn't ask.

After one night in the beautiful ocean-side city of Vancouver, we flew out to Toronto. The flight was uneventful, thankfully so.

The next chapter in our lives waited for us.

CHAPTER 8

Charles's cell rang as we touched down in Toronto. We were headed to pick up our luggage, and as soon as it sounded, he snatched the phone from his pocket to read the caller display. He frowned when he saw who was calling.

He snapped the phone open and pressed it to his ear. "Yes."

His expression hardened upon hearing the person who answered. I turned to Eli, and he was looking at Charles with a frown on his handsome face. I suddenly felt as if I had been stung, and belatedly I realised it was Charles emitting a residue of anger.

"Why are you calling?" he asked through tightly clenched teeth. "Why should I believe you?"

By then I was beyond curious. A lilting female voice was coming from the other end, but I couldn't discern exactly what she was saying. Whoever it was, Charles was not pleased to hear from her. "Fine. Where?" He paused and gave the three of us a sideways glance. We had all stopped just short of the luggage carousel. "Right, I'll be there in thirty minutes."

"What's going on, Charles? Where are you going?" I asked with worry.

"I'll explain when I get back. You have the address and the security codes. I'll meet you there as soon as I can. Should any problems arise, you can reach me on my cell phone." Then he strode off, leaving us completely in the dark. "Take my luggage," he called back to us, before disappearing into the crowd.

"What was that?" Micah asked, taking in the worried looks on both our faces.

"Not sure, but Charles is smart and sly. He's not likely to get himself into something he can't get out of."

"Yeah, let's just let him take care of whatever that was and get ourselves over to the house." I spied my suitcase making its way around and continued toward the carousel. Eli and Micah joined me, and between the three of us, we picked up our luggage.

Outside the wind was bitter, gusting off a frozen Lake Ontario. It was so strange to be back in that part of the world. I hadn't set foot in my native land in almost a quarter of a century. It was bittersweet and stirred up myriad feelings and distant memories. Several taxis waited out front, so we all piled into one and gave the driver the address.

The cab stopped in front of an elegant townhouse, which had been restored to its original beauty. The structure was most likely built back in the time when Toronto was still known as York. A tall, wrought-iron gate surrounded the small but impeccably neat front yard, and the walk was recently shovelled. As I stepped out of the car, I noted stained glass windows on the upper levels and smoke curling from a chimney at the rear of the building. The exterior was a smoky brown, and the front door gleamed with a freshly applied coat of red paint. *Good feng shui.*

The front door opened onto a small foyer with an accompanying closet. A staircase to the upper level was to the right, and a straight shot down the hallway led to a back den and living room area, where the fireplace was located. The kitchen and dining room were to the left, a small office to the right. Like the house in Oregon, few rooms contained any actual furnishings, and the ones that did, held items that were obviously new and expensive.

In the living room, I settled onto a camel-coloured sofa covered with the softest leather I'd ever felt. Micah sat across from me on an oversized armchair, and Eli went to stand close to the fireplace. We were all drained and on edge. Charles's mysterious phone call and subsequent departure did nothing to improve our collective mood.

I looked to Micah. "You must be hungry?"

"Yes, I guess I am. Do you think it would be all right if I ordered something?"

"I don't see why not."

He rose and wandered back down the hallway in search of a phone and computer. He called out that he found both in the small office close to the front door. I watched Eli as the firelight danced softly over his strong profile. Standing there that way, he looked like a normal, attractive young man lost in thought. Knowing his thoughts stole from the serenity of the moment. We stayed in separate but comfortable silences until Micah rejoined us.

"That man thinks of everything," he said and resettled into the chair. "He had a couple of take-out menus from nearby restaurants waiting by the phone."

"He does think of everything," Eli agreed.

When the doorbell rang about thirty minutes later, Eli made Micah let him answer. We had become so paranoid, seeing danger everywhere we looked. We had always been aware before and diligent about our safety, but no longer was there a chance to enjoy any part of our lives without fear hanging over our heads.

The stench from Micah's take-out Italian food was nauseating, but I did not comment. I imagined our diet was equally unappealing to him.

The clock ticked off minutes like years of our lives lost. We talked; we didn't talk; we fidgeted; all the while too aware what we were really doing was waiting for Charles's return. At last I felt the cool psychic whisper hailing his approach, and I almost cheered. I heard the door, and all three sets of eyes locked on the doorway in which he would appear. When he did however, he was not alone.

He was followed silently by a small, flame-haired beauty who emitted no supernatural air at all. Yet, by looking at her, I could tell she was a vampire and a very old and powerful one. Her wide-set eyes were as green as jade, and her hair fell past her waist in thick ropes of curl.

She was as white as any I had seen of our kind, but up close there was the slightest hint of freckles across her cheeks and the bridge of her nose. A psychic invisibility cloaked her presence. She could have walked right up behind any of us and placed a hand on our shoulder before we knew she was there. While Alessandra's unavoidable waves of power were frightening, this creature's ability to keep us shut off from everything about her was truly terrifying.

I noticed Charles stopped with several feet between him and his companion. He looked almost sick and, if I didn't know better, flustered. He used a slight turn of his head to indicate her when he finally spoke. "This is Sorcha, my maker."

No wonder he seemed so rattled when he received the call earlier. If my memory served me correctly, he'd had little contact with her since shortly after his change.

"Hello all. I am pleased to make my acquaintance with you." She had a gentle lilt to her voice, indicating her Celtic roots.

"Hello, Sorcha," I found myself answering without the conscious thought of speaking at all. Her gaze made me feel strangely warm, and I imagined she could get me to do just about anything, including terrible bodily harm to myself, all the while with a pleasant smile on my face.

Micah sat with his mouth gaping, his eyes glazed. Mentally he was lost, captured by her disguised power. He did not speak or move, but I was aware of his heart thundering with loud, rapid beats. She looked toward him, neither pleased nor displeased. His body relaxed even further, and I suspected that if she didn't pull back from her effect over him, he would eventually slip from the chair onto the floor. It was amazing how much she was affecting all of us, yet she was completely non-existent on my supernatural radar.

"Keeping company with humans now, Charles? Allowing them into your home, your inner circle even? I'm amazed."

Micah's body suddenly became rigid, and it was apparent that he was in control of himself once again. Sorcha must have released her undetectable hold over him. His look to Eli and me was, *what just happened*? But we both kept our answers to ourselves.

"Yes, this is the company I keep. They are my friends." His voice was impatient and defiant, with an undercurrent of anger.

"This is who you would be working with if you choose to assist in this conflict."

She came over to us, and there was no other way to describe her movements except to say that she glided. There was no obvious movement of her lower body, and the sight of her approach was mesmerising. It was like being caught it in the spider's web, yet somehow glad to be there, glad to be the prey. Her presence was not threatening or menacing, even though it would have been impossible to turn away. "Now let me guess. You are Rachel?" She looked back to Charles, who nodded. "And that would make you, Eli."

We both managed to stammer out monosyllabic replies then just stood there under her blatant scrutiny. She fingered my hair gently, almost lovingly, before turning to Eli. She cupped a tiny hand under his strong chin and turned his face to one side then the other. Then she stepped a short space back from us. "Lovely, just lovely."

I couldn't explain it, and, for reasons I still don't understand, her approval thrilled me. I could only imagine what the consequences would have been if she hadn't. Then she turned her sights on Micah. "And who is this one?"

"My name is Micah Lazenby," he answered, without the slightest tremor in his voice.

She smiled.

He was still sitting, his height not much lower than hers when standing. She leaned forward until their noses were all but touching. "Again, lovely. This one is strong. He would make a good vampire."

None of us reacted, though I suspected Micah was in agreement with her.

"Well, we're all pleased that introductions have gone well. Have you come to any conclusions about your possible role in all of this?" Charles took a seat on the couch, and I quickly joined him. Eli remained standing but moved closer to the fireplace. Sorcha settled on another armchair, close to where Micah sat.

She took her time answering. "You mean do I intend to join your cause?"

"Yes."

"And what is it you would have me do exactly?" Her voice was peaches and cream.

"Kill. Something I know, for a fact, you are good at and take great satisfaction from."

"You do know the right buttons to push, Charles. You always were a keen observer and a quick mind, even before the change." Then she gave him an eerie, private look that chilled me to the core. He did not react in the slightest.

"And you would help avenge the destruction of another of our kind." My voice was steady.

She turned to me then. "One you held dear, one you loved?"

"Yes, my love, Giovanni." His name hung there as a painful presence among the gathered vampires.

"But he was someone special to Charles and Eli, as well. I can feel their pain at the mention of his name, and I see both the remorse in Charles's memories and the joy in Eli's. He touched all of your lives in some way." A slight note of incredulousness could be heard in her voice.

"He was a father to me, a mentor, and a friend." I also felt Eli's pain when he spoke.

"And I want the chance to right some of the wrongs that I brought against this man, this vampire that I created…and abandoned." It was the first time Charles ever acknowledged what he did out loud.

She seemed to give these statements some thought. "Let me see some of the details of the plans, and then I will give you my answer."

"How can we be sure that you will not interfere in our plans, should you choose not to assist us?"

"Because I give my word, Charles." Her face was equally blank, and the two seemed at an unspoken standoff.

After what seemed like a terribly long moment of silence, Charles relented. "Very well then. Why don't we all go to the office, and I will let you know what plans we have made."

We all stood and, with Charles leading the way, moved to the other end of the house. The office was smaller than the family room and less comfortably furnished, holding only a small desk with a computer and other equipment. Charles sat in the chair behind the desk. Two stools were on the closest side of the desk, which Sorcha and I took, leaving the two other men to stand. Amazing how even under those unusual circumstances, chivalry still survived.

We collectively listened to detailed surveillance notes, reviewed files compiled on the people employed to facilitate the attacks, studied maps and building plans, and any other additional information Charles had carefully collected. It was an impressive undertaking to say the least. I felt completely convinced for the first time that we would succeed. Just as we were about to wrap up, a cell phone rang. Charles looked at the screen fleetingly before snapping it open.

"Charles." He listened for about two minutes before saying, "Wait, let me put you on speaker."

He propped up the phone on the desk after hitting a button on the phone's body. Alessandra's voice emerged with its usual chilly caress. "As I was saying, Charles, I have managed to persuade an impressive number of vampire allies to your cause. Some knew Giovanni fleetingly, some well. All assembled are strong and true in their allegiance. A few you know well also, *il mio vecchio amico*. I believe by the time of the attack, we will have at least twenty."

"Perhaps twenty-one. I have made contact with an even older friend than you, Alessandra."

"Is that so?"

"Yes, Sorcha stands before me as we speak. I believe the two of you are acquainted?"

"But of course. Hello, Sorcha. It's been a very long time."

"Too long, my dear. I am pleased to know that you are well."

"And I you."

Their exchange was cold and I suspected not quite sincere. There was a story there, but it was for another time. Alessandra's voice cut into my thoughts as she swiftly resumed her end of the conversation. "I bid you all good night for now, and I will see you soon." A chorus of murmured goodbyes answered. "And Charles, the place and time still stands."

"Good, and thank you."

Charles returned the phone to his pocket without comment.

The room was silent as we all contemplated the information been presented and the effects our future actions could have on the existence of all of our kind. Not only would we put ourselves out there, risking our existence, but we could change fates for countless others. With my beloved Giovanni's destruction an all-too painful reminder, I realised the outcome of this confrontation could either free us from an enemy sworn to the destruction of vampires, or it could usher in a new era of a more urgent and relentless pursuit of our kind.

Sorcha sat quietly, her warm envelope of nothingness frustrating me to no end. Charles was staring at her, waiting for her answer, as we all were. She did not react in any way to his obvious impatience, but since she was a complete nil for all of us to read, there was no way to know whether she was dragging the moment out to be cruel, or because she was considering her participation thoughtfully.

At last she spoke. "It's been a long time since I was moved in any way, either positively or negatively. Most of the time I give little thought to the consequences of my actions on the lives of the humans around me, and feel nothing except the most passing comradeship toward the others who reside in the darkness as we do, but I must confess that the sense of loss and anger Giovanni's death stirred up has touched me somehow." She turned to me, and a look of incredulousness spread across her delicate face. "It's a strange sensation, this feeling I'm experiencing, and I don't know quite what to make of it."

"Will you help us?"

"Yes, I will. I almost don't believe I'm agreeing to it, but yes, I will help you." She pulled the map Charles spread out across the desk toward her. With one tiny finger, she touched a spot marked as a Desmarais site. "I would like to take this spot. It's quite close to where something powerful happened to me once." Then she dreamily lifted her head to meet the face across the desk from her. She and Charles exchanged a look, and something passed between them that was for their understanding only.

"As you wish, and do you require assistance?" His tone was even, but he was shutting himself off from the rest, letting nothing betray what was going on behind those emerald eyes.

"I think not. It's a small location, and I do better on my own." A double meaning was in the words she uttered, but I understood it was not my place to offer comment.

"Indeed. It's decided then. Will you be travelling over to Europe with us then?"

"No, I will meet you there. I'm giving my word to you here, Charles, and likewise to the rest of you. It is not something I would ever do lightly." She rose to her feet, as did Charles. Despite his long existence and power, he still held the vestiges of the man he had once been, such as his tendency toward formal manners. Without seeming to have moved at all, she was at the door to the hallway, her slight frame haloed by the overhead light. "I shall see you soon. Keep safe." Then she was gone.

I heard the soft click as the door shut behind her, but instead of feeling relieved, I was unsettled. "Do you really think she'll come through?"

Charles regarded me with his blank, unreadable expression before nodding. "Yes, I do. Why she will help, well that's an entirely different matter, but I must impart to you, that even though she made no mention of it, her help will not come without a price. Someday she will need, or want, your help, and she will collect the debt as she sees fit."

"But she contacted us." I hated when he spoke to me with his face devoid of expression, especially when I was so affected. It made me feel weak and frustrated, though in his defense, I knew it was a persona of sorts he adopted over the years. In truth, any extreme reaction at all on his part would disturb me more. His coolness was a safety blanket to me. Seeing Charles lose control would be more than I can handle.

"She did come to us; it's true. At first it was simple curiosity and nothing more. Then the more she heard and the larger the number that committed to our cause, the more she was intrigued. It was hard for her to fathom how any one vampire can care enough about another to risk their own security. These types of thoughts and feelings are foreign to her, as she has never been motivated by anything other than her own gratification."

"Can she not understand that if these people are left

unchecked, they could discover ways to eliminate all of your kind, even ones as old as she?" It came from Micah, whose silent presence I started to take for granted.

"Perhaps it is her motivation. Maybe she is remaining true to her self-interest after all. She is a strong and cunning creature, and no doubt she would be able to see the ramifications of this group continuing their assault against our kind."

I sat back, taking a moment to absorb all that had happened that evening. I believed more strongly than ever before that our victory was all but inevitable. Charles somehow aligned the most powerful and lethal of both human and vampire kind. It was going to be a massacre.

"What are you thinking?" Eli asked.

I turned toward him, somewhat surprised he could not read me clearly. "I'm just suddenly certain it is going to work. I don't see how it can fail, and it will mean freedom for all of us. Even though I know it will not change what has happened in the past, the idea of revenge is becoming more and more appealing to me."

"And of this revenge may come some closure." Charles's words were kind, but the implication was much harsher and far-reaching. It could be closure for the three of us—Charles, Eli, and myself—and perhaps a real beginning for two.

"May I ask what the significance of the location that Sorcha picked is?" I asked.

"It's quite close to the location where she and I met many years ago."

"I see." I took it to mean it was close to the place where he once lived as a mortal man and where he experienced his change.

It was a long night for all of us, and with nothing further to accomplish at that time, Charles led us to where we would spend our daylight hours. He had made the basement a secure space, divided into two separate rooms. He indicated he would share one with Micah, to which Micah did not outwardly react, yet we all experienced his immediate anxiety. He ushered Eli and me into the other room, again as though our co-habitation was a given and did not need to be inquired about. I chose not comment, as there was enough conflict that night already. In all honesty, nothing sounded better than the possibility of falling asleep in Eli's arms.

As usual, Charles did not give much thought to ambience or even comfort, providing only the most Spartan of needs. The room contained a narrow bed with a blanket and nothing else. The walls were solid concrete, unpainted and unadorned. The floor was similarly barren and nondescript. It had all the charm of a prison cell, but it would keep us safe. The construction was fireproof, and the outermost doors that led to the stairwell were monitored by the best security system money could buy. Charles was, if nothing else, practical.

I awoke with a sudden jolt of consciousness, my body tight with terror. Beside me, Eli was thrashing about. He was murmuring incoherently, yet every few seconds he shouted Giovanni's name in a clear, strong voice. Like the evening before, my body was bruised and noticeably thinner. I hurt and was consumed by a hunger verging on madness.

I reached out my trembling hands to wake Eli from his dream when he jerked into a sitting position. His eyes popped open. As the cover slipped from his body, I saw that he too had obvious damage to his body. The face that turned to me was full of horror and pain. He then put his powerful arms around me and pulled me into a bone-crushing embrace.

"Oh God, Rachel! It was horrible…the pain…how could anyone survive?"

Tears slipped down my cheeks. "You had the dream, too, didn't you?"

He was also crying. "Yes, at least I think so."

His mind was wandering back to the slumber-evoked images, so I shook his shoulders to bring him back to the present. "What did you see? Tell me everything!"

"I saw darkness and a laboratory, maybe an operating room. I saw strange faces." He stopped, looking at me for reassurance. I nodded. "I saw, and felt, someone being starved and tortured and being left alone in complete darkness where there was no sound, nothing. I felt pain and hunger like I never imagined there could be, and fear, anger, sadness...it was most terrible."

He hugged me again.

"That's exactly what I have been dreaming about. So, you understand that it's more than a dream. It's inside someone else's head, feeling their pain and fear."

"Yes," he agreed quickly.

I had to know. "Did you see his face?"

I didn't have to explain who *he* was. Eli took a long time before he answered. "Yes, I saw his face. I don't understand it, but it was like I was feeling and seeing things from his eyes, terrible things that can't be true."

I didn't have an answer or an explanation that sufficed. How could two people, even creatures like us, share the same dream? Maybe Eli was correct, and the dreams were simple manifestations of the resurfacing guilt and anger we felt. Certainly, as the day of the attack neared, the more vivid the dreams became. Now Eli experienced one as well.

"I can't explain what's going on any more than you can. I only know that I want it to be over! I can't keep feeling it and reliving it anymore. I need it to stop."

"It will all be over soon," Eli said softly. He tried to reassure, but his voice was strained.

"I mean all of it. I want everything about my past just to be gone. No more anger and grief and regret. I thought when I became a vampire that I wouldn't have any more of it. I want to stop feeling—" My words broke off on a strangled sob.

"Rachel, don't say it, please. I understand where it is coming from, but not all feelings are bad. Think about how you feel about me, about how I feel about you. Hang onto it when all the other stuff springs up."

"What if it's not enough? What if I always have it churning around inside of me, forever? And, in our case, it's what it actually means." My fear was turning to anger, and I felt Eli reacting to my outburst.

"Stop. Let's deal with one thing at a time. Let's get through the next few days, and we'll see if the dreams go away. If they don't, we'll deal with them after the attack. I'm sure they're just the stress of what's coming up that's intensifying all these negative feelings. Soon there will be some closure and revenge and a chance really to start again, fresh, maybe a real chance for the two of us."

"Maybe." A sudden thought occurred to me. I jumped on it, desperate to push away the lingering vestiges of our shared dream. "But there's something I need to do first, before I go to Europe and face those bastards once and for all."

He sat quietly as I told him what I planned to do. I knew he didn't think it was a good idea, and the timing couldn't be lousier, but he didn't try to talk me out of it. That won him mucho brownie points.

"If you must do it, then let me go with you, please."

I was torn. It was something I felt I should do myself, but I thought I would worry as much about Eli as he would undoubtedly worry about me if we were separated, especially at a time like this. "All right, I could probably use the moral support, and there's no one I trust more than you."

We sealed the deal with a tender kiss.

When the sun went down, we immediately went out to feed. The blood wiped away the physical traces of the disturbing dreams but could not erase the fear. The time had come finally to leave the past in the past.

CHAPTER 9

We arrived in Kingston from Toronto on the train. The ride was uneventful, the cars more empty than full. The dark winter landscape passed by in a monotonous blur, though with each minute my anxiety gained a deeper hold.

All too soon we were pulling into the station, and I was stepping out into the city that was my home for the first twenty-six years of my life. I knew instantly that everything and nothing had changed. The night was as cold as the sudden dread in my heart. What did I think I would accomplish by coming here? Eli took my hand, and together we went to retrieve our luggage.

Before arriving, I made contact with the Mead family and arranged for use of the space where, a quarter-century before, I experienced my own change. Gerald, who was the operator of the funeral home at that time, passed away several years before. His son, David, was in charge and had been instructed on the long-standing agreement between his family and Giovanni.

David met us at the back door, which did not changed at all since the last time I saw it. He eyed us with apprehension as we approached but had the good sense to greet us with respect.

"And will Giovanni be joining you?" he asked in a quiet, deep voice.

I cringed inwardly. "Not this time."

"I see." He opened the door then followed us down the narrow flight of stairs. The whisper of memories past tingled over me as we made our way down the hallway. "I've cleaned the space as best as I could on short notice. No one's been down here for years. My dad always locked it and didn't explain why until he got sick with the cancer."

"I'm sure it's fine," Eli answered for the both of us.

We stopped outside the wooden door, and if I had a heartbeat, it would have been thundering. David unlocked the room and stepped aside. He placed the key in Eli's hand before retreating quickly back toward the stairs. He probably hoped never to receive the call he had that night. I didn't begrudge him his reaction.

The room was just as it had been the last time, except the books and artwork were gone. Most of it we recovered, as Gerald sent it on to a pre-arranged destination. In fact, much of the artwork was hanging either at our home in San Francisco or at the gallery in London to which we donated it. The shelves still stood but were barren. A chill rode through my body as I crossed the threshold, as though the time we spent there left a ghostly imprint.

Eli placed the suitcase at the end of the bed. With his back to me, I could imagine him as the specter of Giovanni. He turned and frowned upon seeing my intense scrutiny. My hands felt suddenly slick. When I looked down, I realised I was clenching my fists so tightly they were bleeding.

He came to me and placed a kiss in the palm of my hand. There was a slight smudge of red on his lower lip when he made eye contact. "So, this room is where it happened?"

"Yes," I answered, because there were no other words to say.

He nodded but let the matter go. "It's close to sunrise. I don't think we should chance feeding tonight."

I agreed. I let him take me to the bed, and, without words, we undressed. The sheets smelled of lemons but did not entirely mask the odour of disuse. As Eli's arm wrapped about my body, I flashed back to that night, that moment so long ago.

I remembered myself as the mortal woman I had been. I remembered the look on Giovanni's face, the intensity of the physical reactions in my body, and the power of our love. Then I remembered the terrible pain of his bite and the ravaging of my body as I died, then…Seraphine's face. I pulled away from that image as quickly as I could.

I turned to Eli. "Do you remember what happened the night that you changed?" I had to know what he had felt.

He paused before responding. "I remember some of it. I mean I remember us…being together. I remember asking you to change me and the bite, the pain was terrible…and then I remember nothing until the next night." He raised his hand to his neck as he relived the moment that changed everything. A self-conscious smile came over his face, and he turned to me. "Are you remembering your own change?"

"Yes, at least more of it than I have before, but it's still not clear. The memories are jumbled and confusing, and some of the things I'm recalling, I don't think were ever real, if that makes any sense, at least not to me."

"It makes as much sense as it can, considering what we are really has no explanation."

"Good night, Eli," I said, too tired to speak about difficult subjects any longer.

"Good night, my love."

As I opened my eyes the next evening, for a moment I couldn't believe what I saw. I snapped awake and sat bolt upright on the bed. Eli flinched at my abrupt movement, also sitting up. "You okay? Did you have another dream?"

Surprisingly, I hadn't. I surveyed the room. So, I was back to where it all started. What would it mean for the future? "No, actually I don't think I dreamed at all. If I did, I don't remember anything."

"Me either."

We were one day closer to the "big" event, which also meant time was precious for what I wanted to accomplish. Since I didn't have a clear idea what it was, I needed to get my butt in gear. I lowered my feet to the floor, experiencing a shock as my brain recalled the familiarity of the cold stone against my feet.

I led Eli to the bathroom, guilt and pleasure both itching at my brain. The first time I walked this same course after my change, the sensations I experienced almost overwhelmed me. That night swam through my mind. It was wonderful and tortuous to relive the feelings.

After dressing, I took Eli out the back door and into the first stage of reconciliation with my past. I showed him many places:

my childhood home, my elementary school, the studio where I took dance lessons, the hospital, and finally the condo where I lived when I met Giovanni. The place was dark and the driveway empty when we approached. It was close to midnight, and the neighbourhood was still. An eerie wave of déjà vu washed over me. As I looked back over my shoulder to the park adjacent to the complex, Eli followed my line of sight.

I closed my eyes, and I could see him as he appeared to me that night, when the out-of-control party attracted the police. I shivered as though experiencing his voice again, as it came out of the darkness and over my skin. I traced my fingers over my lips, remembering his kiss.

"Rachel?" Eli asked softly.

"Sorry, just remembering…. It's so long ago, but it's so clear in my memory."

"Some things can never be forgotten." His words held a double meaning I immediately understood. I knew he held on to his memories of me, like I did with mine of Giovanni.

"You're absolutely right." I pressed a quick kiss to his cheek, and he smiled. "Do you want to go in?"

"If it's what you want. Just remember we only have one more night, and then we need to get back to Toronto. Don't you want to check on your nephew and try to see what happened to Shannon, visit your mother's grave?" His expression was soft, and in that moment, I could not imagine how anyone could have a better friend than he had always been to me.

I knew he was right and turned away after one more wistful look. "Okay, why don't we check in on my nephew, Michael, then see if we can scrounge up some info on Shannon? We'll leave the cemetery visit to the end." My voice sounded strange, almost nervous.

"Lead the way."

The first stop was my nephew's house. I got the address from Danica a few months earlier, though I never really thought I would make it there during my nephew's lifetime. Yet, there I was. As I stood before the typical suburban bungalow in a quiet, middle-class neighbourhood not far from where we grew up, I was at a loss as to what I thought I would accomplish. It wasn't that I didn't miss my family. It was simply that I made a choice I embraced fully.

Still, I moved up the shadowy driveway and around the side of the house. Our movements were swift and silent. At the back, we found another door that opened onto the darkened kitchen. Eli broke the lock, and the door opened inward. I had a brief moment of hesitation before I stepped inside.

Eli closed the door soundlessly behind our entrance, and I took a moment to orient myself with the layout of the house. I was aware of two distinct breathing patterns and two heartbeats slowed by the natural effects of sleep. Two exits led from the kitchen to the main hallway and to the dining room.

I chose to enter the shadowy hallway. The house was as quiet as a tomb. Everyone in residence was deeply asleep. I glanced at the pictures along the hallway: weddings, Danica's graduation, my parents, and my brother. All were faces from a past I had long since divorced myself from. I pushed aside the unease that started to rumble and continued. The first door I encountered was the bathroom, which I passed. The next was a small bedroom, the door slightly ajar. I prodded the door further open and peered into the stillness.

I could clearly make out the shape of a child's crib, changing table, and other assorted baby necessities. Danica didn't mention they were expecting, and the sight of the room gave me a momentary shock. A small pang of longing and jealousy clenched in my chest. I brushed it aside. I made my decision a long time ago, and I came willingly into a life that means never having children of my own. I looked to Eli at my side and knew I already had the privilege of experiencing motherhood. That thought brought a wave of guilt and thrust forth the lingering shame I harboured over the recent state of my relationship with Eli. I had to accept what was happening between the two of us or stop it once and for all.

A dark look crossed Eli's face, and I knew he must have picked up my thoughts. Jesus, I needed to get better control. I continued without any acknowledgement of what came to mind.

Behind the next door lay my nephew and his wife. She was

nestled along his back, her face slack from the depth of her sleep. His was much as I remembered it but stronger and leaner from the twenty-five years that passed since I last laid eyes on him. I was expecting so much from the moment of actually seeing him again, I was let down by my reaction. I simply felt as though I didn't belong anymore. I expected sadness, homesickness, something more that what I did experience. I guess the old saying was right: one can't go home again.

I cocked my head in the direction we just came from. Together we made a quick survey of the remaining areas of the house, poked through bills and other assorted records, and generally snooped. I found a few pictures from a recent family event that showed my brother as he currently was. It was so strange to see he had changed, aged, now appearing much older than his elder sibling. I stuffed the photos back in the drawer, not allowing myself to think on it any longer. After coming up clean, we decided to move on to other things.

Silently we retraced our steps until we were once again outside in the bitter winter air. I gave the house one last look before hurrying down the empty street. I stopped a few moments later, taking a seat on a deserted bus stop bench. Eli joined me, waiting for me to speak first.

"I don't know what I was expecting or hoping for, but it wasn't there."

"Were you and your nephew close?"

"Not particularly, I guess, but we weren't not close, if it makes any sense. I've just been questioning everything since Giovanni was killed, and I thought that going back to the place where it all began might help in some way. I don't really know what I'm looking for though. Closure, peace, maybe…"

"Rachel, you're so hard on yourself. You need just to accept what happened and move on."

"So, I can be with you?" I snapped a little too quickly.

"It's not fair, but you know what, maybe, if it's going to make you happy. I could accept just about anything for you right now, if it could stop you being so miserable all the time."

I made myself count to five before I spoke again. "I'm sorry. I didn't mean to snap at you. I'm just on edge here."

"I know," he answered, giving me his best Eli smile.

"So, everything looks fine here. There's no sign of financial problems, health issues or anything illegal, and with a baby on the way, life seems good."

"Yep. Your conscience is clean as far as your brother's family goes. So, where to next?"

"Feel like some breaking and entering?"

"Aw shucks, you sure know how to show a fella a good time."

The bitter wind ate our laughter. Fifteen minutes later we found ourselves on the street outside City Hall, where all the pertinent information on Kingston's inhabitants resided. We slipped around the side of the building to a smaller, dimly lit entrance to force our way inside. Eli popped the door open, and, like restless phantoms, we both slipped inside.

Within minutes a guard appeared, alerted by the security monitor to a disturbance at the entrance. When he was within a few feet of the door, Eli stepped behind him, coming from the shadows of a nearby vestibule. He caught the man's arm and whirled him around until they were face to face. Almost instantly the startled man's expression began to soften, much like his waistline had some time in the preceding years. Eli caught his mind. "How many others are in the building right now?"

"Just one. Lorraine Alexander is working upstairs in her office." His voice was a little too slow, imitating a drugged effect. His eyes never left Eli's face.

"Take us to where the financial and business records for the city are."

He smiled as the man started walking and offered his arm to me. I linked mine through his, and we strolled along behind the guard as though we had every right to be there. He led us to the lower level of the building, which I vaguely recalled from a school trip during my elementary school years. If I remembered correctly, it was the jail in a former existence, back when the city was still under British rule. He unlocked the door for us then stood aside, as though waiting for further instruction. Eli kept an eye on him while I rifled through files until I found what I was looking for. Honestly, I was glad to be away from the guard's blank stare. It was creeping me out.

It only took me a few minutes before I had the information I wanted in hand. Good for her, I thought, as I absorbed the records before me. Shannon had made something of herself.

I slipped back out and found the guard slumped on the floor. He had two tiny marks on his neck but no other visible injuries. Eli shrugged, unapologetic for his actions. "There's still Lorraine upstairs," he offered.

After a quick trip to the upper level, where a lone employee was soon unconscious at her desk, we returned to the outdoors. The address I needed was just a few blocks away. I looked up into Eli's face, and before I could speak, he pressed his lips down onto mine. I melted into him, wishing everything between us could be so easy. I broke our embrace after a few minutes. "Wanna hit the clubs?"

"I'm assuming it has something to do with the information you just found?"

"Yep, looks like my old friend moved on from being a manger to an owner of a nightclub. The owner of three, actually, so I figured we would just start with the closest, and we only have a few hours until last call, so we should get a move on."

"Your wish is my command."

On our second stop, we hit pay dirt. It was a smaller establishment, more of a pub than a nightclub, appealing to an older crowd, which made sense since Shannon was fifty-one. Once inside, we found the place almost full. A large central bar dominated the space, with servers on all four sides and booths that lined the outside walls in a U-shape. At the end, farthest from the bar, was a small stage, but there was no live entertainment that night. The sound system was playing a mix of old-school rock and newer pop music.

A few women moved away from the bar, and Eli and I took over the newly empty space. A young girl appeared before us for our orders, and I had to lean in until my mouth was all but pressed to her ear before she could hear me. "Is Shannon working tonight?"

"The owner?"

I nodded.

"Yep, I think she's in the back."

"Thanks."

"So, can I get you a drink?"

I smiled at her innocent question and felt a wave of fear roll off her. It had been a long time since I really enjoyed a feeding or killing. Eli leaned around me and pressed a bill into the girl's hand. He pulled me from the bar and led us through the crowd toward the back of the bar. In the narrow hallway where the bathrooms were located was an entrance marked "Employees only." Ignoring that order completely, we pulled the door open.

The music was all but silenced when the door closed behind us. I stopped, getting my bearings, and felt for any movement. I caught one strong heartbeat coming from farther down the hall. The door was open, and a soft light spilled out into the interior hallway. At the end of the space was a clearly marked exit, where we could make a hasty retreat if needed.

I paused so suddenly Eli stepped on the back of my heel. "What are you waiting for?"

What was I waiting for? I felt decidedly…nervous, a strange, alien feeling that rarely, if ever, reared its head. I continued without comment, barging straight through the door into the office. Without looking up, the woman seated at the desk spoke, "April, I need you to do a count of the wine stock before you leave. I don't—"

The voice was so familiar, I felt a shiver of remembrance across my skin. As her eyes lifted from the sheets of paper on her desk to my face, she cut off her thoughts mid-sentence. It was the same lovely face I spent many years looking into, being jealous of, but fuller and ever-so slightly softer than I recalled. The expression was caught between shock and joy, momentarily frozen as the realisation of who stood before her sunk in.

"Rachel?" she asked.

"Yes," I replied, waiting for a cue as to whether or not my presence was welcome.

She stood, walking around to the front of the desk, and I was not at all surprised to see she kept her fabulous figure. She stopped within an arm's reach of where I stood, looking me over intensely. "How can it be? You look exactly the same as the last time I saw you...and it was, what, twenty-five years ago?"

I pretended she didn't ask me anything. "You look fantastic. I'm only passing through, and I want to make sure that you were okay."

Her attention flicked to the doorway as Eli stepped in behind me. "Who's he? What's going on here?"

Eli moved inside and swiftly shut the door behind him.

"I just want to speak with you, Shannon. When I left, we were on bad terms, and I have always been sorry for it."

She started to speak then seemed to think better of it. I felt her hesitation and experienced a hazy memory from her of one of the last times we spent together. "So, you just show up here, after all this time, after no contact and not knowing what happened to you?"

"Yes."

"Why?"

It stopped me for a moment. I looked back at Eli, leaning against the wall, and he gave a slight shrug indicating that he didn't understand why we were there either. *Thanks*, I thought. His only response was a slight smirk.

I turned back to Shannon. "I don't know if I can really explain why."

She placed a hand on her hip, showing some of the attitude I loved. "And I'm just supposed to take it all with a grain of salt. I mean we were friends, very good friends, and you just disappeared, and it really sucked, Rachel. If it's who you really are."

I couldn't help but smile. "So, you missed me?"

"Sure, I missed you, and I worried about what happened to you. I spent lots of time looking for you, talking to your mom and the police.... It was one of the toughest things I ever went through." Her tone became defensive.

"Well, I'm good, fine, as you can see, and it looks as though you've done well for yourself?"

"Yes. Are you really not going to offer an explanation for where you've been all this time?"

"Rachel," Eli said, warning me to choose my words with care.

"Honestly, I have been all over the world. I've lived in many different places. It's a very long story."

"I imagine, and why did you leave in the first place? Was it about that guy you were always mooning about just before you left?"

I caught Eli's face as he mouthed "mooning" and forced myself to look back to Shannon. "Yes, it's why I left. I fell in love with someone and, for a very complicated reason, we had to leave."

"It's all you're giving me?" She eyed the two of us with undisguised contempt.

"It's all I can give you. I'm sorry."

"Okay, well thanks for the visit, but as you can see, I'm busy." She turned on her three-inch heels and walked back to the other side of the desk. She sat and returned her attention to the pile of paperwork before her. When she next spoke, she didn't look at me. "Please shut the door behind you."

"Shannon, please…"

Eli grabbed my arm and pulled me from the room. The door made a sharp bang as it closed behind us.

"What are you doing?" I snapped, yanking my arm from his grip.

"Stopping you from making an even bigger mess. She obviously wasn't happy about you being here." Eli grabbed my arm again and forced me out the back door into a narrow alley behind the club. "Let's get out of here."

I was still fuming as we made our way onto the lightly populated streets. I walked as quickly as I could without drawing attention, and Eli didn't try to stop me or speak to me. When a sufficient amount of time passed for me to calm down, I stopped dead in my tracks. "Sorry, I know you're right. I don't know what I was thinking or expecting."

He hugged me tightly and kissed the top of my head. "I don't know that you've been thinking clearly since Giovanni was killed. You're treading water, looking for some way to make sense of something that you'll never be able to. Making sure that people you loved once are okay or refraining from taking lives when feeding isn't going to make up for the loss of Giovanni from your life. I've been trying to get it through your head for the past eighteen months." He was firm but not unkind, yet I still bristled at his words.

My anger roared back to life. "Okay, I get it. Stop the damn lectures." I started walking again. "Let me say goodbye to my mother, and we can leave."

Needless to say, our tense and angry conversation didn't stop there. In fact, it progressed to the point of all-out fighting, something that never occurred between us before. Sure, we exchanged angry words and ticked each other off, but we never were as seethingly, all-consumingly mad as we were that night.

The snow swirled and danced about the deserted graveyard, draping the headstones in icy lace. The cover on the ground reflected the bright moonlight, the elongated shadows cast by the various monuments interrupting the vast expanse of white. We stood inside a small clearing, where members of my family were buried for as long as Kingston was a city. I felt unnaturally warm, flushed with a rage so intense it was all I could do to contain it.

"Jesus, Eli, you have to stop it! I'm not perfect; I screw up. I'm not an angel or this fucking goddess you've put up on a goddamned pedestal. I make mistakes, a lot of them. I don't know everything." I was so mad by that point, my blood streamed in response to my temper.

"I never expected you to be perfect." Eli's anxiety was also high, and he clenched his fists at his sides.

"You just don't seem to get it! I have this huge ball of hurt inside of me; all this guilt and anger is eating its way out of me, and I just keep taking and taking from you, always needy but never able to give anything back... I'm so sick of it!"

"You do give back. I know that you love me, and I also know that you're not over Giovanni, and I can understand that!"

"No, I'm not over him, and I don't know if I ever will be, and I'm so weak, and I keep using you for comfort, and you keep letting me! I can't be what you want me to be, and I can't keep hating myself for letting you down. I need to be okay with me, with Giovanni's death."

"I want you to be okay, too. It's all I want—"

"Stop, stop being nice to me. Stop letting me take from you. You need to stop."

"And what? Go find some pale version of you? Pretend that I don't want you, that I don't crave your touch? Maybe I should. There are lots of girls at the university who like me; I'm sure one of them would love to spend eternity with me."

It stopped me cold in my tracks. "It's not funny. Changing someone, turning them into what we are is not something you should ever do lightly and never out of anger or spite. There is no turning back from a mistake…"

"Just like the mistake you made with me?" he spat out.

The knife twisted in my heart. "What are you talking about?"

"Haven't you regretted changing me every second since that night? Don't you wish you could take that decision back? Don't you wish I was growing older, and one day I will die, and you will finally be rid of me?" Eli's fury radiated from him, the energy hot against my skin.

The thought of him being dead hurt more than any physical pain ever could. "Eli, don't say stuff like that. Don't even think it. The only thing I'm sorry for was not being able to bring you into this existence like Giovanni did with me. I gave you eternity with no security that I would be a real partner to you, and it's what haunts me."

"I knew what was at stake when I asked you to change me. You have never lied to me."

"Haven't I? Don't I give you false hope every time I come to you or let you into my bed? Aren't I making a mockery of your feelings for me or even my feelings for you, as muddled as they are?"

He was quiet then, eyes as pained as any I had ever seen. "I never expected you to be perfect or to have all the answers. I never expected you to be anything but yourself. I'm not perfect either. I'm smart and loyal, and I know you're attracted to me, but I'm not perfect." His voice cracked with the heaviness of his emotions before he was able to regain himself. "But you know what is perfect? My love for you. My love *is* perfect. It can't be swayed, cheapened, tainted, or broken. It just is."

"Eli…"

"And you know what?" His voice rose slightly, deepening with anger. "You're an ass for not realising how solid my love is, and you should just accept it. Jesus fucking Christ, Rachel, the situation is what it is! Being miserable for the rest of your life isn't going to bring him back! And isn't it what this trip is all about? Isn't this another way to stir up more bad feelings to keep you miserable?"

"What are you talking about? You know why I came here."

"Yes, I know what you said. You said you wanted to make peace with the past, with all the bad things that happened and all the choices you made, but isn't coming here just making you feel guilty and sad? I don't see you making peace. I see you moping about, regretting things that you can't change. Just go with what you have, embrace the good things in your life. I'm standing right in front of you!"

"Eli, I've had enough of your pressure to be and feel how you want me to."

"And I'm done pressuring you."

We stood there in the dark, cold night, staring silently at each other. Soft snowflakes fell, landing on his dark hair, and I could not stop myself from thinking back to a night so long ago. Then, with a face clenched in anger, he disappeared in a gentle whoosh of wind, and I was alone.

What brought us to this moment exactly? There was no internal argument strong enough to deny the truth of Eli's words. I knew a long time ago that by joining Giovanni, everything else would be left behind. Our love had been worth the sacrifice and still was. I needed to hang onto the resolve I felt then and keep it bright in the present. There was no reason to look back or to fill up with regrets.

Eli was right. I was the only one keeping myself miserable, and misery did not honour Giovanni's memory. Any thoughts I kept of him should be of love, lust, and pride. He would want me to carry on and be happy. I would certainly want it for him, should our roles have been reversed.

I sat on the cold tombstone of my mother's grave and gave myself a mental ass-kicking. For whatever reason, as I remained there in the silent and deserted cemetery, I had finally seen the light, figuratively that is.

The things that passed between us were ugly, though painfully true, and they were words that would forever alter our relationship and our way of interacting. They were words that may someday be forgiven but never forgotten.

I pressed a kiss to the cold stone and bid a final goodbye to my mother. As I looked up, I caught a fleeting glance of Giovanni and quickly closed my eyes against the pain his vision invoked. When I opened them again, the specter was gone, as the real Giovanni was from my life. Then I returned to the dingy room beneath the funeral parlour, alone.

CHAPTER 10

He returned the following evening, obviously still angry but much calmer than twelve hours earlier. He didn't offer where he had been, and I didn't ask. We both gave our apologies then didn't say more than a handful of words to each other as we packed and headed to the train station.

It was a long and draining trip home, filled with uncomfortable silences, the likes of which I never experienced with Eli before. So much happened to me, so much grief and pain scarring itself deep within my being. As a result, it not only changed me, but it altered who I was to others. I think Eli recognised it and was doing his generous best to make amends with that fact. His love for me would need to adapt if it were to survive. There were a million things I wanted to say but couldn't put into words. I was in free-fall, spiralling down a path that seemed to have no end. It was a ride I desperately wanted to get off of.

As we pulled into the station in Toronto, I reached for Eli's hand, and once our bodies made contact, I gripped him as a painful substitute for the emotional connection I desperately wanted to make. He squeezed back, and when he met my eyes, I knew he understood. Putting things into words could not make the connection between us any more real or powerful. I leaned into his shoulder, drinking in his scent, and, at long last, felt some peace.

We took the opportunity to hunt new grounds away from the familiarity of San Francisco. It didn't take us long to find worthy candidates in one of the seedier areas of downtown. We passed the throngs of prostitutes, runaways, and unfortunates suffering from one type of mental illness or another. I picked up on a particularly depraved montage of thoughts that included images of previously committed violent rapes, and I followed the disgustingly sick trail to its source.

The man was sitting on a low window frame of a darkened store, looking about nonchalantly while the stream of vile memories continued to parade through his twisted mind. When he caught sight of me, he gave me a cursory once-over, deciding absently that I wasn't his type. I thought I might be able to convince him otherwise.

I calmly took in his filthy hands, red-rimmed eyes, and the salt-and-pepper stubble covering the lower half of his face. His body odour was pungent and sour, even through his thick winter coat. He licked his lips, anticipating his next atrocious act. I gave Eli a look he knew well, and he silently disappeared to find a victim of his own. I returned my attention to the ferret-faced man, both repulsed by his existence and excited by his impending demise.

He turned to look at me again, and I cocked my head in the direction of a worn pathway across the street, which led to a series of abandoned buildings. It was a mecca for the homeless, drug addicts, and the criminally inclined. He hesitated, but his nature got the better of him.

I heard him close on my heels as I began down the uneven ground, the sounds and smells of poverty all around us. The whole way, he thought of the pain and humiliation he wished to inflict on me. I didn't stop until I found a building from which I picked up no signs of life. I leaned my back on a wall littered with graffiti and waved the man closer.

He approached, eyes twitching about with suspicion. The closer he got, the more terrible he smelled, and the more intense the barrage of violence in his head became. He repeatedly returned to an event that caused him particular excitement, an especially degrading and cruel sexual assault of a mousy, pre-pubescent girl. I kept her petrified face trapped in my mind, ensuring he, too, would meet an excessively painful end.

"What the fuck do you want?" he asked, when we were finally face to face.

"To taste your fear," I said in a hard and controlled voice.

The realisation of danger crossed his haggard face, and I smiled coldly. I grabbed his arm in my hand like a vise, and with the other, I deliberately bent each finger backward. The snapping of each tiny bone was absurdly loud, as were his cries of pain. There were no signs of reaction to our exchange, so I continued. "The more sound you make, the more painful I'll make it." My words were soft, but the sight of my exposed fangs made his eyes bulge with terror. "It is for everyone you've ever hurt."

I spent approximately fifteen minutes systematically breaking the bones in his body, but to him I'm sure it felt like days of unending pain. Several times I slapped him across the face to jolt him back into consciousness. Then, when I felt I pushed the chance of interruption long enough, I sank my teeth into his neck and drank greedily. His blood was liquid ecstasy. Just before his heart stopped, I pulled away. I made sure he was aware as I opened his belt and pulled down the grubby jeans he wore. I reached between his legs and, with undisguised glee, viciously removed the part of his anatomy with which he had inflicted so much torment. I left him to die in a pool of his own blood on the snowy ground littered with used condoms and dirty syringes.

When I emerged from the path, Eli was waiting on the same window ledge where I found the man not thirty minutes earlier. He crossed the street in a blur of dark clothes and white skin, not worrying about what anyone might think they saw. No one would believe a group of junkies and whores when they tried to explain that the attackers were a pair of vampires. He took my hand, and we made our way back to a main street to hail a cab.

We hadn't spoken since we fed, and as we merged onto the highway that led home, he finally broke the silence. "Feel better?" His voice was neutral, but I picked up on his concern. It had been a brutal attack on my part and a way I had not acted since before Giovanni's death.

"Yes," I answered, "and he deserved it."

"Oh, I don't dispute that fact. It was impossible not to pick up on the images he was processing. They radiated from him like a beacon. It was disgusting."

"He's the type of person who deserves to cross our paths."

"Agreed."

We returned to Charles' borrowed car, where I flicked through the radio stations until I found something I could listen to. As I settled back, I picked up on a sensation of nervousness from Eli.

"But it's not all I was referring to."

I knew what he meant. He was talking about us, trying not to push or appear too anxious after all that happened between us in the past few months.

"Yes, I do. It will be a real fresh start and hopefully a real chance…for us." Emotion in my voice choked the last two words, but I knew he heard.

The ride home was dark, yet comfortable. I felt calm and oddly content. The time passed easily as I watched over the passing traffic, letting my mind wander where it would. About halfway there, Eli pulled out his cell phone and made a call but didn't identify who it was. "Yeah, it's Eli. We're back. How about making tonight the night?" He paused briefly, obviously receiving a response, then ended the conversation with the quick, "Cool, see you soon." He snapped the phone shut.

Soon enough the city came into view, and it was a pleasing feeling to be going home. I wasn't paying very close attention and didn't notice that we weren't immediately heading back to Charles's townhouse until we were pulling into the parking lot of an unfamiliar nightclub. I followed Eli to the front entrance of the club, where he gave the bouncer his name, and he let us in without resistance. He was smiling the whole time, and I knew he was up to something but keeping a tight block on his thoughts.

"You know I hate when you do this stuff." I pulled the door closed behind me.

"I know," he agreed happily then led me over to a spot where Micah waited for us. He waved hello without speaking to me, then the two men turned to leave. "Wait here," Eli said.

I stood there alone, people-watching. Instruments were set up on the stage, indicating some type of live performance was to happen. I assumed the band that would play was one

Eli enjoyed, and it was his purpose in taking us there. He was probably talking his way backstage to meet the musicians. A pretty young waitress brought the white wine I ordered, and I took a small sip, letting the taste allow me to feel "normal," a wonderful reprieve, even if it only lasted for a few minutes.

The usual chatter and thoughts floated about, most trivial and harmless. A few I picked up on were there to drown the sorrows, but for the most part, the crowd was anticipating the performance and simply looking to have some fun.

Then the band took the stage, and the crowd clapped enthusiastically at their appearance. Lights danced behind the band, spelling out "The Ferocity of Sadness," which I guessed was the name of the band. Catchy. The singer was a young woman with wild purple hair and a rail-thin body. The band must have been well liked because the crowd greeted the sight of her with thunderous applause, to which she broke out in an adorable grin.

"Now we have a bit of a change here tonight. A friend of a friend has called in a favour, so we're going to have someone else come out to sing a couple of songs with us. I'm going to fall back on guitar, and let's give him a nice welcome, everyone!"

Eli came up from the back of the stage, swiftly raising the microphone stand up to the correct height. Micah followed behind him, ready with a bass in hand.

"Thank you, this first one is a personal favourite of mine." He looked directly at me when he spoke, and I experienced a warm fluttering in my stomach. When the band broke into a heavy version of "How Soon is Now?" I could not keep the enormous grin off my face. I had no idea he could sing and sing as well as he did.

As the song ended, he spoke again, chipping away at whatever blackness might have remained in my heart. "Now, Rachel, this one is for you! I think you'll know why." He looked at Micah, who nodded, before locking eyes with me again. "I love you. Always."

He began a song I had been listening to a lot in the previous weeks, "Fall for You." When my dark times overtook me, I often retreated to the library to read and obsessively listen to songs of heartbreak and loss—nothing like rubbing salt in the wound to make myself feel better.

When the music started, and I realised what it was he was about to sing, I cracked. Any walls that had been still standing within me, blocking the way to me being able to let Eli into my heart, crumbled. It was odd how one gesture or the right setting or tone of voice could change everything. Music, art, and the written word could often be the catalyst to a change of heart. There were messages in the lyrics of that particular song that could apply to both of our points of view and our unbreakable devotion to one another. We both caused each other a lot of hurt but also were source of strength at the same time.

We connected on such an intimate level, it was hard to discern sometimes where one finished and the other began, and I knew I was not only aware of his thoughts and feelings but experienced them as my own. It was more than just the nature of what we were. It was the basis of *who* we were. It took everything I had not to let the tears fall, but I knew I couldn't risk the chance of anyone noticing the colour, even in the relative darkness of the club.

The crowd was incredibly moved. I could feel the outpouring of emotion: love, sadness, and jealousy, and I couldn't help but be amazed that this performance was for me alone. The lyrics could be interpreted to mean many things but seemed particularly true of our situation. "...won't live to see another day...it's true...a girl like you is impossible to... You're impossible to..." As far as I was concerned, there was no point to anything if I didn't have someone to love.

I stood as his voice began to die out, fearful and exhilarated at the same time. He leaped from the stage and walked straight toward me, not acknowledging anyone in his way. The sea of bodies parted then roared with delight when he took me in his arms and kissed me as if he would never stop.

When our lips parted, I whispered in his ear, "I love you, too, and I will never again let anything keep me from being with you."

"I'm going hold you to it."

The band kicked in with a bass-heavy number that

invigorated the crowd. The bodies around us began to dance and jump to the tempo, and we quickly moved back to where we stood earlier. Micah soon joined us, and together we escaped into the waiting darkness.

Nothing could ever be the same after that night.

CHAPTER 11

We left Toronto the following night to meet with an assembly of allies the likes of which the world never saw before. Charles, either through his direct initiation or through Alessandra, was able to persuade twenty-three vampires of varying ages and strengths to support us in our attack on the Desmarais forces. We touched down in London, where our new comrades were waiting in a nearby home of Charles.

The plan was simple. We would divide into three main groups and five smaller ones to hit the main compounds and associated meeting places. There would be five vampires in the group for each of the main sites, and the remaining would split among the smaller targets. Allies of the human kind would augment each group: ex-soldiers, mercenaries, and assorted professional criminals. Some were privy to the real nature of our existence, others simply lured by the big payoff. The humans were already in place, and travel arrangements were set for the vampires

Being back in England was bittersweet. It was a way to reconnect with happy times from my past, and it was also the scene of my greatest hurt. Sitting between Eli and Charles in the car en route to the meeting house, déjà vu overtook me, both wonderful and agonising. The next phase in my life was just within reach, and it made me smile even as it broke my heart.

"You okay?" Eli asked, for what seemed like the thousandth time.

I forced myself to smile reassuringly and bit back the first remark that came to mind. "Uh-huh. I'm good. Please stop asking me, or I will get upset."

The vaguest of smiles slipped across Charles's lips, but he wisely did not comment. After a dreary ride through pounding rain, we pulled up in front a small manor house set on a hundred-plus acre estate behind a colossal stone gate. Trees rising tall enough to challenge the heavens and obscure a clear view of the house lined the drive. The car skidded to a stop in the slimy mud, and I got my first glimpse of where we would meet.

Eli stepped out from the car and popped open an umbrella, which he held above me as I followed him from the backseat. The house was mostly dark. Only a single outside light had been turned on, but my eyes clearly made out the charming details of the craftsmanship.

"It's lovely," I said as Charles appeared at my side. I was peripherally aware of the driver taking our bags from the trunk up to the front door. As he returned to the car, Charles put some bills into his hands and thanked him for his service. Micah joined us, his elevated heartbeat giving away his nervousness.

"Come on then. Everyone is waiting inside." Charles was at his cool, prim best, just what I needed.

Eli slipped his free hand into mine, and we followed Charles up to the front door. There was an alarm system panel, of course, into which Charles punched a code. The door swung open, and once inside Charles locked it behind us. I smelled a wood-burning fire and caught a murmur of voices. Brief, intermittent flashes of thought touched me, all too fast or vague to have any meaning. I suspected the group assembled locked down their minds as solidly as their age and individual abilities allowed—a vampire show of bravado. *I'm too strong to let you touch my mind.* I shivered.

We hung our wet coats by the door, and Charles took the lead to a room at the back of the house. In its day, it was a grand entertaining room with double fireplaces, walnut panelling, and ornately designed windows. It contained two separate sitting areas with chairs, couches, and tables, yet most of the room's inhabitants stood. Suspicious, powerful eyes followed our approach. It couldn't have been more somber if we were marching to our deaths. There were a few surprised reactions upon the realisation that we had a human with us.

Charles nodded and murmured, "Hello," to several people as we passed, all met with polite acknowledgement. I spotted Alessandra standing with an Asian female at the far end of the room. She smiled as she saw me, and I reacted with both a terrible chill and an inner calmness. Standing in the farthest corner, completely alone, was Sorcha. Her wild red hair gleamed in the firelight, and her slight frame was preternaturally still. The expression on her face was impossible to read.

Then a strange sensation surged through my body, a warm whispering, reminiscent of the way the spread of blood felt when I fed. A soft tingling pulled at my brain, and I was compelled to look off to my right.

A young man a few feet away pulled my attention. He stood with two other men and an exotic-looking female, whose power radiated like a slow boil. Our eyes met, and a strange familiarity passed between us. His brows puckered, and I was sure he experienced it, too. I caught the back of Charles's arm, indicating in the man's direction. "Who's he?"

"His name is Kieran. Giovanni was also his maker."

I was surprised and somehow not. Kieran smiled in my direction, and I caught a glimpse of Giovanni's face as seen through his eyes. It was a warm, fond memory, yet it hurt rather than touched me. Something about the affection with which he thought of Giovanni sparked a hard, jealous, and spiteful response in my mind.

As I forced myself to look away from Kieran, another small grouping of vamps on the other side of the room drew my attention. A striking woman stood with several men, one of whom she was all but glued to the side of. She made eye contact with me, and her power lashed out. She was thin, of medium height, and looked to be of Eastern European descent. The man she pressed so closely against was as close to the perfect Aryan male specimen as ever existed. He had the blond hair, blue eyes, and fair skin combination that was a cliché, and also exquisite yet masculine features. I could see his face plastered on Nazi recruitment posters: If you look like this, sign up *here*!

The woman's demeanor reeked of possessiveness, which

did not seem to please the man. I could have been mistaken, but when our eyes met, I thought I saw a silent plea in their depths. I looked back at the woman, and her eyes narrowed in a decidedly unfriendly manner.

Eli slipped his arm about my waist and nodded in the woman's direction. She nodded back, then looked away. The man's eyes followed us as we continued further into the room.

Charles stopped as he reached Alessandra, the two a formidable union no matter what the occasion. He turned to address the assembled group. "First, I must thank you all for coming here tonight. I know it is not our nature to meet like this, especially under the circumstances, but I think that by attending, you have shown your agreement that the situation, as it is, represents a threat to all our kind."

A murmur of approval circulated through the room. We spent the next hour answering questions about the circumstances of Giovanni's death, the nature of the Desmarais vendetta, and the scope of their power. When all inquiries seemed to be satisfied, Charles suggested breaking into smaller groups to discuss the specifics of each attack.

He, of course, would lead one, joined by myself and four other vampires. Alessandra, with Eli's assistance, would take the second group. The third was to be led by a male vamp named Jeremiah, whose face bore strong Native American features. The smaller sites were led by individuals or pairs, Sorcha going her assault alone, as requested. I took notice of the fact that the blond vampire and his mistress joined Eli's group.

Every site was studied meticulously, and it was in quick order that our immortal army understood the plans. Charles's human contacts were briefed before our arrival and would meet with the leaders at a pre-assigned location the following evening.

With a few hours to sunrise, the groups broke up, and a reserved type of mingling started. A few retreated immediately from the house, with the majority staying behind to familiarise themselves with their newfound allies. I scanned the room until I found Eli talking with Alessandra and another female vampire. I felt his voice in my head, *I love you*, and returned the sentiment. Just as I was about to attempt to rescue him from Alessandra's clutches, a cool hand touched at my elbow. I turned to find myself face to face with a brother I never knew I had.

CHAPTER 12

Kieran was about the same height as Eli with a slightly thinner build. He had medium brown hair and blue eyes, and the clean lines in his facial features reminded me of the classical movie stars of the golden age of film. When he smiled, which he did easily, it lit up his whole face. His smile turned him from someone who might be passed unnoticed on the street to someone to stop for another look at. He appeared to be in his early twenties when he was changed, forever unspoiled by the ravages of time.

He regarded me as intently, without any obvious self-consciousness. Finally, he stepped forward and placed an old-fashioned kiss on the back of my hand. He was still smiling, and I realised the look on my face was not as warm as his. The fact that he knew Giovanni long before I was born really bothered me. I couldn't explain or rationalise it. It was a reaction that simply was. Yet, however off-put I felt, I still wanted to know everything about their relationship.

"I'm happy to share my story," he said to the question I thought. "Do you want to talk here, or would you like to go somewhere more private?"

His kindness and sincerity were killing me. Though he had done absolutely nothing to incite my anger except exist, I had to fight to stop from snapping at him. His gentleness made me wonder what attracted Giovanni to him in the first place. I always believed Giovanni enjoyed my spunk, my dark side, and I didn't see any of it in Kieran. If it was good, bad, or irrelevant, I wasn't sure. It did make me question, for the first and only time, exactly what it was that had existed between Giovanni and me.

"I prefer for us to speak alone. Though, with this bunch, it's going to mean moving some distance from here." It would be impossible for us not to be overheard with the crew of immortals assembled. I might have no chance of reading them, but there were some who could see into my mind no matter how hard I tried to control my thoughts.

"Very true." He paused then smiled again. "Why don't we head down the road to that dilapidated barn I passed on the way in? We should have lots of privacy there and be out of scope of any who might overhear or have access to our thoughts."

"Sounds perfect. Just let me tell Eli where I'm headed."

"Of course, you wouldn't want him worrying." He was still smiling, though I could have sworn there was an undercurrent of sarcasm to his words.

Eli was eyeing us from a short distance away. When he saw me moving in his direction, he closed the space between us with a few, quick strides. "Everything okay?" He looked over my shoulder in Kieran's direction as he spoke.

"Yes. Kieran and I are going to step out for a bit to talk. Don't worry; everything's fine. I have my cell phone if you want to get a hold of me."

He was smart and didn't argue with me. "Fine. I'm right here if you need me."

His eyes burned the back of my head as I turned toward Kieran. He followed, without a word, as I passed him and made my way to the back door of the house. Keiran's energy was soft, tickling the back of my neck like a warm summer breeze. We made short order of the several miles between the house and our destination.

There was not much to see as we silently moved down the dark, country road, only wide-open fields devoid of life at that time of the night. The nearest neighbour was several miles on the other side of the barn where we headed. Such isolation was the point, to have a private, secure place for the group that came to meet.

The barn appeared like a black, misshapen entity on an otherwise flat and empty expanse of land. Most of the roof had fallen off, and one of the front double doors was missing. The wooden fence about the property sagged, the laneway overgrown with weeds and grass. It was the type of place that would appeal to wild animals and teenagers looking for someplace to do questionable things out of the view of adult scrutiny.

We crossed into the main part of the structure, where once upon a time a farmer stored his feed or perhaps farming equipment. Then it was barren but for a rusty rake and assorted garbage. I could hear mice and some larger mammals scurrying around. Somewhere overhead a bird fluttered.

"Better?" Kieran asked.

"Much. Thank you for humoring me."

We stood together in the darkness, both privy to a relationship with Giovanni that was separate from each other's. A strange connection, for as close as we both were to him, we were complete strangers to each other. Kieran was very open; a stream of warmth washed over me, and I was exposed to flashes of happy memories during the time he spent as Giovanni's companion. His smile was wide and easy, and a smile tugged at my own lips in response. Why was I fighting so hard against liking this man?

"It seems we have much in common and, at the same time, are completely different. We're from different parts of the world, different time periods, even different sexes, yet we both share the same maker..."

I experienced a strange discomfort as he pointed out that we were of the opposite sex. I wasn't sure whether he was implying something or simply stating as a fact. "And you two were close? I mean what type of relationship did you have exactly?"

He smiled even wider then. "You mean, were we lovers?"

Did I want the answer to it? "Yes, it's what I'm asking."

"No, we weren't intimate, not sexually, at least, but we were close. I came to look upon him as a father figure and, after we had spent many years together, as a brother." The smile faltered ever so slightly.

"How long were you together?"

"About seven years, and then we went our separate ways. We did meet up from time to time and kept in contact, but we never resided together again."

"I see. What made you go your separate ways?"

He didn't respond immediately, and, after a few minutes, I wondered if he would answer me at all. Then I felt myself being pulled into a memory of the two of them together. I recognised both men immediately, though the setting was unknown to me and their style of clothing was something from long before I ever existed. They were sitting in a cosy den, with a fire snapping brightly in a nearby hearth. Giovanni's face was dark, a brooding expression I remembered well.

"Something happened to make Giovanni start to pull away from me."

"He got very quiet and didn't tell you what was going on." I was familiar with the experience.

"Yes, exactly, though I didn't understand it then, I suppose he received word the Desmarais had caught up with him. I imagine he thought the best thing for my safety and survival was for us to part ways. He rather abruptly gave me access to a large sum of money and several properties, then bought me a ticket to the Orient by sea. When next I heard from him, he had taken up residence in America. I didn't see him again for nearly thirty years afterward."

"And he never shared with you anything about the Desmarais or Seraphine?"

"Not a word. He didn't speak much about his past, in general, not even his mortal life. He was always very generous with his money, his attention, and protection but not with his past. That type of thing he kept very close to his heart and did not share."

"But you were close?"

"Yes, very close. I knew him peripherally before the change, at least his reputation. He was one of the few who, at the time, paid his house staff and field workers well. It was a very hard time then, with much of the country out of work, and the poor potato crops causing a widespread famine. He was not seen often but was known to be polite and generous."

So, we had arrived at the moment of truth. "And how did you come to be changed?"

"Not from the best of circumstances, I must confess. As I

said earlier, it was a bad time for the country. My father died when I was a young boy, and there was only my mother to look after me and seven siblings. She worked long hours as a field hand and also took in laundry, but there was still not enough money to feed all those mouths. As soon as one of us reached about the age of ten, we also went out to work. We took on any number of jobs, if there were any to be found."

His mind was alive with memories of a tired-looking woman and many dirty-faced children. All were dressed in worn clothing and looked much too thin. I saw images of a small house with a dirt floor and paper stuffed in the many broken windows. The house was surrounded by fields, and far off in the distance was the outline of a great manor.

He began to speak again. "I had taken up with an unruly bunch, poor young men like me who were sick of the conditions in which we lived. We were angry with the failing crops but angrier still at the government for its seeming lack of ambition to help their people. Many landowners did not even live in Ireland themselves. They were landlords and farmers in name only. They charged outrageous rents and paid poor wages, compounding the problem even more.

"And these men I came to view as my new family, they were nothing more than a bunch of hooligans. They stole and flopped in abandoned buildings. Any money they did manage to get they spent on liquor and women, and it was during one of our night-time pilferings that I crossed paths with Giovanni. I wasn't of the mind that what we were doing was making our situation any better and tended to be a passive participant more than anything else, which usually meant I was the lookout.

"So, there I was standing in the dark, fidgeting from nerves and trying to keep myself warm, while the others broke into a large home that belonged to a family known to have money. I couldn't see more than a few feet in front of me, and the night was deathly silent. Then, out of nowhere, a man appeared standing not five feet from where I was.

"To say I was startled is an understatement. I about jumped out of my skin when his face appeared. His skin was so white, he all but glowed in the darkness. My heart started hammering, but as scared as I was, I didn't run away. He stepped close until we were just about nose to nose, and I remember thinking I never saw eyes so blue in all my years. 'What are you doing here?' he asked, though I know he was aware of what was happening.

"'Waiting for my friends,' I managed to stammer out. My shirt was suddenly drenched in sweat, though moments earlier I was shivering from the cold.

"'Maybe not the wisest choice in friends?' he said, and I could not look away from his face. I was shaking and feeling slightly ashamed of my seeming cowardice.

"'Maybe not,' I agreed.

"'Now's your chance to make a smart decision. If I were you, I would leave and never look back. There's more to life than thieving and drinking.' It was an order, no doubt, but his tone was even and kind.

"I didn't need another prompt. I took off running, and, like he had said, I didn't look back, not even when the night was suddenly full of the screams of my former comrades. The dirt path was slick from a rain earlier in the evening, and I had trouble keeping on my feet as I tried to escape. I was concentrating so hard on getting as far away as possible that I wasn't aware of the approaching wagon until I was almost on top of it. The horses whinnied loudly as the driver pulled them to an abrupt stop. 'Who's there?' he shouted.

"'Just someone on their way home, sir. I didn't mean to frighten you.' My breathing was heavy and tight in my chest.

"'You're trespassing, boy, you know that?' He stepped down from the wagon, and dread filled me when I saw the pistol he clutched in one hand. I was trapped between being shot and whatever happened to the men I deserted. I decided to take my chances on getting shot.

"I burst away from the man with as much force as I could muster. I heard him snort in surprise, then his heavy footsteps pounding in the mud behind me. A loud shot rang out, and there was a bright pain as the bullet grazed my right shoulder. I clutched at the wound and stumbled slightly. It was enough for the man to catch up with me.

"The next shot hit me right between the shoulder blades. I fell face first into the mud but oddly didn't feel any pain. The man roughly rolled me over onto my back, and, though he was mere inches from my face, I could not see him clearly. I was already slipping away.

"'That'll teach ya. I'm sure it's no coincidence to find ya here on my land in the dark, after all the robberies been happening lately.'

"My throat started filling with blood, and I was drowning in the heaviness of it. I coughed, and my heartbeat suddenly thundered in my ears. I heard the man begin to speak again, but the sound of his voice was hastily cut off. Then Giovanni's face appeared in the space just above my own. He smiled and said, 'Do you want to live?'

"I couldn't speak but did the best I could to nod. I felt his mouth press to the hole in my chest, and the closing greyness came more quickly, but I was no longer choking on my own blood. Then a thick liquid trickled into my mouth, and the most curious sensation began in my body. I became aware of his wrist pressed against my mouth, and it was his blood spilling down my throat. I remember struggling internally with it, feeling both repulsed and yet unable to stop drinking. Then there was nothing."

I trembled with the feeling of my own remembered experience, mingled with the psychic tickle of his.

I was so drawn into his story that it took me a moment to realise he was done speaking. "So, he saved you?"

"Yes, both from my wounds that were undoubtedly fatal but also from myself. If it not that night, certainly some other terrible fate would have befallen me. I was doing all the wrong things, putting myself in one stupid, dangerous predicament after another."

"He saved me, too, not from any immediate risk to myself, but he saved me from a lifetime of nothingness, if it makes any sense."

"It does."

We looked at each other in a comfortable silence, then Kieran reached forward and pulled me into a brotherly embrace. He placed a chaste kiss on my cheek, and the last of my reservations melted. It was good to have someone else to call family.

"May I ask you a question now that we have cleared the air?" he asked. He pulled out of our hug.

"Of course." I already knew what the question would be.

"Is Eli your partner now, your lover?" His tone was easy, non-judgmental, but I still felt that rush of predictable guilt.

"Yes," I answered.

"I see, and may I ask how he came to be one of us?"

I tried to stop it, but the memory of the night of Eli's change surged through my mind. "He was our son; Giovanni and I raised him from a child. After Giovanni was killed, I made him a vampire." I knew my words sounded defensive, but I couldn't help myself.

"Then he is like a brother to me also, having come from the same bloodline."

"I guess you could look at it that way."

"The other whom you arrived with. Charles?"

"He is Giovanni's maker."

"A father to us all then?"

"Sort of."

He was quiet for a few moments again, seeming lost in thought. Then the bright, irrepressible smile returned, and I could not help but grin in return. "We should head back before anyone worries."

I followed him out toward the road. It was so quiet, the darkness so solid, like one who lived in the brightness of a city could not understand.

About halfway back, he spoke again. "Perhaps, when it is done and things settle down, I might come for a visit, give us a chance to get to know one another?"

I was surprised at how intense my reaction to his question was. I really did want him to come, and for us to get to know one another better. "Of course, for you my door will always be open."

"Good. It's a plan then."

Kieran picked up the pace and we made it to the back entrance in less than a minute. I paused on the back veranda, a myriad of emotions chugging through my brain. When he noticed I no longer followed, he turned back. "You coming?"

"I just need a minute."

"Sure, I'll see you tomorrow then." With it he vanished back into the house.

I had just sat on the rain-damp steps when I heard soft footsteps approaching. "Eli?" I called out, not surprised that he would be waiting anxiously for my return. He did like to hover sometimes.

"No, I'm sorry. It's not Eli." The voice was male and one I was not familiar with. It had an accent I could not place, still quite sharp, as though not too many years had passed to smooth it away.

"Who's there?" I peered into the darkness, discerning a male figure dressed in dark clothing coming from around the side of the house. An injection of strange images jumped into my brain as the figure closed the space between us. I saw scenes of war, men in dark uniforms, blood, and death, then the face of the unfriendly woman loomed large, just as his face became clearly visible. It was the handsome blond man I noticed earlier in the evening.

"My name is Aldous. I don't mean to intrude, but I would like the opportunity to speak with you if I may?" Up close his features were even more impossibly perfect than I initially thought.

"Sure. What can I help you with? Charles is the more ideal person to speak to, if you have questions about the attack tomorrow."

His face had been impassive up to that point, and my words triggered a look of pain. "It has nothing to do with the attack. It's, well, it's of a personal nature." He shot a worried look at the house as he spoke.

"Okay."

"Could we perhaps move away from the house a bit? I don't want Tatiana to find me speaking with you before I get the chance to say what I need to."

His panic touched me. I reached a hand out to him, which he took after a brief hesitation, and together we moved to the far side of the property. We stopped when we met the stone wall, at the farthest edge of the house's main horse field. "Far enough?"

"With Tatiana you can never be sure." His tone was grim.

"Well, let's get to it then. What is it you wanted to speak to me about?"

"Now that I'm here, I feel at a loss for words, but I simply cannot go on as I have been."

"It has to do with Tatiana. The woman I saw you with earlier?"

"Yes, she is my maker, and I have been what amounts to her slave for the past sixty years. In every way, physically, sexually, though I cannot rightly say emotionally, because I do not think her capable of any real emotion. I am certainly not someone that she cares about in a romantic sense. I am her property."

I swam in his anguish as his words tumbled out. I thought the abandonment that Giovanni experienced with Charles was terrible, but this was a fate equally, if not more, grim. "And you want to leave her?"

"Yes, God, yes. Being alone until the end of time would be Heaven after the years I spent with her. Can you help me?"

I touched his cheek and absorbed an awful and demeaning moment he experienced at her cruel hand. It involved choke-collars, studded paddles, and painful-looking items I didn't even have names for. "I will do everything I can to get you out of this."

"You are as wonderful as I've heard tell."

"Flattery will get you everywhere."

We both seemed to realise suddenly just how closely we stood to one another. He took a small step back then seemed unsure of what to do with his hands. "I think to be fair, you should be aware of who I was in my human life. Perhaps you might think me deserving of the lot I received."

It took me aback. "All right."

"I was born in Germany." Ah, it explained the accent. "I became a soldier during World War Two, leaving university to enlist. I was not part of the SS, just a regular soldier. My family wasn't prestigious or wealthy enough to be higher than that." He paused, and I choked back a bout of inappropriate laughter. I was kidding when I mused about his outward Aryan perfection. It didn't cross my mind that he might *actually* have been a part of that horrible episode in German history.

"And I was just a young man following the wishes of my parents and trying to be loyal to his country, but I did horrible things. Even worse, I didn't stop atrocities when I could have." The expression on his handsome face was as genuinely remorseful as I ever saw.

"And yet aren't we all killers here?" I answered honestly.

He nodded stiffly. "Yes, but by nature, not necessarily by choice."

"Well, I could argue with you there. We can leave our victims alive."

"Sometimes," he agreed with the barest of smiles, "but somehow I cannot seem to let go of what I did as a mortal man. It haunts me more than anything I have done or seen since."

"How does Tatiana fit into all of this?"

"Tatiana enjoyed the war immensely, lots of easy, weak victims, and she relishes inflicting pain upon others. Naturally, she ingratiated herself into the higher ranks of the SS and Hitler's inner circle. She got off on the sickness that bred there. I imagine she contributed some of her own ideas, as well."

I shivered as I remembered pictures I'd seen of concentration camp victims, of the destruction the German army was responsible for. Though it was long before my birth, the effects were still felt. "How did she get a hold of you?"

"I was injured and brought to a hospital for surgery. She liked to have her pick of victims from among the young men. Whomever she happened to find attractive became her next target. One night I awoke to find her at my bedside. She was so beautiful, like nothing I ever saw before." I remembered my own feelings the first time I laid eyes on Giovanni. "Everyone else in the room was asleep. She offered me her hand, and, without even thinking, I allowed her to help me from the bed and down the corridor to an empty surgical theatre. Once inside, though, her beauty changed into something cold, demonic. She bit me, draining me to the point that I could no longer even stand. Then she asked me 'Do you want to live?' I used my last ounce of strength to answer, 'Yes,' and that was it."

"Have you ever tried to leave?"

"Many times. She always finds me, and she is much too strong to fight for long."

"Why do you think I can help you?"

"I thought you might persuade her that there is another way to exist, that it is possible for our kind to have friendships, even love." That last word brought with it an image of a delicate woman I fleetingly saw earlier in the house.

"You have someone in mind?"

"Yes, yes, I want a chance before she crushes the last remaining goodness from me, like she did others before me."

"She's done it to others?" I was incredulous at the thought.

"A few times. Two whom I know of became so sick that they had to be destroyed. The one remaining vampire I have met is as twisted as Tatiana herself, if not more so."

"Do you know if Charles is aware of this situation?"

"Tatiana's reputation is well known."

"I see..." I was just about to continue when he launched himself at me, wrapping his hard body around my much smaller one. It was not a sexual or romantic advance in any sense."

"Please help me," he whispered against my ear. I hugged him back.

"Aldous," a strong female suddenly called out.

Aldous pulled away from me like I was on fire. "Scheisse! It's Tatiana. She never lets me out of her sight for long." He let out a harsh stream of unfamiliar words.

Quicker than a blink of an eye, Tatiana was right in front of us. Her presence filled the space around us like a foul odour. I almost expected acid to shoot from her eyes, as she angrily took in what she could assume was a compromising situation. Aldous's hand twitched in my direction then clenched firmly into a fist.

"What's going on here?" Tatiana asked in a much too-loud voice.

I willed myself not to bolt. "Nothing. We're just chatting, getting to know one another."

"I guess we didn't notice how far we wandered away from the house," Aldous said.

Tatiana whipped her head in Aldous's direction at the sound of his voice.

He gave me a quick sideways glance, which I took as an urging to go along with him. I forced myself to hold that thought in my mind as I felt the icy tendrils of hers reach out to me.

"Yeah, geez, we were just chatting up a storm and lost track of time."

She didn't even pretend to be civil. "Let's go, Aldous, now." Her tone was one reserved for naughty children and misbehaving dogs. She turned away, and Aldous followed in hostile obedience at her heels. He disappeared from sight with one last pleading look.

I was left alone in the darkness, confused, overwhelmed, and a little helpless. How could I help Aldous against *her*? I was working different scenarios about when a hand unexpectedly touched mine. I just about fell over from the surprise.

Eli's face broke out into a huge grin, and he leaned over with hands to his knees in laughter. "Jesus, sorry, Rachel. I didn't mean to scare you."

"Well, you did, you ass. God, if I were human, I would have peed my pants."

One hand rose to his chest. "Sorry."

"How long have you been out here?" I snapped to overcome my embarrassment.

"Long enough. I was worried when Kieran came back into the house, and you weren't with him. I came out to check and saw you leaving with Pretty Boy."

Pretty Boy? "Yeah, well, he wanted my help."

"I know, I overheard."

"You mean you were spying."

"Yes, I was spying. I was worried, so sue me. Anyway, what do you think you can do about it? I don't know much about vamp politics, but it doesn't sound like something I want to get involved in."

I agreed but didn't say so out loud. "How can I just leave him like that? I know we don't really know him, but he is here helping us. I think the least we can do is talk to Tatiana."

"Or have Charles talk to her."

"It's an idea."

"And here's another." Eli scooped me up, hoisting my legs up around his waist. The force of his kiss pressed me back against the wall, where the creeping vines snagged my long hair. We each responded with ardour, and I burned with desire as I felt the front of my shirt ripped open. Eli's hands roughly caressed my breasts, and my nipples hardened with pleasure.

I used my own strength to push Eli back and, in one fluid movement, came around the side of his body, in essence reversing our positions. I landed on my knees, and before he could react, I reached up and yanked down the zipper of his jeans. I tugged his pants down below his hips and brought my mouth to his body in a way I knew drove him crazy. He moaned quietly and pressed his back into the wall.

Eventually we ended up in the damp grass, clothing more off than on. He pounded into me, and I bit my lip to hold back my screams. His tongue lapped at the blood, and I tasted it as our mouths pressed eagerly together. Then, just as I was reaching the crescendo of my climax, the sound of someone screaming my name filled my brain, blocking out all my other senses.

The scream tore through my mind, paralysing and blinding me. *"Rachel! Rachel! Rachel! Rachel! Rachel! Rachel! Rachel! Rachel!"* It screamed in an endless, agonising succession. The pressure was so enormous, I thought the top of my head would blow off. I don't know how long it lasted, but it felt like eternity.

I came to with Eli's face but an inch from my face and his hands gripping my shoulders like iron vices. For a few seconds, his features swam out of focus, and I thought I might pass out. He shook me again, and my eyes snapped open. I sat bolt upright, realising I was mostly naked, muddy, and screaming at the top of my lungs. My screams died with a whimper, and I clutched at Eli for comfort.

"God, Rachel... I know I'm good but probably not good enough to make a bad-ass vampire like yourself pass out from pleasure." He was trying to make light of the situation, but his voice was too shaky to be convincing.

Several vampires came racing from the house, including Charles and Kieran, only to be waved off by Eli. He let them misunderstand the reason for the screaming.

I was trembling, confused, scared. What the hell was happening to me? "Sorry, Eli, but it had nothing to do with you. It was just like back in San Francisco or in Toronto, only worse. It was much more intense. I was completely paralysed by the pain…. What is happening to me?" I started to cry, and Eli immediately pulled me back into his embrace.

"I don't know," he murmured softly. He rocked me in his strong arms, "but I'm going to find out."

CHAPTER 13

SWEET REVENGE

I didn't get much rest that day; the after-effects of the mental attack left me with a throbbing, relentless headache, which made it all but impossible to sleep. The fact that Eli was restlessly tossing beside me didn't help either. With several hours left before sunset, I gave up and wandered downstairs. I didn't need to worry about the sun, as Charles locked down the house, much like our house in Europe had been.

With no destination in mind, I entered the large room where our unprecedented gathering occurred a few hours earlier. The room was dark and the hearths cold. I was just thinking about starting another fire when I became aware that I was not alone. *Please don't be Tatiana*, I thought with a shudder.

"Don't worry, it's not." The voice was female and soft, with a vague English accent.

I turned to meet the owner of the voice, finding myself before a woman of about my height with a lovely heart-shaped face. She reminded me of a porcelain doll, all kewpie eyes, pouty lips, and delicate features. Her soft brown hair, which fell to her waist, had a clean center part. She was lovely but in an understated way, the type of girl who as human might have seemed mousy or plain. It was also the woman Aldous thought about during our conversation.

"Thank God. I have to admit that she scares the crap out of me."

"She scares all of us."

"Aldous most of all, I suspect," I agreed.

"Yes," she said sadly. She then reached a tiny hand out to me. "I'm Emmaline."

"Nice to meet you." Touching her hand was like a warm summer breeze. There was nothing outwardly cold or dark about her, not even when I felt her touch me psychically. Her contact with my mind was a gentle massage, a subtle sweep through my brain. "You're not like many of the others I've encountered."

"I'm going to take that as a compliment, considering the company that we keep."

I laughed. "Yes, an interesting and an incredibly scary bunch."

"So, what are you doing up at this time?"

"Probably the same thing as you—worrying. Maybe just not about the same thing?"

"But the same sentiment. We are both worried about the men we love—you about avenging your partner's death, and I about the possibility of even having a chance to be together."

"Does Tatiana have any idea?" The fact that she was still standing before me should have been answer enough.

"No, for all her formidable strength, she has limited ability to read minds. Much to her frustration, I can assure you. Aldous, on the other hand, has a very strong mind. I tend to keep close enough that we can communicate somewhat that way."

"How did you meet?" I asked.

"Tatiana and I have the same maker. We met a few times over the years. I have known Aldous since he was first changed. I knew instantly that he is different, that he is not as black as Tatiana herself is."

"Is your maker cruel like Tatiana?"

"No, not at all. She is a bit cold, distant, as a lot of the older immortals are. The elders are not good at relationships or emotional connections. They are of the mind that our kind are solitary creatures, not capable of friendships but only of alliances and civility when needed. It's hard for them to change their way of thinking."

"Yeah, I get it. Charles was like that when I first met him. Even now, as he deliberately tries to change, it's very difficult for him. He still can't show emotion or connect very well. It takes great effort."

"Then you know what I mean, but even as cold as Samaria might be, even she does not approve of Tatiana's actions. You know the saying 'keep your friends close, and your enemies closer?' I think she looks on Tatiana in the same vein."

"Have you and Aldous had any chances to be alone together, away from Tatiana, I mean?"

"Not really. We've spent only one night together, during a time he managed to slip away and get on a plane before she was the wiser. I met up with him before she did, but of course it quickly came to an end. She found him, as she always does, and I fled before she knew he had not been alone."

A forbidden vampire love story? "I promised Aldous I will do whatever I can to help."

"I thank you for it; we will both be forever grateful."

"Yes, we will."

I turned, as did Emmaline, to find Aldous in the doorway. He came to her side and kissed her with unabashed desire and need.

"I thought maybe you couldn't get away."

"I had to be certain that she was soundly asleep. I'm sorry you've been waiting so long."

"I will always wait, as long as I have to."

I suddenly felt like the cliché third wheel, a guilty voyeur to the lovers' precious intimate moments. "I'm going to let you guys have a moment and go and see if I can't get Charles to come speak with us."

Aldous couldn't even take his eyes off her as he answered me, "Thank you, Rachel. We'll be right here."

I slipped out silently and made my way toward the basement, which housed Charles's daytime resting place. He had a thing for basements, a remnant of his past where vampires didn't live the way many do now. Then, it was a matter of serious concealment: basements, crypts, secret passages, and the like. Distant, nearly impossible to access castles and fortresses were the all-time favourites.

I tapped lightly on his door, not wanting to disturb the

occupants of the room next to his. Zhongxing and Mengmei, a couple far older than even Charles and Alessandra, were resting there. They, with Aldous and Tatiana, Emmaline and a few others, chose to stay at Charles's home rather than make their own accommodations. I suspected they didn't want to go to the trouble, as they would leave immediately after their part in the attack was over.

After a few seconds, Charles called out to me. "Come in, Rachel."

I pushed open the door and stepped into the intense darkness.

Charles was already standing, pulling on a coat from a nearby chair. "Trouble sleeping, my dear?"

"Something like that. I'm actually wondering if you can come with me. There's a situation I can use your help with." It felt inappropriate somehow to be standing in Charles's space like I was. Had Charles ever been in love?

"Let me guess, Aldous and Emmaline."

Was there anything this guy didn't know? "How did you find out?"

"Well, if I couldn't read you like an open book, which I can," he said curtly, and I inwardly cringed, "I picked up on some longing thoughts from her earlier this evening. I must say it was very brief, but I still got something. Aldous, on the other hand, he's like a tightly shut vault, sort of like our young Eli."

"And you know about the situation with Tatiana?"

"Of course, I've had the displeasure of her company on a few occasions and have heard many stories over the years. She is the type that the legends of vampires are based on: sadistic, remorseless, a true killer. And you thought I was bad?"

It was possibly the first time I ever heard Charles make a joke, and I wasn't sure how to take it at first. He smiled, but his smile always seemed to alarm rather than reassure me.

"Well, we've come a long way since those days."

"True enough, and what is it that you are asking of me? Would you like me to approach Tatiana to see if she will willingly let go of her pet?"

"Yes, it's exactly what I'd like you to do. You're probably the only one besides Alessandra who is strong enough to do it and come back with all their limbs still attached."

He didn't comment on my bungled attempt at flattery. Even though I was certain Charles was on our side, he still flustered and intimidated me sometimes. It was like being friends with a pet lion, and time would tell if or when it would turn. The lurking danger could be fun, but it was also more prudent to keep a stuffed version rather than the live one. "I'll see what I can do, but it would be to our advantage if we had something to offer Tatiana in return for her relinquishment."

"Like what?"

"I'm not sure. Should we go chat with the lovebirds and see if they have any ideas?"

Of course, he picked up on the fact they were waiting upstairs. Damn my inability to shut my thoughts off! "Yep, sounds good to me."

The two sat on a small sofa in a cosy corner of the room when we returned. Undisguised guilt and need were plastered across their unnaturally lovely faces. Aldous tapped his foot lightly, his nervousness over being discovered all too apparent. Charles and his power swept into the room, humming over all of us and making us keenly aware of the pecking order. I took a seat opposite the couple, and Charles remained standing. As I looked at Charles's ramrod straight posture, I filled with an affection and admiration not normally associated with our friendship.

"Well," he said, finally facing the two of them like an old-school headmaster, "It is quite the predicament."

"Yes, we understand that there is only a slim chance for success here," Aldous said.

"Slim would be generous. Tatiana is a fearsome creature and not one to bend to other people's needs. You better have something good to offer up in return."

They looked at each other, and I shifted uncomfortably from their obvious distress.

"Like what?" asked Aldous.

"Like something she wants or something she does not know. I am very aware of her limited psychic abilities, as are others who might have used it to their advantage against our dear Tatiana."

"I don't know of anything, I would tell you if I did…" Aldous was starting to unravel a bit, and he shot a nervous glance in the direction of the hallway as he spoke.

"Try harder, boy. If it means as much to you as you wish us to believe, you will think of something."

"I know something that could help us," Emmaline whispered.

"Well?" Charles said.

"If I give it to you to use, it will most likely mean the death of two others."

Charles paused, pursing his thin lips. I remembered the Grinch, from the Dr. Seuss classic, but not in a pleasant way. "Well, I guess you need to decide if your desire to be together is worth the sacrifice of others' existences."

"Emmaline, be careful," Aldous warned, but she looked back to Charles.

"I take it on myself, please be sure of it. A while back, Tatiana, Samaria, two other immortals, and I were in the company of a particularly powerful family in Vienna. It was a wedding celebration, with many members of royal and other wealthy families in town for the weeks leading up to the actual day. Tatiana enjoyed feeding off the many well-to-dos, as she did on other occasions, and had her eye on a set of handsome young twins as the ultimate prize. Unfortunately, the twins disappeared one night, causing a huge upset and almost delaying the wedding. It was eventually decided that the two met an unfortunate end while out in the unfamiliar wilderness or on the water, but I unintentionally became privy to the real truth." She looked down as she spoke her last few words.

"And the real truth is?" I prompted.

"The other two immortals lured them away from the estate one night with promises of sexual indulgences the likes of which the twins never even heard of, let alone experienced before. They were led out past the edges of the property, past an abandoned house on an adjoining property where I was hiding from Tatiana, Samaria, and the bore of polite society we were a part of for several weeks by then. I picked up on their plans and followed then until they reached their intended destination. It was an old hunting cabin, which was long forgotten. There those two ill-fated boys endured some of the most horrendous tortures that I have ever seen."

"Names." Charles words were a command, not a request.

"Chantal and Ameera."

"It was before my time, but Tatiana mentioned it several times. I know it always bothered her not only that the boys got away, but also that she never conclusively knew what happened. She never mentioned any names to me. I believe she has always suspected something other than an accident or other coincidental happenstance." Aldous watched Emmaline's face intently as he spoke.

"Now that would be something to bargain with. What were the twins' names?"

"Michel and Hans."

"Good, now I think you have pushed fate enough today. You should return to your rooms, and I will pull Tatiana aside before she heads out for the attack."

Aldous placed a quick, firm kiss to Emmaline's mouth. "I'll see you soon, love."

"Yes. Be safe." She watched as he slipped out of the room, back to his unwanted place in Tatiana's bed. She placed a tiny hand on my shoulder and gave me a knowing look before departing herself.

I came to Charles's side and gave him a playful punch in the arm. He smirked.

"You old softie, you," I teased.

"Don't push it. I can still squash you like a bug." Another joke, I hoped. "In all seriousness, you need to keep focused. There are dangerous times ahead, and you need to be exclusively dedicated to the matter at hand. The other will sort itself out, and I will do my best to help it along."

"Yes, believe me, I'm very aware of what the next few hours mean."

"I'm sure you are, but remember it is not only your revenge we are after here, but the elimination of a possible threat to all of our kind. The Desmarais have grown strong and wealthy over the years, and they cannot be allowed to continue."

A clear and perfect image of Giovanni's face appeared in my mind. I allowed myself to cling to it, losing myself for a moment to something that could never be again. "I agree one hundred percent. I won't let you or Eli down."

"Good. Now I'm going to go back to my room and think on the best way to approach Tatiana. I will see you and Eli soon when we meet before embarking on our individual tasks." He looked at me with a strange expression, wavering, and I took that hesitation to my advantage and threw my arms around him.

With some reluctance, he returned the hug and patted my back, obviously uncomfortable. "Now, now, you know me. I can only take so much sentiment at one time."

I wiped a wayward tear from my eye before it had a chance to fall. "Yep. Got it under control, grand master."

He vanished without another word, and I experienced a violent wave of fear as I stood there in the silence, alone. I raced back to the room where I was staying and crawled into the bed. I pressed myself tightly against Eli's side, and his arm automatically curled around my body. The shaking did not stop, and a flood of tears threatened to spill forth. To block the pain, I began to kiss Eli, hoping that finishing what started earlier outside could push the torment away.

"Whoa, let a guy wake up first, would ya?" Eli did not move away from my advances.

I slipped my hand inside his boxers, finding more evidence that he was not protesting. "Do you want me to stop?"

His eyes snapped open, and before I could blink, he was on top of me. "Not for anything."

Afterward, we lay in the bed, talking softly about everything except what was at the forefront of our minds. Soon, the sun would set, making it time to meet with the others before heading out on the most important and perilous night of our existence. The darkness called out to its children, and the chance for revenge lured me like a siren's call. After that night, everything would change.

A few hours later, all assembled again in the same room as the night before. Charles divided us into the groups for our individual targets. I was introduced to my team, and they were all curious about me and my relationship with Giovanni. They made polite inquiries and expressed their condolences. It was a strange group with both ancient and very new vampires included, consisting of Charles, Zhongxing and Mengmei, Donovan, Kieran, Saskia, and me. Besides me, Kieran and Donovan were the youngest of the immortals. Donovan was changed in the early sixties and, like me, was not as adept at reading or controlling minds.

"You're cute," he told me by way of introduction. He was very warm and outgoing, not at all possessing the dour personalities of a lot of the older vampires. He wiggled in his seat and hummed softly, reminding me of a hyperactive child pushed beyond the limit of his attention span. A few times he made a funny face in my direction or gave me a sly wink. I remembered him dancing about the room the night before, as though we were at a rave and not in a room of immortals who could kill the two of us without effort.

Zhongxing and Mengmei couldn't have been more different. They were both ancient, originating from a time and culture far removed from the realities of the modern world. They had small, compact bodies and glossy ebony hair that gleamed in the moonlight. Their movements were precise, and when they were still, it was the eerie, absolute stillness only the elder vamps could accomplish. They spoke very little to each other and even less to the rest of us.

Saskia was a lovely, ashy blond who took her dark kiss just past her sixteenth birthday. She had pale green eyes and a distinct crescent-shaped scar on her throat, a wound that must have been inflicted during her mortal lifetime. She was certainly older than me but younger than Charles. Together we formed a formidable and frightening company to behold.

Aldous and Tatiana were on the same team as Eli, and Emmaline was in the third large group. Every now and then she cast a curious look in my direction, but I had no information to give. I hadn't found the chance to talk with Charles again, though I passed him speaking with Tatiana in the hallway on my way down. A few minutes later, they swept into the room together, and if I were to make a guess, I would say Tatiana appeared pleased. Micah was grouped with the human allies, who'd keep watch over the perimeter of the sites we'd hit.

We discussed the plan, then Charles called the head of the human allies to confirm that they were standing by. The groups departed for their various targets, and, as I fell in step alongside Charles, I took the opportunity to quiz him. "So, what happened?" I didn't need to clarify.

"She agreed to a trade. I told her that Aldous wants his freedom and that I have some information she wants. She barely hesitated, and I could tell her curiosity was getting the better of her. Besides, she had no real attachment to him. He was simply a plaything for her."

"And there will be no repercussions to him or Emmaline?" I had a hard time swallowing that.

"Well, I told her about that part after she agreed to the trade, and she already had the information. There was no going back then without it turning into something personal between her and me, also, and, of course, she had to save face and act as though she couldn't care less."

"Save face, as in she didn't appreciate a lesser vamp like Emmaline getting the better of her?"

"Exactly, not that she was hurt that Aldous wants to be with another woman. She doesn't think that way, and you think I am cold."

"Uh-huh, I hope this works out for them." We left the matter at that.

Fate waited for us with open arms.

CHAPTER 14

We parked the van several miles away from the target, leaving it at the side of a rural road that led to a scattering of residential homes and small farms. The human army Charles assembled, consisting of both men and women, was already in place. They waited for our initial sweep to take place before advancing on the compound. It made sense that the vampires make the first strike, as we could approach silently with our unnatural speed. That way we had the element of surprise on our side, and it was easy to take out the people guarding the gates, entrances, and surrounding area. The next wave was a combined force of vampires and humans with immense firepower. Once the facility was cleaned out, the humans went on to the homes of any who were not on site. No one was overlooked.

Charles, Donovan, Kieran, Zhongxing and Mengmei, Saskia, and I flew over the snow-covered landscape, an army of death descending upon the unsuspecting members of the Desmarais legion. Moments later, the compound came into view, the grey industrial building and twenty-foot fences topped with vicious barbed wire looking exactly as it did in the photos.

"We all know where we're going?" Charles asked.

Six pairs of vampire eyes looked back at him, but there was no need for answers. We all knew our places and could feel each other's intense concentration on the task at hand. Zhongxing and Mengmei took off with incalculable speed, seeming just suddenly to be gone. Donovan, Kieran, and Saskia departed next, with Saskia giving me a small shrug that said "Here we go."

"Ready?" Charles questioned me softly.

"Absolutely. Let's do it."

We swept down the steep hillside to the bottom of the north-facing security tower. We scaled the two-story height of the structure with ease, even though the outside was almost perfectly smooth and vertical. We both hopped over the metal railing encircling the top level where the command booth was stationed. Inside were two armed guards, with easy access to alarms that they could trip with the simple touch of a finger. We didn't intend to allow them that much time.

In one swift movement, Charles grasped the handle of the solid metal door and ripped it from its frame. We were both inside before the two men even had the chance to blink. Charles pulled the first man by the back of his jacket, upending the chair he was sitting in, and clamped his mouth over the man's neck to drain his body of blood. A fraction of a second behind him, I had the second man in my own grasp. I used one hand to twist his head around one-hundred-and-eighty degrees, enthralled with the sharp snapping sound his neck made as I broke it, thus ending his pathetic life.

From there we dropped onto the ground inside the compound's fence. I saw Zhongxing and Mengmei at the bottom of the east-facing tower, and Mengmei nodded to indicate their success. From our vantage point, we could not see the others, because the sprawling building blocked our view of the southern tower. We waited in the shadows until Charles received the okay on his cell phone. Then we advanced toward the main building.

From there we split up to move out individually. Two freestanding buildings stood apart from the main structure, which housed vehicles and supplies. Only one man patrolled back and forth between the two, and Kieran was in charge of his elimination. The main building had four entrances, two delivery bays, and two outside flights of stairs to access the upper levels. During surveillance it was noted that the one flight of stairs and the smaller of the two delivery bays were used infrequently and never at the time the attack was set for. During Charles's surveillance, he established when the compounds were most vulnerable and when the others who were not at work would most likely be home in bed. We could pick them off like flies.

The remaining five fanned out to cover the four main doors, the large delivery bay, and the staircase. Once cleared, Charles accessed the interior control room to open the gates and allow the waiting human team to enter. Then all hell broke loose.

I veered off in a northwesterly direction to approach a door leading to the facility's main research labs. The door opened onto a narrow hallway that ran the full length of that side of the building, opening onto a series of doors that led to stairwells, labs, storerooms, and other spaces. It was supposed to be all but deserted at that hour, though all parts of the building ran at least a skeleton crew on a twenty-four-hour basis. Of course, the building had topnotch security, and all personnel were well-trained, but, when possible, the Desmarais favoured attacking during the daytime when vampires were more susceptible to harm.

An outside security pad waited for me, which required a viable code to open the door. We all memorised the codes we planned to use for access. We could have easily broken the doors, but it would have set off the alarms, and we wanted to penetrate as deep into the structure as possible while still undetected. I punched in my code and waited for the eternity-long three seconds it took to clear. I opened the door, careful not to make a sound, focusing on controlling my trembling hands.

The hallway was lit at intervals by a series of overhead fluorescent lights. All doors were shut, and the space was as quiet as a tomb. I ran to one end of the hallway and started opening successive doors. I encountered very few humans and killed them all on the spot. I closed all doors behind me with the utmost care, in case a wayward soul made their way into the area. All appeared normal and secure.

In one room, I found two men, both seated before surveillance screens, monitoring what appeared to be several empty rooms. Each space on the screens showed rooms devoid of life, holding only operating-type tables or large storage containers. One man reached for a red button on the control panel, but I snaked out a hand to catch his arm and removed it from his body. A thick stream of blood shot out and splashed onto the control panel and closest screen.

The second man barreled into me before I had a chance to reach back to get a hold of him. We crashed to the ground, his partner's broken body and the rolling chair both falling on top of us. The man struggled to reach the alarm, and, for a few panicky seconds, I thought he might make it. At last I emerged from the tangle of bodies and equipment, knocking the man back with a quick jab to the throat. The back of his head slammed against the tile floor, and he looked up at me, stunned.

With a solid grasp about his throat, I pulled him up as I stood, careful not to slip on the now-bloody floor. His shoes rattled against the arm of the chair as I pulled him toward me. Then, with as much strength as I could muster, I smashed his head against the heavy desk, reducing it to a mushy, bloody pulp. The ruined mess made me think of a smashed pumpkin. For some reason, this thought brought a cold smile to my face.

Suddenly my phone vibrated in my pocket, and I dropped the bodies quickly to answer the call. "England, thirteen twenty-seven," the male on the other end stated.

"Canada, nineteen fifty-eight," I answered.

"Good, everyone has been successful. I'm heading to the control room as we speak. Meet at the designated area." The phone clicked off. My eyes slipped closed, and I took a moment to regain my composure. It was close.

As I started to retreat from the room, my gaze flashed across the monitors, and I experienced a violent sense of déjà vu. I stared at each screen in turn, trying to determine what initiated the sense of recognition. I couldn't put my finger on it, but my body tingled with anticipation. Leaving the room, I locked the door behind me and backtracked to where I had started. At the far end of the hallway was the door leading out to a larger passageway which, if followed, would bring me to the facility's main entrance. The control room was located in this open area.

I ran into a young woman in a starched white lab coat as I stepped from the hallway I cleared into the larger passage. I was surprised she caught me so unaware, belatedly realising I was more rattled by the strange experience in the lab than I initially thought. I grabbed her by the arm, spilling the cache of file folders she was clutching to the floor. She whirled about in surprise, and my expression must have just about matched hers when I saw her face full on.

The resemblance was so close it was shocking. She had the same wheat-coloured hair, pale hazel eyes, and fair skin. Even the shape of the face and the slope of the nose were perfect matches. "Don't scream," I ordered. I was so surprised I wasn't sure what to do with her.

"Don't hurt me." She spoke with a heavy French accent.

I responded with silence. Her mind was clear and open, and though she was afraid, she did not harbour any ill-will toward me. She knew what I was and what I was capable of doing to her, but she was not filled with the black hatred I expected from one of the Desmarais ranks. In fact, she seemed curious and awed.

I clamped my hand around her thin arm, forcing her slightly ahead of me as we made our way toward the front of the building. I willed myself to remain focused, and I did not sense other life in that part of the building. Overhead and to the south, I picked up snippets of conversation and a jumble of random thoughts. In less than a minute, we were stepping out into the building's front waiting area. Zhongxing and Mengmei were already there when we exited. Seeing me with the girl, Zhongxing shook his head in disapproval.

Charles stepped out of the control room, closing the distance to me with three long strides. He stopped short, meeting first the woman's gaze, then mine. I could read nothing from Charles, as was his intention, but his expression was hard. "The resemblance is remarkable."

"Yes." I was still rattled.

"*Comment t'appelles tu*?" he asked sharply.

"Genevieve." She raised her chin in defiance

"Desmarais?"

"*Oui.*"

Just then our human allies burst through the door. They did nothing more than nod in our direction as they continued to their pre-established destinations. I watched fifteen men and two women in impeccable physical shape jog by, automatic rifles gripped in their capable hands. From somewhere in the rear of the building, gunfire erupted.

"What do you plan on doing with her?" Charles asked.

"I don't really know."

"Well, you can't be carrying her around while the place is under attack." He turned from me to Genevieve and deftly struck her across the face with a closed fist. She crumpled instantly to the ground. "Now, put her in the room over there and hurry up."

Without waiting for a response, he was gone. I dragged her to the closest room, tucked her inside and closed the door behind me. Even if she woke before I returned, I knew she could not escape. Troops were posted all over the area surrounding the facility, watching for any who might try to flee. I hurried down another hallway on the main floor, carefully snuffing out every life whose path I crossed along the way and acquiring a few small wounds for my trouble. Within minutes, I arrived at the back of the building. Ahead was a set of swinging double doors that led to the largest of the building's many storage spaces.

Just as I was about to push one of the doors aside, I experienced a psychic attack so brutal my knees buckled, and I crumpled to the floor. *Rachel!* I wrapped my hands around my head in a fruitless attempt to ward off the pain, but the calling became more insistent and intense with each utterance. Vile images of an emaciated male form strobed behind my eyes. I ground my teeth so forcefully, I feared some would be crushed. Then, as suddenly as the image had come, it vanished.

Footsteps pounded the floor, heading in the direction where I lay. I looked up into the barrel of a rifle aimed at my head. The leader held up a hand to the men close at his heels. He took a few tentative steps forward and, recognising me, came to my side. He offered a hand, which I gratefully took. The shots wouldn't have killed me, but they would have hurt.

"Are you okay?" he asked with a strange accent I could not identify. He was about forty, with close-cropped hair and rugged good looks. I thought his name was Kurt, but I wasn't positive.

"Good. Carry on. There're several ahead."

They continued with the sweep, bursting through the doors in a blaze of gunfire and machismo. I felt an insistent tugging in my mind, luring me away from my assigned course. I turned toward another set of doors I believed led back to the same area I cleaned out earlier. I looked through a round window, seeing no one and picking up on no signs of life. I hesitated, knowing I should stick with the course I was supposed to follow, but I was unable to shake off a call only I seemed to be able to hear. The door swung open and still there was nothing.

I started to run when my phone rang, causing me to miss a step and knock into the solid concrete wall. I snapped the phone open without looking at the number, assuming it would be Charles confirming that my second sweep was complete. Instead it was another voice I heard.

"What's going on?" Eli asked, each word dripping with concern.

"What do you mean?" He was miles away at another location, and I didn't think he would have been aware of me at that distance.

"I felt something terrible. I've been picking up on you here and there, enough to know that you're okay. A minute ago, there was a sharp cut-off, and then an intense pressure like someone was literally inside my head, screaming your name, so don't act like nothing is going on."

"You felt it, heard it? Whatever. I've been trying to tell you that something has been going on, something connected to my nightmares…" I stumbled over my words.

"I'm sorry we didn't talk with Charles about this."

"I think you'd better get over here."

"Things are under control here. I'm on my way." I was debating whether I should continue alone when the pain struck again. I pressed my back to the wall, legs bent at a slight angle to help keep myself upright. A thick liquid dripped over my upper lip. When I pulled my hand back from wiping it across my mouth, there were streaks of blood. Terrible stinging sensations erupted all over my body, as if I were being branded over and over again with a red-hot poker.

Unfamiliar faces swam in and out of focus before my burning eyes. I heard a terrible moaning and voices speaking in unfamiliar languages. I choked as my throat seized. What was happening to me?

Rachel! Rachel! Help me!

My legs gave out, and I fell unceremoniously to the floor. Using my last bit of strength, I rolled onto my stomach and forced myself to my hands and knees. I was attempting to move forward toward the source of the attack when Charles found me. He pulled me to my feet. I couldn't speak for several minutes, and Charles waited with limitless patience. Zhongxing and Mengmei checked in on his cell when their sweeps were complete, and still I was fighting the effects of the psychic attack.

Eli burst through the doors, the shushing as they wound down their swinging momentum enough to close again seeming absurdly loud in the silence. He took in Charles's arm about my waist to keep me steady and immediately replaced him as my crutch. His presence and his familiar touch dimmed the torment in my head. Belatedly I saw he was not alone, and the flash of blond hair made me realise it was Aldous.

"What the hell is going on here?" Eli demanded. His voice echoed ominously in the hallway.

"I'm not sure," Charles answered. "When Rachel didn't follow through with her final sweep, I became alarmed and went looking for her. I caught a bit of what it was she was experiencing and then found her lying on the floor. I didn't get enough to be certain of what's going on, but it seems to be a psychic attack of some kind..."

"A psychic attack? Who would be capable of that but another vampire?" Eli asked.

"Not...an...attack," I managed through gritted teeth.

Rachel!

All three men and I instantly reacted to the outburst. Everyone was affected to varying degrees, from discomfort to agony, with me taking the brunt of the force. Aldous raised his hands to his head while Eli stiffened at my side. My body became rigid at the initial contact then sagged heavily. Charles squinted and seemed to be tracking the direction from which the power emanated.

He started trotting down the hallway. "This way." Charles motioned in the direction of the far end of the hallway.

We followed like lame dogs. It was difficult for me to move, even with the men's assistance, as my limbs felt paralysed. Ahead, Charles smacked open the next set of doors with the flat of his hand. Immediately after passing through, he snapped around a left-hand corner and disappeared from view. I still had enough of my senses to know we were heading toward the back of the building where I made my initial sweep.

We came through the doors, and as we turned to follow in the direction Charles went, the force increased ten-fold. Hot, urgent tendrils of energy reached out to us, snagging us with phantom barbs. The overhead lights seemed to dim and blaze at intervals timed with our footsteps, though it could have been a trick of my mind.

Rachel!

Again, the force snaked out, and I stumbled at its ferocity. I pulled Eli along with me.

"What's going on?" he asked.

I shook my head, the space around us spinning like an out-of-control carousel. "I don't know, please..." I felt Aldous at my back and we became one joined line as we continued on to whatever lay ahead.

One step. *Rachel!* Another and my mind countered the call, *No!* The men were carrying me between them by now, as I was defenceless.

No! Rachel! No! Rachel! No! Rachel!

Charles skidded out into the hallway from a door about ten feet from where we were. The expression on his face was terrifying, his usually empty eyes alive with alarm. He waved his hands in our direction. "Wait. I don't know if she should go in there!"

"What the fuck is going on, Charles?"

"Eli, come here, now!"

He turned to Aldous, who nodded and adjusted his hold to take on the full support of my sagging body. Eli let go of me and raced ahead in a blur to meet Charles. Their figures disappeared into the unknown room, and my stomach dropped. Several agonising seconds passed before I heard Eli call out, "It can't be! It can't be! Oh my God, what have they done to him?"

A muffled response came from Charles that I could not make out, and in my state, I was not able to pick up anything from the other vampires around me. My fragile brain could not make sense of anything except the incessant, throbbing call of my name, pounding out like a heartbeat in the cold night. Eli shot out of the room as though it were on fire, pausing with his hand on the open door. He shook his head with vehemence, as though trying to dislodge something that would make sense of whatever it was he had just witnessed.

When his face finally met my own, it held the strangest mixture of emotions fighting to take their place: horror, anger, sadness, and fear. Then, without being conscious of the fact he moved, I found myself in his arms. "Oh God, Rachel," he moaned in an odd voice. "I understand. I'm sorry, so sorry. I understand now." He pulled himself a few inches back from me, a flood of tears streaming down his face.

"What are you talking about?" Aldous asked. The sound of his voice startled me. I almost forgot that he was there.

"She has to see it for herself." Then the two men guided me to the open door. With each step, the more the entrance resembled a yawning maw, waiting to suck us all to Hell.

Rachel!

We all turned the corner together, stopping just short of Charles's still figure. He was standing, his back to us, staring down into a rectangular concrete structure on the floor. It was an immense storage container, unadorned yet menacing. The top lay on the floor, where it was obviously pushed aside in haste. There was nothing else in the sterile white room except for several video cameras surveying the space with electronic eyes.

Charles turned in slow motion. When I saw tears also streaming down his face, I collapsed to the floor. My body smashed against the cold tiles with enough force that a shower of stars appeared before my eyes. It took everything in me to get onto my hands and knees and begin to crawl forward. I had to know, yet was deathly afraid of what could evoke such a response in a stoic creature like Charles. I remembered a room eerily similar to this one was on the monitor in the room where I killed two men earlier in the evening. Is it what they were watching?

My hands made contact with the cool, rough surface of the container, and I jerked back as the force struck out again. It slammed into me like a bolt of lightning. *Rachel! Help me!*

Charles was suddenly at my back, lifting me from the floor to deposit me back on my feet. The contents of the container swam into view. I reeled back, almost losing my balance again as the comprehension of who lay before me struck deep in my brain. I gripped the sides of the container.

"Giovanni!" I screamed, but my voice was far away and detached from that moment in time.

CHAPTER 15

There, in that nondescript box, lay the body of my beloved Giovanni. It was he, I was sure, yet what appeared before me was a grotesque and violated version of the man with whom I spent twenty-five years of my life. His face was sunken, almost mummified; his body nothing more than skin stretched over bone. The only thing that remained untouched was the brilliance of his sapphire blue eyes, which stared out sightlessly from his face.

As I reached out a hand to touch what I was certain was a figment of my imagination, Eli grabbed my arm and prevented the connection. "Rachel, don't…"

I shook him off and leaned over the container until I was mere inches from the body. "Giovanni?" I asked, my eyes now clouded with tears. My voice met silence, and I stepped back from the horror before me. I couldn't believe what I was seeing. After two years, the nightmares, and my never-ending grief, seeing his body was more than I could handle. "What are they doing with his body?" I managed to get out.

Both Eli and Charles shook their heads. Aldous came to stand beside Eli and was visibly disturbed when he saw what we were all looking at. He shuddered and looked away. Then the force struck again, and we all cried out in pain. I fell forward against the container, and my hand brushed the leathery skin on Giovanni's arm. For one crazy, terrible moment I thought I felt the limb move.

I jumped back from the contact, knocking into both Eli and Charles, before taking one tentative step forward again. The body *was* moving. It twitched pathetically, then those beautiful blue eyes that once captured my soul moved to meet my own. I saw recognition there, lurking in the depths of the unspeakable torment he must have endured.

"Giovanni!" I cried. I cupped the skeletal face with my hands. The eyes blinked, once, twice. "Oh my God, he's not dead!" It took both Charles and Eli to restrain me from throwing myself into the container with Giovanni.

"Be careful, Rachel. He's in a terribly fragile state right now. Too much shock could kill him." Charles's voice returned to its usual strong, commanding resonance.

I let them pull me back, but I couldn't look away from Giovanni's face. "What are we going to do, Charles?"

"What about the girl, Genevieve? She must have some idea of how to help him."

"He needs blood." Eli's voice was odd, almost cold.

"Yes, he does. You three give him some while I go back and get the girl."

Charles barely moved, and I was already ripping up my sleeve. I gouged my wrist across the edge of the container with enough force to rip open a wide gash. Blood sprang to the surface, bright and red. I pressed my wound to his mouth, pumping my fist furiously to make the blood flow faster. Giovanni's lips were slack and cold, an alien waxy texture against my skin. As he fed, my mind swam through a restlessly shifting spectrum of emotions.

The amber of my love for Giovanni, which I buried deeply in my attempt to carry on after his loss from my life, flared brightly and forced its way to the surface. The fire burst forth, throwing aside my fear, hesitation, and shame. I understood then, looking down onto my love's wasted body, the pain I often felt when trying to embrace my relationship with Eli was sparked by this feeling, a feeling that would never die.

When I began to feel dizzy, I pulled my wrist back and surveyed him for any sign of improvement. I might have been mistaken or simply desperate, but I thought his face seemed slightly less gaunt.

"Eli." I pulled my eyes away long enough to see that he stood there like a statue. I grabbed his arm and shook it harshly. He seemed to come around and hastily pushed back the sleeve of his dark shirt. Following my example, he ripped open a wound against the container's edge. He pressed his wrist to Giovanni's mouth, and I saw a small twitch of Giovanni's lips.

Aldous had his wrist at Giovanni's mouth when Charles's power surged ahead of his entrance into the room. He had the woman, Genevieve, clutched in his arms. She was struggling unsuccessfully against his grip but stopped when she realised she was before an audience of vampires. He released his hold on her, setting her onto her feet. Taking in the figures before her, she seemed to resign herself to the fact that there was no use in trying to escape.

"Help him," I ordered. I closed the space between us before she could utter a sound and snatched her from Charles's grip. She gasped in surprise and pain.

When I let go of her, she immediately crossed the room to a small door I did not notice before. She pressed the upper corner and the door sprang open to reveal a refrigerated storage space. She removed several bags of blood, an intravenous line, and other necessities. Her movements were quick and efficient, exemplifying how many times she did the same thing as she set Giovanni up to receive blood. She left the gauge open wide, so an entire bag of blood was released into his body within minutes.

A second replaced the first before she dared to speak. "It is only the start," she said. "He suffered a lot of damage over the past two years. Some effects may be permanent."

I took Giovanni's hand in my own and pressed it to my chest. "What have you done to him?"

"Not I, them, those bastards who run this place. I'm here to keep him alive and study the unique qualities of your vampire blood. I don't condone this…this torture."

"You didn't answer her question. What has been done to him?" Eli's voice was strong, and he obviously recovered from his initial shock.

I was filled with strange detachment, much as I had on the night I believed Giovanni was killed. I reasoned with myself that I must be in shock, but in a way, it was a welcome reaction.

I was able to think clearly and rationally and not be swept away by overwhelming emotions. "I know some of what has happened here. I have been dreaming about it."

Eli closed his eyes and turned away from me when I said those words. He did not believe me, but I couldn't think about his anger with himself. The only thing that mattered at that moment was that Giovanni needed me.

Genevieve looked at me, curious. "You must be Rachel?"

I nodded.

"I thought so. He used to speak of you often, before the experiments got so bad. He spoke of his love for you, described you, and often demanded to know what happened to you. He loves you very much." Her voice was gentle, but it was difficult to look at a face I equated with the source of all our troubles.

Giovanni's hand twitched and I squeezed back. His eyes were closed, but his face was noticeably fuller. "What can help him?"

"Time, most of all, and blood. It's hard to say definitely because no such instance has ever occurred before, at least to my knowledge, and, of course, many of the scars of this ordeal will be psychological." Then she made direct eye contact with me. "I really believe that the only reason he didn't go completely mad was because he never stopped believing in your love for him."

Eli rubbed a hand along my back, trying to be reassuring, but it made me sick with guilt. If what he went through at the hands of the Desmarais weren't bad enough, when he regained himself, he would have to face the ultimate betrayal of his partner and adopted son. My shame and anger with myself grew to gargantuan levels, clouding what should have been the most joyous moment of my life. My love was returned to me, and all I could think of were my feelings for, and actions with, another man. My weakness disgusted me.

Charles's cell phone rang, cracking the building tension. It was enough to snap me out of my self-loathing and refocus myself on the importance of tending to Giovanni's needs.

"Yes," Charles answered. "Everything is fine here. Yes, I'll come out and meet you, and you can tell me. Front lobby." The phone snapped shut and disappeared into his pocket. "I am going to meet the others and regroup. I will be back in a few minutes. Don't leave here."

"If you can, get word to Emmaline that I'm all right?" Aldous asked before he retreated.

"Of course," he answered then fled from sight.

I turned my attention back to Giovanni and, more specifically, to the care Genevieve was administering. The blood bag ran dry, and she was not replacing it.

"What's going on?" I demanded. She flinched from the harshness of my voice.

"I think he's had enough for now. Though he is weak and malnourished, I am worried that too much blood after this long period of starvation will do more harm than good." I remained silent as she pulled back his eyelids and peered into them with a small light. "His pupils are reacting to light, and it's a good sign." She sighed and ran a hand through her hair.

"I think you should listen to her, Rachel. She's our best hope right now." Eli's words were low and full of sadness.

"Can we move him?"

"I suppose so, but it's risky. He has been in here for years, being taken out only occasionally, and even then, it was to inflict some type of pain or research."

"We can't stay here, just in case. We need to take him somewhere safe." Eli started pacing, and we were all silent. The graveness and shock of the situation were finally setting in. A tight panic was building in my brain, and I wanted nothing more than to take comfort in Eli's arms. As soon as the thought crossed my mind, I guilt flooded me again. What had I done?

"Rachel," someone called out. When I realised it was Giovanni who spoke, I leaned down over the container. I felt Eli at my side, also leaning in. Giovanni moaned, and his eyes flew open then closed again. I waited to see if he would speak again, but his body was still and silent.

"I think he's dreaming," Genevieve offered.

I met her eyes and nodded. "Is there a gurney or something we can transport Giovanni with?"

"Yes. If you will permit me, I can get it and my research, my files, disks, videos. It might be helpful for Giovanni's recovery.

I've learned a lot about vampire physiology over the past two years."

"Aldous, you go with her. Make sure she doesn't pull anything," Eli directed.

"Let's go," Aldous said, and she complied without argument.

I kept my eyes on Giovanni's still form as they retreated from the room. I had what I wished for since Giovanni's supposed death, yet I didn't feel the exhilaration I would have expected. I felt...conflicted. I was happy yet afraid. After all that happened in the preceding years, nothing could ever be the same for us. Perhaps Giovanni would not be able to forgive me. More likely, I would not be able to forgive myself.

"You couldn't have known, Rachel. None of us could have, and I don't believe Giovanni would have wanted you to be unhappy or alone." Eli's voice was low, cracking under the burden of his emotions.

"You say that because you are just as guilty as I am. For all intents and purposes, he is your father, and it makes me nothing more than a cheap, incestuous whore."

"And me as well, I suppose." He sounded as weary as I felt. "What are we going to do?"

"You are going to be with your real love, and I am going to back off. I always knew I was second best, and I'll find a way to deal with this."

"Just like that?"

"What choice do I have? I have friends I can lean on, places I can go."

"You're going to leave?" My voice rose and echoed in the nearly empty room. I turned to meet his blue eyes with my own. I'm sure the pain I found there was reflected on my own face. I finally came to terms with Giovanni's loss and the quality of my love for Eli, then the tables were turned again. There was no denying Giovanni was the love of my life, but my feelings for Eli were just as real. "You can't..."

"What would you have me do, hang around in the background, watching the two of you live your lives together, be your son once again? How can we ever go back after what happened between us?"

"We can't, but we can go forward, just in a different direction, and it's not just me or us here. Giovanni is going to need all of our support. I mean, he doesn't even know about Charles and the turnaround he made or the connection we made with the other immortals. The last thing he'll remember is the three of us and our life in England. The past two years that we've been together he's been trapped in this box in this horrible place!"

"I will stay if I'm needed and if Giovanni wants it but not forever. I couldn't bear it. I'll need to have some distance if there's ever going to be the chance of me getting over you. I mean, you're the only one I've ever really loved." Strangely, a flash of Micah's face came from his thoughts.

"Maybe that's not entirely true." Charles's return interrupted my thoughts. I turned and watched as the others, except for Zhongxing and Mengmei, filed in behind him. They approached the container with a mixture of caution and disbelief.

"Holy shit!" cried Donovan.

Saskia, with her wintry beauty, turned to me. She was obviously stunned. "He's alive?"

"Yes!" I cried. "He's alive!"

Charles was at my side, anger tight on his face.

"Yes?" I asked.

"I have Jean-Claude."

It took me a moment to register what he meant. Then the significance of the name slammed into me, sparking the rage that never entirely died. Charles had the man who did this to Giovanni. His face flashed in my mind, and my hands clenched tightly at my sides. "Where?"

"Zhongxing and Mengmei have him in the main storage area."

"Make sure they make his suffering last until daybreak. I want him to go to his grave in as much pain as is humanly possible."

"You don't want to have a hand in this yourself?"

"No, there are more important matters to attend to now."

I turned around and surveyed the faces in the room. Eli

watched me, his anguish like a scarlet letter. Charles was stoic and controlled, just as I needed him to be. The others wavered between shock, happiness, and anger.

The only thing that mattered in that moment was that Giovanni returned.

CHAPTER 16

The next two weeks were a blur of blood transfusions, worry, and waiting. We brought Giovanni back to Charles's home in England via armoured car and private plane, while all of the attack sites burned to the ground. Once back, we settled him in a ground-floor room with a king-sized bed, where I could lie at his side, watching over every excruciating minute of his recovery. He had endless nightmares, which he forced upon me with our proximity. Often, he screamed and writhed about in pain, with no comfort possible. It was disturbing and uncomfortable to all in the house, but in a sick way it made us all the more certain the massacre we took part in was beyond justified. How he survived was a miracle.

Most of the assembled immortals stayed for the first few days, but, as time rolled on, they slowly began to depart to wherever it was they came from. All played their parts successfully, but Giovanni's condition overshadowed the mutual satisfaction.

One of the very first to go was Tatiana, whom no one was sorry to see leave. Yet Charles made the attempt to remain on good terms with a humble, "Thank you." Soon after, most followed suit, until only Charles, Eli, Kieran, Donovan, Aldous, and Emmaline remained and, of course, Micah, and our new human companion, Genevieve.

Strangely, Genevieve made no attempt to leave, or even ask for her release. She attended to all of Giovanni's needs without prompting and seemed most sincere in her desire to help him regain his strength. We learned that she was a hematologist by education and spent all of her post-education days in research. Most interesting, though, was the fact that the majority of her time away from Giovanni's care was spent with Charles. She often spoke to me of her time at the compound with disdain and did not seem at all troubled by the destruction of her family. The implication was that she had been as much of a prisoner as Giovanni.

Giovanni had brief moments of lucidity during his early convalescence, when we talked or lay together in comfortable silence. The others fluttered in and out, offering kind words and brief respites for me to feed and bathe. Eli was distant with me during this time, almost never appearing at Giovanni's side without Micah as his shadow. The two men were obviously getting closer, as evidenced by the tightness I saw in Micah's eyes each time he came into the room. It could have been nervousness at my reaction to his presence in Eli's life or fear I would take the relationship away from him again. The feelings from Micah I stumbled across in San Francisco were obviously more than wishful thinking. I now knew they were longings for something he already experienced.

One night, as I lay on the bed, a book I could not concentrate on open on my lap, Giovanni suddenly sat up. I jumped in surprise, and the book slipped to the floor. I found myself face to face with those ocean-blue eyes and a face that was almost fully fleshed out to what it was in my memories. His hand rose slowly and reached across the chasm of space that had been our years apart.

When his hand made contact with the upper part of my arm, I was choked into silence by myriad sensations and emotions coursing through my body. Soon the hand cupped the back of my neck and pulled me forward. Then my lips pressed against his, something I did a thousand times before and was sure I would never do again. I had kissed him, of course, since his return, but it was the first time he really had the strength to kiss me in return.

"Rachel," he whispered.

"My love, Giovanni... I can't..." I couldn't put coherent thoughts to words.

"I love you," he said.

All my emotions clenched like a giant fist in my chest. "I love you, too, always." My brain flooded with images of times past: places we lived, things we saw, our years in England. Then thoughts of Eli crept in, and I pushed them away with violent ferocity. Giovanni trembled against me, a reaction, I was sure, to my psychic outburst. I wrapped my arms more tightly about his body, refusing to allow myself to think of anything but Giovanni. He slipped back down onto the bed.

"My brain is muddled. I can't make sense of things. I don't know if what I'm picking up on are dreams or memories or some mixture of both. A few times I have been aware of you thinking of Eli, and then there have been some things I don't understand, like just now. You reacted very harshly to his image."

"I don't think now is the time to get into it, Giovanni…"

"Why? I feel better than I have since you found me. I need to know about the time I lost, about what happened. I still don't understand really how we came to be in Charles's house, under his protection, or how Eli was changed…who all these others are. Please, Rachel…"

Each day that passed brought me closer to this moment. I knew there would be questions, and, more accurately, he would demand answers of me.

"Charles came back to warn us about the Desmarais attack, that night in England. Unfortunately, he didn't make it until it was too late, and you had already been taken. I thought you'd been killed, and I was a mess. I was devastated. He helped Eli and me get away from the house and then helped us slip out of England. He's stayed with us ever since."

"And how long has it been? I can't make sense of my time there…"

"It's been just over two years."

"Two years? It doesn't seem possible."

"I know it's hard to comprehend. Some days it seems like yesterday, and others it seems like an eternity."

"And Eli? How did his change come about?"

Shame rattled through my body, and I bit my lip to fight back tears. "I changed him before we left England. He wanted me to." My voice was quiet.

He surprised me by not pressing for more. "And the three of you went where?"

"Well, we moved about a bit for the first few months, and then we settled in San Francisco. We've been there about a year and a half."

"And how did you come to be at the Desmarais compound?"

"Charles devised a plan to attack them. It's what all the immortals were doing here. He assembled a massive army of vampires and humans to strike all of their known meeting spots and facilities, and, while I was there, I heard your call to me. I've been dreaming about you, and now I know it was more than that. It was you, your mind reaching out to me for help. Somehow you must have known how near I was because your call became so intense all the vampires who were close heard it."

"I never stopped thinking about you." Those words were a dagger through my heart. "I knew when you were near, and I used my last ounce of strength to call out to you."

I couldn't speak again without my voice betraying me, and, instead, I pressed my mouth to his. A knock sounded at the door, then Genevieve entered to check on her patient. To be honest, I was grateful for the interruption. How could I tell him the truth without ruining everything?

"How's the patient today?" Genevieve asked with her pleasant bedside manner, to which Giovanni gave his usual response—apprehensive silence.

"He seems much better, stronger. He sat up on his own and moved about without help," I offered, after forcing back the lump in my throat.

"Yes, I feel much better. I think I would like to try and get out of the bed today." It was the first time he spoke directly to Genevieve, though on all their encounters she had attempted to converse with him. Her resemblance to Seraphine was explained, but her appearance always rattled Giovanni nonetheless.

"Okay, let's take a look at your legs first. One thing at a time." She snapped a bag of blood into place and he reacted like a junkie taking a hit. Genevieve then came around the side of the bed and flipped back the covers to expose Giovanni's lower body. I stood and joined her on his side of the bed.

He wore men's pajama bottoms and his feet were bare.

The last time I checked, his feet were still quite skeletal in appearance, and he was too weak to control his movements. Then he pulled his knees up to his chest and stretched them back out again. He wiggled his toes with a slight smirk on his lips. Genevieve had a serious look on her face, and she wasn't about to be swayed by his show. She pushed up the legs of the pajamas and took her time looking over the skin and the muscle condition in his calves.

"Okay," she said at last. "Let's try it with Rachel and me for support."

She watched as he raised himself into a seated position and helped turn him so his legs dangled over the edge of the bed. She sat at his side, placing his arm about her shoulders, and I mimicked her actions. Together we helped to get him into a standing position. We took a few steps before he pulled away from our support. Then, in the blink of an eye, he raced to the window at the far side of the room. He stopped and leaned over, like a runner after an intense workout. Then his legs buckled, and he collapsed to the floor.

When we got to his side, he was laughing. "I never thought I would do it again."

I sat on the floor with him and couldn't help but join in his obvious delight. He leaned forward to embrace me, and we both tumbled onto our backs on the floor.

Genevieve loomed over us, but she had an amused expression on her face. "I think I'll leave you two alone. I'm sure you can get him back to the bed, Rachel?" She raised her eyebrow knowingly and gave me a sly wink.

I nodded. Just as I was melting into Giovanni's kiss, I heard her call out, "You've got a visitor, lovebirds."

I sat up, and Giovanni refused my offer to help. He struggled a bit but seated himself in short order. Eli was coming across the room. His expression was neutral, one that he wore a lot lately, but he was surprisingly alone. "Having fun, you two?"

Giovanni grinned. "For the first time in a long while."

"I'm glad to see you're feeling better, Giovanni. You gave us all quite a scare." Eli's words were filled with genuine warmth and love, and I was glad to see him making the effort.

He joined us on the floor, where we chatted for a few minutes about inconsequential matters. Soon Giovanni showed signs of fatigue, and the two of us helped him back into bed. His eyes were closed as I pressed a kiss to his cheek, but he murmured, indicating that he wasn't quite out. "You two need to talk... make everything okay." Then he was asleep.

"He's right," Eli replied.

I pressed the button on Giovanni's bed, and Aldous and Emmaline appeared in a matter of seconds. They took over my watch, and Eli and I made our way outside to finally clear the air.

The night was cold. We wandered far from the house, with no destination in mind. We found ourselves in a small clearing in the woods that surrounded Charles's property. I brushed aside a light covering of snow from a fallen tree and sat. Eli sat beside me, a noticeable space left between us.

"I've made a decision," he said.

"Yes?"

"Yes." He turned to me, and, for the first time in weeks, I saw real emotion on his face. He was sad and also resigned to what he about to tell me. "I am going to change Micah, and he and I are going to be together. For now, at least, and we'll see what happens."

"As a couple, you mean?"

"Yes, as a couple. You were right. I do have feelings for him. Whether they're strong enough for us to last, I don't know, but they're strong enough that I can't deny them anymore. If none of it had happened, I would have happily spent eternity with you, but now it seems to be where I should go."

I took a moment to let it sink in. When changing a human, it was never something to be taken lightly. "It is what he wants, Micah, I mean, to be changed?"

"Yes, we've discussed it every day since we found Giovanni. He loves me, and he wants to be with me."

"I want you to be happy, Eli. You must know it."

"I do, and I want the same for you. I know that you will only be truly happy with Giovanni. He's the other half of your heart. There's no denying it."

"I could have been happy with you, too."

He closed his eyes tightly against the pain of my words, and I was sorry. "I know it, Rachel. I really believe we could be happy, but it isn't meant to be. Now you have Giovanni back, and I have my chance with Micah. We can all go on from here and be happy." He was thinking of Micah, and I absorbed a memory of one of their nights together in San Francisco. The sexual heat of the memory overpowered me, kicking my own libido into action. I pushed myself away from the feelings his memories were eliciting.

"Are you planning to leave San Francisco?" I managed to force aside the residual excitement from the intensity of Eli's feelings. The memory must have been significant and intense enough even someone as controlled as Eli couldn't completely contain it.

"I'm not sure about it yet, not right away, at least. It's a big house, and we always have Micah's place if things get too close for comfort." His feelings cut off sharply, and he avoided eye contact with me for a few moments.

"Are you mad at me?" I asked.

"Not at all. Being with you was like skating on thin ice. I was bound to fall through sooner or later. It is just a struggle for me, I don't know why…I mean I do. It is weird talking about anyone else with you, but it's especially difficult because we're talking about me being with another man. "

"I'm not sure I understand. Are you embarrassed?"

"No, not embarrassed, I've just never had feelings like them before. I have never been attracted to a man before Micah or ever even considered the possibility. There was only ever you and other women I used in place of not having you."

"Love is love, and even just lust is not something that you can effectively hold off. We want what we want, and there is not always an explanation for it. It's just like how I feel about Giovanni. It simply is. I love him, need him, crave him."

"I know, and now with these feelings for Micah, I'm starting to understand what I never could before. I don't know how I can go on without him."

"It shouldn't be the end of our relationship or friendship.

I can't bear not to have you in my life, Eli. No matter what the circumstance, I will always love you. You're very important to me."

He pulled me close and swept his lips across mine. "And I will always love you. It is just the way things have to be. It's the way they're meant to be."

We sat in the cold for a very long time, not speaking, not touching, just accepting the truth as it was between us. The walk home seemed like a journey from the farthest reaches of the earth, yet I knew the hardest moment was still to come. I had to tell Giovanni the truth, everything that transpired. I was heavy with dread for what his reaction might be.

Eli and I heard the commotion long before the house came into view. There were shrieks, angry voices, and pounding footsteps. Eli grabbed my hand, and we raced ahead to the unknown conflict before us. As the path to the back door appeared, I discerned several distinct figures then heard a voice that chilled me to the core. I knew her reaction was too subdued, and then it was the time to pay for stealing her prize.

"You honestly thought I would just hand you over to this little bitch? You go only when I am done with you." Tatiana's voice radiated icy hatred, smothered in contempt.

She had Emmaline's arm in her iron grip. It was twisted at a viciously unnatural angle, which even to a vampire would have been agony.

Charles and Aldous were at the base of the back steps, mere feet from the two women, and two strange male vampires stood close by. As we came into view, all eyes flickered our way. Tatiana looked annoyed, Aldous relieved, and Charles's expression never wavered. In the upstairs window I saw Giovanni's outline, Genevieve at his side. I shook my head, "No." He was still too weak, and worrying about him would be too much of a distraction for me to be of any help to the situation.

"Let's just calm down here, Tatiana. I'm sure there must be some way to work it out." Charles was smooth but not condescending, a smart move on his part.

"Please, Tatiana, let her go." Aldous pleaded with his one-time mistress, but his eyes never wavered from Emmaline's face. The pain was tightly stretched across her delicate features, but she didn't utter a sound.

"Save it." Tatiana cast a look at the two goons at her back, and the one broke out in a ridiculous grin. He flicked his greasy hair out of his eyes and turned his smile in my direction.

"Tatiana, be reasonable. There are more of us," Charles said.

"Yes, that may be, but I can assure that my associates are much stronger than those you have at your back." She tipped her head, and the greasy-haired man was before us, grabbing Eli about the throat. I made a sharp sound and lunged at the attacker. Peripherally I was aware of the second man appearing before Charles and Aldous. Emmaline screamed and the battle began.

I jumped on the man's back, pulling with all my strength at arms like steel, which held Eli in their grip. One arm suddenly released and his elbow made solid contact with my stomach. I fell to my ass, and the momentum carried Eli and his attacker to the ground. There was movement to my right, and I looked up just in time before Charles and his sparring partner crashed on top of me.

As I scrambled out of the way, Emmaline screamed again, and it was a sound of utter agony. Instead of getting back on my feet, I dove at Tatiana's legs and managed to knock her off balance. I heard a wet, ripping sound and her scream of frustration as Emmaline was pulled from her grasp. I dragged Emmaline toward me and placed my body in the line of Tatiana's next move. There was commotion all around me, grunts and obscenities hurled in rapid fire.

As I braced for Tatiana's assault, I became intimately familiar with Emmaline's injuries. She lay underneath me, broken and wet with blood. Her left arm was almost pulled right off her body and the bony protrusion of her shoulder was sharp against my chest. My hair was lifted in a sudden gust of wind, followed by a loud thud as two bodies sailed over me and crashed to the ground.

I took the opportunity to press my mouth to her wound, aiding in the healing process. Soon the blood flow slowed to a trickle then stopped altogether. Emmaline remained eerily silent throughout the whole ordeal, her face a shock of alabaster in the night, too white for even one of our kind.

Lifting my eyes to survey the damage, I saw Charles managed to destroy his attacker. The man's body lay in bloody, twitching pieces all over the snow-covered lawn. He was just joining in the fight between Eli and the other man, when the touch of Emmaline's hand reclaimed my attention. "Help...Aldous...she's so strong..."

I jumped to my feet in time to see Aldous's body fly past and slam into a nearby tree. The enormous trunk shook from the violent contact with his body, and his pain lashed out at those in close proximity. Blood poured from a wide gash on the side of his face, and he had barely enough time to gather his bearings before Tatiana launched herself at him again. I raced ahead, managing to catch a handful of hair, which only slowed her attack by seconds. It was enough time for Aldous to get to his feet.

Her hand caught me by the throat, and she easily tossed me off. The touch of her skin was living hatred. Her anger soaked me in its poison, gagging and momentarily disorienting me. Staggering, I then came at her again with everything in me.

But Aldous beat me to it. He managed to rip off a large tree limb, which he thrust forward with lightning speed and determined strength. The limb caught Tatiana in the gut, slicing through her torso to erupt out her back in a spray of blood and bone. Aldous kept the movement going, forcing her backward until she was impaled against an even larger tree. The limb penetrated the enormous oak, and Tatiana was trapped. Aldous didn't stop there. He rushed forward with a look of shock that almost mirrored the one on Tatiana's face. Then, with a cry of anger and murderous retribution, he ripped her head from her body. The decapitated body sagged, yet for a few seconds the hands twitched helplessly at its sides.

He tossed the head to the ground, which Aldous promptly squashed under the heel of his heavy, military-style boot. It made a satisfyingly loud popping sound and subsequently reduced to a bloody, meaty mess. He didn't stop pounding at it until he slipped and almost fell into the remains of his maker. His eyes were those of a mad man's, and no one present attempted to stop him. I understood his overkill, and, as far as I was concerned, it was justified.

Then the maniacal light in his eyes vanished, and he seemed to come back to his senses. His hands clenched and unclenched, and with the danger to his partner eliminated, he regained his composure. He turned to where we stood watching, where Charles, Emmaline propped up against his body, cradling her mangled arm. Aldous rushed to her side, crying her name. He dropped to his knees and grasped her good hand with both of his. Her face was slack.

"We need to get her inside and get her arm set before she starts to heal herself. Having to break and re-set the limb would be excruciating, and she needs blood," Charles said

"I can give her some." The words popped out of my mouth.

"Me, too," Eli said at my side. I looked up into his eyes, taking in the torn shirt and the various injuries. He shook his head and smiled. "I'm okay."

I nodded but knew that no matter what the circumstance, I would never stop worrying about him.

Aldous lifted Emmaline into his arms and carried her up the steps into the open back door. We followed him to the dining room, where he laid her atop the enormous table. I took off my coat and tucked it as gently as I could under her head. She murmured something I couldn't understand, but I stepped out of the way to allow Aldous to be by her side.

Genevieve hurried into the room and everyone stepped back without being asked. She surveyed the damage with a clinical eye and ordered Eli to get her medical supplies. As he ran to fill her request, Giovanni and Micah appeared in the doorway. Eli brushed his hand along Micah's face then disappeared to get the needed supplies.

"What happened?" Giovanni asked.

"I'm not totally sure. When Eli and I returned, Tatiana and her thugs were already here," I answered.

"Aldous, Emmaline, and I were just talking on the back step when they appeared. Genevieve was with Giovanni. There was no discussion. Tatiana simply charged us and snatched Emmaline away," Charles explained.

"I knew she took Aldous's desertion way too easily."

"When she left, I searched her mind vigorously. She had no firm plans for revenge, or I would have said something. She was angry and felt cheated, but she honestly seemed as though she only wanted to get away as fast as she could, nothing more."

"Well, somewhere along the way that changed. Who were those other two anyway?"

Eli reappeared as the words left my mouth. He handed the supplies to Genevieve, who immediately went to work.

"One was another child of Tatiana's, named Ivan. He was just as twisted and cruel as she. The other I'm not sure about," Aldous answered.

Eli stood at Micah's side. Micah was obviously worried as he looked Eli over for injuries.

"I'm fine, nothing serious."

Micah didn't look convinced, but he stopped his examination.

"Why don't you two go ahead? There's nothing you can do here. Emmaline is in capable hands with Genevieve." I looked to them both as I spoke.

Eli frowned. "You sure?"

"Yes, go." *Be with the one you love.*

He took that last part without comment and gave me a bittersweet smile. They left, Eli's arm around the other man, and I knew the next time I saw them he really would no longer be mine. I pulled my gaze away from the empty door, back to Giovanni's face. The exertion of the walk from his room and the time standing had taken its toll. I slipped my hand into his and led him to nearby chair. After I shared some of my blood with the needy Emmaline, I took Giovanni back to our bed.

I felt the pressure of the whole world on my shoulders, as I came to my love's side, and as gently as I could, I lay down beside him. I savoured the quiet and serenity of being alone with Giovanni, drinking in his scent and allowing myself to be conscious of nothing but my love for him. I pushed aside what was going on in the other room, my conversation with Eli. My mind just started to wander in search of memories of our time along the Mediterranean Sea, when he snapped me back to the present.

"Have you settled things with Eli then?" His voice was husky, a harsher version of its usual sound.

My heart seized with pain, and guilt flooded my brain at the sound of Eli's name. "As best we can, I suppose."

"You two became very...close after you thought I had been killed?"

An image of me lying naked in Eli's arms flashed through my mind before I could stop it, and I was powerless against the sickening waves of remorse washing over me. I couldn't not be honest with Giovanni, yet I feared what the truth might do to him and to us. I had to face up to what I did, for eventually he would learn the full truth, either from a slip of words, an angry outburst, or a glimpse of my memories. "Yes, we were very close, and in a way always will be. Without him, I don't know how I would ever have gone on..."

"And you were lovers?" The pained tone of his voice shamed me terribly.

"Yes," I answered. There was nothing else to say.

"And you loved him, like you do me?"

I rolled up onto my elbow and looked down onto the face I loved beyond all reason. "I could never love anyone as I love you! But yes, I did let Eli into my heart, as a partner and my best friend. I thought we would be together."

"And it is why you changed him, to be with you?"

"No. Yes. I mean, I would have changed him at some point, if it's what he really wanted, but it came about from a position of grief and desperation to hang onto him. I couldn't lose him, not after I lost you. I could never have gone on then, but things got so mixed up. I knew Eli had feelings for me, feelings above a family connection or a friendship. I knew he thought he was in love with me, and it was wrong what I did, but I can't change the past."

"No, you can't, and neither can I. What has happened, has happened, and being angry or resentful will change nothing. I don't blame you for anything. I am glad you found a way to go on. You'll just have to let me work through it. It hurts, even though I don't want it to. Do you understand?"

"Yes, I would understand if you thought I had betrayed you, if you were disgusted with me."

"I could never think badly of you, Rachel. You are my heart, my reason for existing. Without my memories of you, I would never have survived what the Desmarais did to me, and nothing can take away from the happiness I feel being reunited with you. We have each other, and we've proved nothing can destroy our love. We have a second chance at forever."

"I have not and never will love anyone the way I do you. I gave my life once to be with you, and I would do it again."

"Nothing will keep us apart now."

A tear escaped my eye and slid slowly down my cheek. Giovanni's finger traced its course, then his hand moved into my hair.

"Please forgive me."

"I already have."

"I dreamed so many times about you, sometimes about the life we shared and sometime about the horror that you were trapped in, though at the time I didn't understand what it meant."

"The very fact that you felt my call despite the vast distance and my condition proves how strong our love is. It is simply meant to be, and no one can ever take it away from us. I owe you my life. I would never have survived if I didn't have you to fight for. There were many times when I thought the pain and the isolation would break me...and then I thought of your face, the sound of your voice..."

"Don't ever leave me again; I couldn't survive it."

"I never will. I promise."

It was the first night we made love, after more than two years of being apart. His touch against my body was fire. I kissed every inch of him, savouring every caress as though it were my last. We brought each other to levels of pleasure beyond description or reason, and when we finished, our faces were damp with tears of thankfulness and love.

We both fell asleep certain the world was right once again.

A few weeks later, after a vast improvement in Giovanni's condition, the remaining vampires met around a dining table in a cosy room not far from the location of our earlier gatherings.

Charles chose the smaller space to facilitate a more intimate atmosphere for our discussion. It was time to settle back into our own lives, which most likely would take us in different directions.

Giovanni no longer needed assistance to move about and was almost back to pre-Desmarais form. His strength had returned, though he did tire easily and still had to be careful not to push himself too hard. The prolonged effects seemed mainly to be in his mind. He had terrible nightmares, moments of confusion, and his ability to connect psychically was deeply diminished. Perhaps these things would work themselves out, but only time would tell.

When we arrived in the room, hand in hand, all the others were already gathered. Eight pairs of eyes regarded our entrance with a mixture of responses. Most were happy, pleased, but an undercurrent of uncertainty existed. Micah had not yet been changed. His face was flushed, but for the first time in weeks, he looked me directly in the eye.

Charles was at the head of the table, with Genevieve to his left. There were two empty chairs to his right, which we took. It put me between Giovanni and Eli, a reminder of the emotional place I lingered in for the previous two years.

Eli squeezed my hand then leaned around me to address Giovanni. "I'm glad to see you up and walking on your own. Your recovery seems to be going very well."

"Yes, thank you. Rachel has been a great source of comfort and strength for me, and, of course, Genevieve has been the most wonderful nurse. I'm glad to see she was successful with Emmaline's injuries, also." He smiled in Genevieve's direction, and she flushed at his praise

Donovan, Kieran, Aldous, and Emmaline were across the table from us, smiling warmly at Giovanni's obvious improvement. Aldous had his arm protectively about Emmaline's slight shoulders. Her splint was off, and her flesh had healed itself neatly, but I knew from personal conversation the joint was still stiff. In a few more days, it would be only a dark memory in her mind.

Donovan gave me one of his not-too-subtle winks, and I had

to laugh. He was bopping in his seat, seemingly in response to a beat only he could hear. I would miss him with all his goofy antics and infectious enthusiasm. Kieran also laughed at his side, and it was a nice sound to hear after all the tears, screams, frustration, and fear.

"Well, now that we're all here, I thought we could take this time to have a debriefing of sorts. As I'm sure we're all aware, the attack was a success, but I have been keeping a close eye out for any signs of retaliation. I sent the human troops out again to double-check all homes, vacation properties, any sites where Desmarais associates were known to spend time, do business, anything. There has not been so much as a peep. I have taken over many accounts, and the rest are being watched for attempted access. To date, there has been no communication or activity anywhere. I will continue to monitor for at least a year, but I think we can safely assume the enemy has been eliminated."

"I still find it hard to wrap my head around all of this," Giovanni responded. "It's hard enough to understand how you came to be an ally, a friend even, to Rachel and Eli, but that you orchestrated this whole scenario to avenge my death?"

Charles's lower lip gave the slightest twitch. "Our encounter in Greece affected me deeply. Believe me, I was more surprised than anyone could have been. I felt…well…badly after I left. I couldn't recall ever feeling that way before in all my years. There were many times I wanted to come back and settle things properly, but I didn't. Instead I began keeping a close eye on the Desmarais, and when I got wind of what they had planned, I tried to warn you."

"I thank you for it, and for staying with Rachel and Eli. I'm glad they had you to count on."

It was a poignant moment, hundreds of years in the making. They spoke a few brief times since Giovanni's return, but it was a real declaration that the past was forgiven.

"I would like to thank all of you here for your help and your loyalty. Please know we are forever in your debt and forever your friends." I looked around the table at all the faces as I spoke and knew it was a new beginning for all. We talked for about thirty minutes, about everything from the past to what led us all to that particular moment in time. There was a wide variance in our backgrounds but a common thread in our hopes for the future.

"So, what are everyone's plans now?" It was from Kieran.

"Emmaline and I will remain in Great Britain. She has a home in Wales, and we will go there for the time being," Aldous said. They both had the biggest of smiles on their faces, but, knowing how I felt about Giovanni, I couldn't begrudge them their happiness. They fought hard to be together and won. It was time to savour that victory.

"Kieran and I are going to head out on a trip across Europe, maybe Asia," Donovan said. "Have some fun." I wasn't surprised at hearing of their plans. He and Kieran became quite chummy over the past few weeks.

"Yeah, I think I can have some fun with this chap, as long as he doesn't get us in too much trouble." Kieran turned to me. "I thought in a few months, after you two have settled, I'd take you up on that offer of a visit?"

"Sounds good. What about you, Eli? What are you and Micah going to do?"

He smiled at the sound of his lover's name, and I was relieved to see real happiness on his face. "Well, tonight we're heading out to another home of Charles's, which he has graciously offered. Tonight is the night." His eyes met mine, and he didn't need to explain. "And then after some time alone, I think we will return to San Francisco with you two. Either we'll stay at the house, or we'll move on to Micah's. For the long term, it's up in the air." He kissed Micah softly on the cheek. That soft, sexual energy touched me again, but it was much more subdued than the night in the woods.

Giovanni placed his hand on my thigh. I knew he was as relieved as I. All eyes returned to Charles, and, to my complete surprise, he was grinning.

"Okay, what's up Charles?"

Genevieve was blushing again, which only made Charles's smile widen. "I think I will be staying here for a while."

"And I'll be staying as well," Genevieve added.

"Really?"

Giovanni pinched my leg, and I tried to hide my reaction.

"And are there plans for you, like there are for Micah?"

"Not at the moment, but you never know," Genevieve said. She gave Charles a sideways glance and let out a small giggle.

"Charles, you old dog." Donovan snickered, and, like most of the things that came out of his mouth, it triggered a laugh from me.

Genevieve's smile faded a bit with what she said next. "I know that my acceptance and loyalty to you may seem strange, but I want to assure you it has been a long time coming. I may be a Desmarais by blood but not by a shared belief. I thought their ways were barbaric, and the more that I came to know Giovanni, the harder it was to align myself with their all-consuming hatred. After knowing one of your kind, it wasn't so black and white any longer."

"Thank you," I said, not only to the words just spoken but also for all that she had done. Giovanni began to remember the early days of his imprisonment, times when Genevieve spoke with him, cared for him, even protested his violent treatment.

Things were looking up. Aldous and Emmaline and Donovan and Kieran slipped out to feed. Eli excused himself to go on his own hunt, giving Micah a firm and lingering kiss before leaving.

Just as he was about to disappear into the hallway, Giovanni called out to him. "Eli, may I speak to you alone?"

Eli hesitated ever so briefly. "Sure."

Giovanni smiled at me then left the room with Eli.

Once they went, Micah gave me a look that mirrored what was going on in my head. "What's that about?"

"I'm not sure, hopefully putting the past to rest." I didn't know what to make of the situation and didn't want to offer hope in case something untoward happened.

"Should I referee?" Charles asked.

"I don't think so. It is something they need to work out, man to man."

"As you wish. Come, Genevieve." He rose from the table, his beautiful lady right on his heels. I still couldn't quite wrap my head around that one.

Then I was alone with Micah, and I didn't think I had been in that circumstance since the night so many months before, when we had talked in my library in San Francisco. "And should we clear the air also?" I asked evenly.

"Yes, I guess we should. I don't like feeling uncomfortable around you, especially considering how close you are to Eli."

"And considering how close you and Eli are," I offered in response.

"Yes, you're right. I never meant to deceive you. I tried very hard to keep my feelings for Eli in check, once I knew you and he were together, but love is a funny thing, as I'm sure you know."

"I know it well, and I can understand completely why you fell in love with Eli. He's gorgeous, smart, fun, caring, almost perfect."

"Yes," he said simply, by way of agreement.

"I have to admit, though, I was aware something happened the odd time I picked up on a memory from you or a bout of intense feelings. You couldn't have been aware of what I sensed, and I did feel bad for that. It wasn't my business who Eli wanted to sleep with, if I wasn't making a commitment to him myself."

"I was terribly envious of you, still am in some regards. I know he loves you deeply, and even if he is ever able to let go of his feelings, I don't know if he can ever love anyone as intensely as he does you."

"You have to understand much of it has to do with him being raised in such a close way to me and his perception of me as some kind of saviour. I came into his life at a time when he was very fragile, and his feelings became very intense because of it."

"Yes, I'm sure some of it is true, but don't sell yourself short. You're very beautiful and smart, and I can see why he's attracted to you."

"Can I ask how you knew he was attracted to you? I mean, he has never shown an interest in men before."

"Honestly, I wasn't so sure. It started innocently enough. He often stayed after class to discuss some thing or another, often challenging my position on different matters. Over time we took these discussions out to a bar to have a drink while we talked, and then one time we ended up at my place. We were sitting together talking when he turned to look at me, and without thinking I leaned in and kissed him. When he didn't pull away, I kissed him again."

"I see, and then you two had an affair of sorts?"

"Yes, for a few months, and then he drifted away. Eventually he told me he was in love with someone else, and afterward he kept me at arm's length. Then I knew it was you."

"I don't think he ever stopped thinking about you. Eli is very closed and hard for even my kind to read, but a few times I felt him return your affection and got a touch of his attraction for you, and, to be honest, it made me jealous."

"Now here we are."

"Yes, a very strange predicament."

"I hope we can be friends. I do love Eli very much, and all I want is his happiness."

"It's all I have ever wanted for him, since the first time I laid eyes on him."

He put his hand out, which I took and shook gently. "A new beginning for all of us then?"

"Agreed."

He stood, looking decidedly relieved. "I'm going to go get ready. It is a big night, after all." He leaned down and kissed my cheek and gave me a quick hug.

"I'll see you on the other side."

I heard him take the stairs to the second level and, a few minutes later, the sound of the shower running. I sat in the dim room, relieved yet anxious. Giovanni and Eli had not yet returned, and my mind wandered through one scenario after another. When I could stand it no longer, I left the house by the back door, using my mind to search for the men. I felt a slight prickling, a spur of power that I set off toward.

I didn't go too far before I crossed paths with Eli. He stopped, hugged me briefly, and whispered in my ear, "It's okay now. He's just a bit farther up the road."

He headed back toward the house while I continued to meet my love. Giovanni stood alone in the road, the wind swirling about him. It reminded me of the times he appeared to me before my change, during that wondrous winter back in Canada. He turned at my approach. I came to his embrace, immediately filling with the certainty that I belonged nowhere else.

He was quiet for a few minutes, and I didn't press.

"I think we've settled things."

"Good, and we'll all remain friends?"

"Yes, I still love him, always will. He is my son and a friend. Despite what happened and what his feelings may have been, the important thing is he kept you safe. He was solid for you, and I know he would have done whatever it took to make you happy."

"Yes, he would have, and he will always be there for both of us."

"I really think he will be happy with Micah. While we were talking, several times his mind filled with thoughts of him, and even with my brain the way it is, I still managed to pick up on it. He loves him very much, and I think he's just confused because of his feelings for you, and because he has never been attracted to a man before."

"I have to admit, it took me by surprise. Eli had worked through a series of different women before we…well, before us."

"It's okay, you can talk about it. Acting like it didn't happen isn't going to change anything. You can't keep feeling guilty."

"But I do. I feel terrible for what you went through and not understanding what the dreams actually were. I feel awful for being with anyone but especially because it was Eli. And, all that time, you were lying there, thinking of me…"

"And now I'm back in your arms, and I'm not going anywhere."

As we kissed under the moonlight, it was the beginning of not only the next chapter in our lives, but for all our kind. It was the night one human joined us as a vampire, another chose to stay as the companion of an immortal, and a love, which was forbidden for so many years, had the chance to blossom. I imagined Aldous and Emmaline felt just as Giovanni and I did, thankful to spend forever in the arms of the one they were meant to be with.

CHAPTER 17

That first night in San Francisco, I awoke to Giovanni's agonising screams. During his recovery in England, many days were punctuated by restless sleep and dreams alive with memories of the torture he endured at the hands of the Desmarais. As his strength grew, the nightmares became less frequent but were not shaken off altogether.

I instantly awoke at the sound of his terror, grasped his shoulders, as I often did in these situations, and shook him until he woke.

His electric blue eyes were wild, but upon seeing me, a smile replaced the pained expression. "Sorry. Haven't had one for a while now."

"Nope." I resettled myself in our bed.

He ran a hand through his rumpled hair. "Why don't you give me something else to think about?"

His hands caught me around the waist and our naked bodies melted together. I drowned in the sensation of his hand tracing its way up my body. His lips found their way from my neck, down my shoulder to my breast. His tongue lapped at my hardening nipple, fangs brushing teasingly, making me warm and wet between my legs. I stroked him until he was hard. He moaned as he snatched my hands away and pinned them over my head.

His grin was devilish and irresistible. All of our sexual encounters were powerful and satisfying in ways impossible to express in words. I was dimly aware of the bed knocking against the wall and my cries of passion muffled against his shoulder. I rode the waves of ecstasy to a dizzying climax, met soon by Giovanni's own. We remained tightly wrapped about each other's bodies, all too aware of how close we were to never knowing that feeling again.

As we were getting up to go to the bathroom to clean up for the night, a sound from overhead indicated Eli and Micah were also up for the evening. They alternated between our house and Micah's and, despite the circumstances, we all settled into the new arrangement with little awkwardness. In fact, the four of us got along very well, and wasn't I the lucky girl to be living with three hot guys?

"You know, I think I'm going to finish that picture now." Giovanni stopped just short of the entrance to the bathroom, eyeing the unfinished portrait of me over our bed.

I looked up and was unsettled by the thought of altering the portrait in any way. "Maybe you could do another one out in the garden or something here? I kinda like that one the way it is."

His eyes glimmered as he pulled me close. "Sounds like a good idea."

We joined the two men out on the patio a short while later. They were holding each other and kissing, oblivious to anything else as we approached.

"You have a room, you know," I teased.

"Yeah, and we have ears, too! Geez, I know you're like on your second honeymoon, but can you keep it down a little?" Eli laughed as he responded to my joke.

"Touché." We were both grinning. "So, what's on the agenda?" I took a seat at the patio table.

"Micah's teaching, and I have a class."

"What's going to happen when it's still light out when night classes are on?"

"We've worked out a share with another teacher. Micah will cover over the fall and winter, when it's dark in the evenings, and another newer prof will cover the spring semester, and we can always figure something out to get him to the building without being exposed. We're both smart guys." He gave Micah a good-natured punch in the arm.

"Ouch. Yeah, I'm good business for the university, so they'll work with me."

"Okay, and what about you two, you know? Has anyone picked up on anything yet?"

"I'm not worrying about it." They both smiled and appeared in agreement.

"What about you?" Eli asked.

"I think I'll go down to the club and check in. I haven't been there in so long."

"Oh, that reminds me. A package came for you, from the lawyer." He jumped up then returned with a small, sealed bundle.

"It's probably the papers you've been waiting for," Giovanni said.

"Sweet!" I ripped the envelope open, confirming what I already knew they were.

"Catch ya later," Eli called as they headed out to the garage. I briefly pulled my eyes up from the papers in my hand to wave goodbye.

Giovanni and I took a seat at the table, reviewing the documents carefully. After all his years of moving between countries and identities, he became very knowledgeable about the law. He understood loopholes like nobody's business and was meticulous in making sure nothing was amiss, which could put a hold-up on his being able to access finances or property. It was a trait that served him well over the years, ensuring no one in his inner circle would ever want for anything.

"Looks good," he finally said. I was relieved to have a way to reward the loyalty of those closest to us and our secret.

Several weeks passed after our return to San Francisco before we approached any of our friends and allies. We stayed mostly at the house, venturing out only in the wee hours to feed. Giovanni made contact with his many lawyers, property managers, and accountants to get the scope of any damage to his assets in his absence. Everything seemed in order, since Charles or myself took over the control of things. Those who served him knew better than to question his reappearance. What he asked for, he got in short order.

I helped him re-familiarise himself with the area as, like Alessandra, he had not been to that part of North America for many decades. We walked the streets while the majority of the inhabitants slept, and were careful not to cross paths with any who would not become a source of food. He was amazed at the growth the city had seen, remembering it as a small mining community and not a center of education and entertainment as it was now.

Several times we passed near Danica's apartment, and I was tempted to see if she was home, but I kept even my niece at arm's length. I told Giovanni about our reunion and about my club and friendships with Jared and Mary-Jane. He took it all in without much comment, but I felt his reservation and amazement at how I adapted after I thought him dead. Before, he had been a part of every aspect of my life, and now many things were foreign to him, many things that were between only Eli and myself. Slowly the edges of our time apart began to fray, and his presence wound its way in. Soon it was like it was before, where we filled the parts of each other that were missing, together becoming something impenetrable to outside forces.

We fell into a natural rhythm, overlapping with Eli and Micah's lives, but also rebuilding our own. Charles kept in touch, calling almost daily to give us updates on his surveillance of possible Desmarais activity and about his and Genevieve's relationship. He assisted Giovanni with financial matters as necessary, and the two men both made attempts to fill in the blanks of their many hundreds of years apart.

Then, one night, soon after we woke, Giovanni asked me to take him to see Carmilla's. It was an innocent and easy request but was also in many ways a double-edged sword. I was proud of my accomplishments there, but it was also an integral part of the life I lived with Eli. I pushed aside all reluctance and agreed.

We slipped in the back door, passing two waitresses on the way in. Both were young, attractive, and dressed to encourage generous tips. They both gave Giovanni appreciative and hungry looks, ones he received from many women.

When they thought we were out of earshot, the one said to the other. "Holy shit, he's hot!"

I caught Giovanni's smirk as we entered my office. I gave him a quick tour through the history of my ownership and subsequent improvement in customer attendance and revenue. He was genuinely impressed, but I caught a brief thought of him fearing my lack of need for him.

"It was never about how much money you could provide; it was only about you." I confirmed the sentiment with a toe-curling kiss.

From the office, I led him down the deserted hallway to the door opening into the employee area of the bar. It was about an hour after opening, and the place was already pretty full. The sound system was pumping out music, entertaining customers until the live act arrived. It was too bad Mary-Jane wasn't playing, but she was hard at work on her first professional album.

I peeked out of the door leading to the bar and found Jared. He made eye contact, and, after a moment of surprise, smiled to indicate his happiness at my return. He watched as I emerged, then the smile vanished as he realised I had someone with me he did not know. I raced over to him, giving him a hug bigger than I knew he was comfortable with. He hugged me back and whispered hotly in my ear, "I'm so glad you're back and in one piece."

"Me, too. Can you come back to the office for a minute?" I didn't wait for a reply.

Jared joined us a few minutes later, not quite entering the room. He eyed Giovanni nervously, keeping his hands clasped defensively in front of him.

"Jared, I would like to introduce you to Giovanni."

He snorted, blinking rapidly several times before he could process the words. "I don't understand. I thought he was dead. I mean I thought it's what all this stuff with the Desmarais was about." He looked back and forth between Giovanni and me, brows furrowed in confusion.

"It's long story. Another day we can get into all the gory

details. I just wanted to introduce you two and let you know that I am okay."

"It's a great pleasure to meet you. Rachel has told me many wonderful things about you." Giovanni offered his hand, and I took in Jared's reaction. He looked at Giovanni's hand as though it were the last thing on earth he wanted to touch, and I couldn't blame him. Besides me, the last time he was touched by an immortal, it was Alessandra. I knew from personal experience how vile and frightening it was.

"It's okay, Jared," I urged.

He shook Giovanni's hand, teeth slightly clenched, then relaxed when nothing untoward happened. "It's good to meet you, too."

His mind was its usual tightly wound coil, but he did let slip a wayward thought about the effects of Giovanni's reappearance on Eli. He was uncomfortable in our presence but was fighting not to be. *Everything's fine.*

"I called you back here for another reason, too."

I approached him and, taking him by the hand, led him to a chair in front of my desk. Giovanni handed over the package, and I pulled the legal papers from the envelope. I smiled and placed them in Jared's hands.

He scanned the documents, looking confused at first, then becoming more animated. He looked up finally, his smile wide enough to show his chipped front tooth. "You're kidding me?"

I giggled. "Nope, Carmilla's is all yours. I told you once that I value loyalty, and I meant it."

"Rachel, you didn't have to do it. I was never going to tell anyone."

"I know, and it's exactly why I did it. You deserve it. You work hard, and you have proven to be a very good friend, and it's not all."

"What do you mean?"

"Remember I told you that if I could help you with your mother I would?" He nodded, and I continued. "Well, Charles pulled some strings and has made arrangements for your mother to be discharged into your care, with nursing support in place. He purchased a new home for you and will cover all medical expenses. She will be ready to go by the end of the week."

He was stunned. "Just like that?"

"Just like that. Now as for how things will turn out once she's released, that's up to you."

"Yep, there are a lot of years to make up for." His eyes glazed over, as though he were lost in thought.

Giovanni and I waited quietly while he sorted the information out in his head.

"Wow, I can't believe it."

"Believe it."

He shook his head. "Sorry, I gotta chew on this a while." He turned to leave then stopped. "I almost forgot. Mary-Jane wanted me to let you know that the album's going really well and thanks, of course. She's gonna want to see you ASAP."

"Good. Tell her to not be a stranger."

"Will do." He left the room, papers in hand.

"Another good deed done." Giovanni pulled me into his lap.

"Uh-huh. Credit should be given where it's due. Mary-Jane and Jared have both kept their mouths shut about what went down here and about us in general. Jared stayed on top of stuff with the club, and they both deserve a break. Hey, it only took one call to get Mary-Jane in front of the right person, and now she's on her way to her dream, and Jared deserves the pride and the financial reward of owning his own club. He's had a rough life."

"We seem to be a beacon for the hard-luck, lost causes."

I was suddenly filled with the image of Eli's sweet face on the night I found him. If ever there was someone who had needed help, it was him.

"And now that debts have been repaid and your conscience cleared, what are you thinking of doing?"

"Well, there's one more thing to take care of, but afterward I thought of returning to Europe, finding another home along the Mediterranean and forgetting about everything else but us. How does that grab ya?"

"Sounds perfect. What's left to take care of?"

I told him about my idea for a farewell and the last person I needed to speak with before we left.

A few nights later we held our "going away" party. Eli and Micah were there, as were Jared and Mary-Jane and my niece Danica. We had a nice meal catered for the human attendees, and we all sat in our little-used dining room. The air smelled of garlic, fresh bread, and flowers. It was a much happier feeling than the last time we gathered at the house. There was no threat of gun-wielding assassins or life on the run.

Mary-Jane looked lovely in a floral sundress, her hair loose. Her smile was as easy and infectious as I remembered. She was so happy to see me, Eli, and Micah, she squealed. She hugged us over and over again, jumping up and down in excitement. I always believed her when she told me she was a true friend, but it was still wonderful to see her reaction.

I was also glad to see she and Jared moved past being friends in our absence. They came in hand in hand, looking very happy together, and more at ease with themselves than I ever knew either to be. After her rambunctious greeting, we all took a seat and filled each other in on what happened in our months apart.

I learned Jared and Mary-Jane were moving into the new house Charles had bought for Jared, and were busy preparing it for Jared's mother. We filled them in on the Desmarais attack, what really happened to Giovanni, and Charles's new relationship. I left out any mention of specific vampires taking part, as some information was best kept vague. Ignorance was bliss in some instances, and I felt it qualified. Soon we moved on to less difficult subjects.

"She'll be coming on Wednesday." Jared answered Micah's question about his mother's arrival.

"And is she excited about being with you?"

Jared turned to me. "Yes, and excited that I finally understand. I hope you'll be able to come and see her before you go. I think it would be therapeutic for her to see another of your kind. You know, to assure her that she isn't crazy. I've talked with her, but I want her to know that I'm not just humoring her."

"Of course. I would love to meet your mother, and I've spoken with Charles about the situation. He's going to see what he can do about finding out who it was that came to your mother all those years ago. He must be around somewhere."

"Yes, I bet she'd like to see him again."

Danica's soft giggle punctuated the silence. "Does anyone else find this situation as odd as I do?"

"I know just what you mean. We're sitting around here with a bunch of vampires, talking about mothers and houses and jobs like it is the most normal thing in the world." Mary-Jane tossed her waves of brown hair and smiled warmly. She was joking but hit the nail squarely on the head.

"Well, it is going to be normal for all of us from now on. It is our reality," Giovanni said. All eyes turned at his voice, and a murmur of agreement met his words.

I seized the break in conversation as an opportunity to make our announcement. "Well, now that we have everyone assembled, there's something Giovanni and I would like to tell you."

Danica smiled, a look both happy and sad. She knew what was coming, as we discussed the situation earlier, on the night I gave ownership of Carmilla's to Jared. Giovanni and I came to her office, where she was working alone, as usual.

I knocked lightly at her door, and when she saw it was me, her whole face lit up. She raced around the desk, threw the door wide, and all but jumped into my arms. She was still hugging me tightly when she became aware I wasn't alone.

She stepped back and regarded Giovanni with a mixture of surprise and awe. She took a few steps forward, touching Giovanni's face as though she couldn't quite believe he was real. Then, satisfied it wasn't a specter or figment of her imagination, she hugged me again. Giovanni smiled in return, before we all took a seat on the lumpy furniture in the office's outer waiting area.

"When did you get back? I've been waiting to hear from you." Her voice was breathy, almost nervous.

"About two weeks ago. We've been keeping a low profile, just trying to settle in. I'm sorry I didn't call; I just thought it was something we should do in person."

"Okay. I'm assuming that he is Giovanni, but I don't

understand how it can be. You told me he was killed."

Giovanni reached across the space to shake hands with my niece. She took his hand, shivering slightly from his cool touch. "It's very nice to meet you, Danica. Rachel has told me much about you."

"It's nice to meet you, too."

I launched into a condensed version of events, the assembly of vampires, the attacks, and finding Giovanni. We explained what the Desmarais did to him and how we found him. Danica listened, visibly affected by the stories of Giovanni's confinement and torture.

"And now you've been reunited, just like a great love story."

"Yes," I agreed. "It is what is meant to be."

"I'm so glad everything has worked out, and I hope everyone else is all right? Eli and Charles, Micah?"

"Yes, everyone is fine, but a lot has changed. Charles chose to stay behind in England, and he found a new companion, and Eli and Micah are together now, and Micah was changed."

Her look indicated that she understood what I meant. "Well, it's interesting."

"Yes, but it seems to work well." Giovanni's expression remained neutral, but I knew there was still a rawness when it came to matters of Eli and myself.

"I know that Mary-Jane and Jared are okay. She's called me a few times since you've been away. In a weird way, what happened at the club that night has made us friends."

"Good, I'm glad to know it. She's a wonderful girl, and I think she could be a really good person to know when times are tough."

"And so, will you two be staying here in San Francisco?"

"It's what we're here to talk to you about." I pulled a bundle of papers from my purse. Jared's legal documents weren't the only ones I received from the lawyer. "Giovanni and I will be going away for a while. I think you can understand that we need some time alone."

"But I've just found you again, and now you're leaving."

"We'll only be a plane ride or a phone call away, and I promise you will always know where we are. We have a present to make sure that staying in touch will be that much easier." I put the papers in her hand and let her read them over.

"Are you kidding me? Five million dollars and deeds to homes in San Francisco and London? Rachel, you guys don't have to do it."

"No, we don't, but we want to. So, now there's no reason why you can't come and visit whenever you want, and maybe you can cut back on teaching and do the research I know you've been itching to do, or fund a new project, make a documentary, whatever you want."

"You're part of our family," Giovanni added, "and we always take care of our family."

"It is amazing, but I'll miss you, Rachel, and I haven't even had the chance to get to know you, Giovanni."

"Plan on a long vacation this summer."

"I will. No summer classes, thank God!"

"So, we're having a dinner on Saturday, and I hope you will come."

"Of course." Then she moved in and gave Giovanni a brief hug. "Make sure you look after her."

"I don't plan to let her out of my sight."

And so now we were before all of our friends and family in San Francisco, and I felt suddenly very panicked at the thought of leaving them. Yet I knew it was for the best because Giovanni and I would have some time on our own. I burned each of their faces into my memory and reassured myself they would all be a part of my life for years to come.

"So, Giovanni and I have decided to take an extended vacation of sorts, probably the better part of a year, and go to Europe."

Eli didn't look that surprised, but the tone of his voice was strained. "I've sorta been expecting this."

"I hope you guys will keep an eye on things around here until we get back?"

"Yeah, we can do that," Micah answered.

"Yep, no problem," Eli agreed.

"Danica will be a neighbour soon. She's got a place just a few streets away."

"Someone's gotta keep an eye on these two." Danica jabbed a thumb in Eli and Micah's direction. Everyone laughed, but a heaviness pulled at the joyous atmosphere. All were aware things were changing, perhaps for the best, but many unknowns lay on the road ahead.

"Yeah, I can imagine the trouble these two could get into when left to their own devices and the mess! I don't even want to think about what the house will look like without me to nag at them." I gave the two men a knowing wink. "That is if they can ever get out of their bedroom."

"Ohhh! You should talk, and there are such things as maid service, you know."

"Of course, I must have been deluding myself to think you would actually pick up after yourself, Eli." I grinned.

"I give my word that I will check in at least once a week and make sure they're behaving themselves."

"Thank you, Danica. I knew I could count on you."

The rest of the evening passed easily. When we broke for the night, many hugs were exchanged, a few tears, and lots of reassurances that we would see each other soon. I made sure Danica had all our contact information and anything else I felt she should know, but, when it came to saying goodbye, I couldn't believe how emotional I became. Danica was my last link with my human life, and I realised part of me wanted very much to hang onto that.

"Call me, okay? Lots, anytime you want."

"I will, Rachel. Don't worry about me. You need to be with Giovanni right now."

"Yes, okay, but I expect you to come visit soon."

"I will. Be happy, Rachel. I love you."

"I love you, too."

Then I watched her as she walked to her car. She raised a hand to wave goodbye, then she was gone. Mary-Jane and Jared had already departed, leaving the four members of our vampire family alone.

I didn't realise I was crying until Eli gave me a hug. "It's okay, Rachel. We'll see you again soon, and we are all happy now, safe and loved."

"Yes, but so much has changed, too."

Micah put things in perspective, and I knew his words were honest and from the heart. "But all for the best. We have all received the blessing of more people in our life to love and to love us back. We will all be stronger for it."

He was right. Everything was good. All my friends and family were safe and doing well in their lives. Somehow, we all managed to make peace with the past, and through it opened the door for our future.

My love returned, and, as he had said to me on a cold, quiet night in England, we had a second chance at forever.

The night was waiting for us.

Look for the series finale,

BORN OF BLOOD AND RETRIBUTION

Book Three of The Dark Kiss Trilogy

About the Author

Liz Strange is the published author of ten novels and several short stories. She has also written multiple scripts for both film and television.

Curious about other Crossroad Press books?
Stop by our site:
http://www.crossroadpress.com
We offer quality writing
in digital, audio, and print formats.

www.ingramcontent.com/pod-product-compliance
Lightning Source LLC
Chambersburg PA
CBHW030132180626
46812CB00002B/655